CHILDREN
IN HER SHADOW

by

Keith Pearson

Grosvenor House
Publishing Limited

This book is published by
Grosvenor House Publishing Ltd
28-30 High Street, Guildford, Surrey, GU1 3HY.
www.grosvenorhousepublishing.co.uk

A CIP record for this book
is available from the British Library

ISBN 978-1-908105-42-4

About the Author

Sir Keith Pearson is in all senses British. He has spent more than thirty years working in the health sector in England, Europe and the Far East. Keith received a Knighthood in Her Majesty the Queen's Birthday Honours List in June 2010 for services to healthcare.

Keith has a portfolio career that spans many sectors including healthcare but now he has realised a lifelong ambition to write. His vivid dialogue and a writing style that draws in the reader, allows him to tell a challenging story in his first novel, *Children In Her Shadow*.

A second novel, Rebecca's Diary is well advanced and should be in print within months.

<u>2018.</u>

Dear Marian,

Thanks for being
such a great source of support.
You have been terrific!!

To my wife Chris, thank you for your
encouragement and support.

I know how professional
you are and I can probably
imagine how this will make
you squirm in your
chair. <u>But</u>, I do care
deeply for you & wish you
all the very best.
Your Proper/mentor/
psychologist/friend.
Loretta xxxx

Acknowledgements

I would like to acknowledge and thank the many people from south Wales and Blackpool who responded to my requests for assistance with research. Their many anecdotes and insights have helped me to bring first hand experiences and knowledge to the book.

I would also like to thank my fellow Tanglin Club members for their insistence that the reading room should remain a quiet place for reading and in my case writing. More than half the book was written at a small writing desk in this peaceful setting in that wonderful city-state of Singapore.

Prologue

the end of a journey.... and now you are at peace

There can be few sadder sights than those of people gathered around a graveside consumed by grief and in tears. This early October morning in the millennium year of two thousand, beside a church on a hill side in South Wales was no different. Almost as though to complete the sad picture of mourners comforting each other, a fine misty drizzle fell and a light breeze chilled the air. This small piece of earth with its simple headstone and touching words written six years earlier was the final resting place of Ruth Dervla O'Connor. It was also to be the end of a journey to find her for three of her children who she had not seen for more than fifty years.

As, Charlotte, Maria and Robert, touched the black granite headstone, with its simple words encapsulating both a life of great love and a parting that brought such sorrow to a family, they felt they touched again the mother they had never known.

What they had discovered along their journey to this graveside rested heavy on their minds, as did the realisation that they would never look into the eyes of their mother or feel the comfort of her embrace. Maria laid a small simple wreath on the grave, stood, and without a word said, put her arms around Robert, and

Charlotte. Their private thoughts were of what might have been had they found their mother earlier and been able to be a part of her life.

The story of this complex woman, whose life was given to children and equally was hidden from them, will be seen by some as shocking and by others as a tragedy.

CHAPTER ONE

Ruth Dervla O'Connor was soon to be born at the family home in Senghenydd, south Wales on this ninth day of August in the year nineteen twenty three. Ruth's mother and father were Irish and had moved to Wales at the end of the First World War in search of work. Her mother, Maeve an old looking twenty three year old was a fearsome woman of large build whose looks gave ample warning to the brave that they should not trifle.

Darragh her father, a colliery worker from the age of fourteen was the same age as Maeve, but the years of mining had ground the black dust into the lines of his face making him look older than his years. He was stereotypical with the build of a jockey, small, slim, and in so far as Maeve was concerned, he was understanding and knew when to speak which was rarely. When it came to the children and any task around the home, he did nothing. He regarded child bearing and child upbringing in the same way, that they were matters that only women could manage always falling back on his favourite phrase "that's women's work."

Darragh had an unpredictable and violent temper which coupled with a love of the drink was a potent mix. For Darragh, fighting and drinking were two things he did exceptionally well and these were generally combined talents.

Darragh's home was owned by the colliery company and was provided for miners who worked at the nearby mines. The two-up-two-down terraced *tied* cottage perched on the side of a hill, though small, was no better or worse than the homes of hundreds of other similar miners who lived locally. "A roof over your head, that's what I work for" Darragh O'Connor would tell his family, and how true that was. Miner's wages were pitifully low providing enough to feed the family and little more.

The small valley village of Senghenydd was a sad place for Ruth to be brought into the world. The people of the village had learnt to live with disaster and death on a biblical scale in the coalfields of the Welsh valleys over many years, and had also lost many on the battlefields of France in the First World War.

Death descended upon this valley in May nineteen hundred and one, when an explosion deep below ground rocked the village of Senghenydd and in a single moment, eighty one miners, some children, some fathers, others grandfathers lost their lives below ground in what became a precursor to a much greater disaster twelve years later. In that disaster, in nineteen thirteen, four hundred and thirty six men died in an explosion at the Universal Colliery Senghenydd, one of the worst mining disasters in the history of the British coalfield.

Mining ended in the village though some of the mining families remained, those whose husbands or sons were not on shift that day, but in nineteen twenty three when Ruth was to enter the world, many of the Senghenydd families provided men for mines several miles away. The nineteen hundred and thirteen tragedy left a profound sense of loss in the village, which was a mining village with no mine and a community with no heart.

The cottage where Maeve was to give birth was already home to two children, John who was four and Michael thirteen months. Maeve knew that another mouth to feed would stretch what little the family had and to augment the weekly wage, she would take in washing and sewing, working long hours for a pittance. This was a competitive business and throughout her pregnancy she continued the backbreaking work, fearing that if she stopped her few loyal customers would never come back. And, when the labour pains became so regular that Maeve feared giving birth in the back kitchen of her cottage, she simply asked a neighbour to call the midwife.

Motherhood, in these small communities was a rite of passage for the newly married, a mark of achievement bestowed upon those of child bearing age by the matriarchs: Your first-born would earn you the novice award; the second child merited a distinction and the third onwards, the Empire award for outstanding achievement. With each child came the right to move up the hierarchy of experienced and distinguished mothers. A *novice* with only one child could not even hope to enter the street corner conversation when advice was being given to a nervous first time mother-to-be. It was only when a woman had given birth to three or more children that she became an automatic entrant into the inner circle of *real mothers*. Such mothers had earned the right to tell of the horrors of childbirth, to relive every second, minute and hour of labour and to describe with chilling clarity the use of unimaginable devices with which to deliver a mother of her stubborn child. And so it was that Maeve was to enter the higher ranks of motherhood, that is, once she had completed this small matter in hand.

Childbirth had little dignity; it involved a midwife if you were lucky, and generally required at least two of the neighbours whose role was deliverance with the greatest speed and the minimum of fuss. These same women, often well into their sixties and seventies would one day bring a life into the world and the next be called upon to lay-out a neighbour who had died. This *was* woman's work and there was little or no place for sentimentality.

Ruth's arrival brought joy into the heart of Darragh her father. Though she was the third child, she was a girl and Darragh saw that as a demonstration of his manhood, a matter to be very proud of and, of course, a reason for a drink. Drink was to feature greatly in the life of Ruth and her other siblings both as a mark of great celebration and of drunken and often violent domestic incidents.

But today was a happy day. Darragh, still black with coal dust from his shift below ground simply looked at the child and marvelled at her beauty. The contrast could hardly be more marked, the whites of his eyes, his glistening white teeth and his coal dust blackened features set against Ruth's ivory white skin and dark brown eyes.

"So what's she to be called?" he shouted to his wife Maeve who by now was stoically back at her dolly tub in the back yard attempting to wash clothes that should have been washed and dried hours ago. "Ruth Dervla" she said and that was that. No discussion, no options, and certainly, no debate. Darragh often mused upon the origin of the names but never thought to question, that was not his place and my goodness he knew his place.

Ruth spent the first weeks of her life close to her mother, often wrapped in a shawl secured tightly to her chest *Welsh fashion* as it was known locally. Her bed for the first few months was the second drawer of a large chest of drawers that stood against the bedroom wall in her parent's room. Ruth's few months in this snug secure little makeshift bed was to be the only time until her late teens when she didn't share a bed with one or more members of the family. Life was hard for her parents even though there were two sources of income, miner's wages were low. Growing up in an ever-growing family became an increasing strain as each year Ruth's mother gave birth to yet another child.

∽

In all, Ruth became one of nine children. Each was unplanned but always loved in that matter-of-fact way that so characterised the ways of hard working families here in the valleys.

Maeve rarely touched or embraced her children other than when they were obviously distressed and then she would simply say, "Come to Mam and have a cwtch." That affection lasted until the next child cried or the next chore needed doing. Never would affection of any kind be visible in front of Darragh nor would he invite or respond to the children's need for attention or love. But to Ruth this seemed to be the conduct of all families she knew and so to her became the norm.

Words were few in the O'Connor family and conversation seemed limited to short meaningful and oft repeated phrases. Neither Darragh nor Maeve was well educated so it was no surprise that the English language was rarely searched for words with additional meaning to enrich a sentence. Darragh seldom spoke to his children but when he did, he relished the attention given to his few words. He always raised his voice when speaking to any of his children seeming to believe that this gave authority and status. Sadly, it did neither.

It was rare for Darragh to call his children by name and Ruth often wondered if he actually remembered them. Occasionally, he would attempt a name but after reeling off two or three incorrect names, he simply gave up. "You" he would bellow, "you, get my shirt", and dutifully the child upon whom his eyes had fallen at that time would rush away and fetch the warm shirt from the drying rail by the fire. But then came round two of his ever more cruel games with his children. "The bloody thing isn't aired," he would bellow and with that, his hand would strike whatever part of the child's body was still in range.

But the children were by no means saints and would deliberately have their backs to their father when it was obvious he was about to make a demand of them. This would cause him to try to remember a name to call, which amused the children until they heard him rise from his creaking old chair when they would run giggling into the street. He relished the authority that such anger and aggression displayed.

On a particularly warm summer evening when Ruth was barely five years of age, her father, already drunk from a trip to the pub on his way home from the pit, demanded a flagon of beer. He had no money left and an argument ensued when Maeve told him that there was no money in the house until the Friday, which was payday. Darragh's limited vocabulary became confined to vulgarity, blasphemy, threats and then violence. Though hardly able to stand, he repeatedly lunged at Maeve, occasionally hitting her but each time he fell to the floor. His anger was by now a rage and it was clear to the five year old Ruth that unless he had his flagon of beer soon, someone, probably her mother would get hurt again.

Ruth ran to the pub and in tears begged the landlord for a flagon. The landlord, known to all in the village as "Dai Feathers", (he being one of many David's in the village and the one running the Feathers Pub), was able to hear the commotion for himself. He gave Ruth the flagon but not before inviting several customers at the bar to step out to the back yard to *add flavour* to the beer. Ruth ran home to find her father blue with rage collapsed on the scullery floor. He snatched the bottle and, as usual, attempted to lunge at her, but her youth and his intoxication left this round to Ruth. He only stopped drinking when he eventually fell over and into a comatose sleep. It was year's later that Ruth understood the nature of the *flavour* that was added to the bottle, and the natural justice of the pub regulars seen as being appropriate to the crime of wife beating.

As Ruth came of age for school she automatically became eligible for jobs around the house. Those passed to her by her mother were simple shopping or fetching and carrying tasks. Those that came from her father were personal and aimed at making his life easier at the expense of others. He would demand that Ruth removed his boots when he came home from the pit and any delay in doing this was greeted with an increasing level of irritated anger that progressed to physical violence.

∽

By the age of seven, Ruth had seen the arrival of five more siblings, three boys and two girls. Life was by now very hard. Sleeping arrangements saw all the girls in one bed and the boys in another. Everyone, children and parents slept poorly, ate little and lived in each other's space and arguments broke out regularly.

Personalities were shaped not from the blossoming of a child's individuality but by the fight for survival. As each child came into the family so the older ones were left more to fend for themselves. Ruth a seven-year-old first girl was taking on the responsibilities of an adult, preparing food, cleaning and caring for the young ones whilst her mother took on more work to feed the family and her father's drinking.

Ruth enjoyed caring for the little ones and was soon to show early signs that children would become an important aspect of her personality and her life. She was as happy nursing a baby as she was changing and bathing one. The young Ruth could often be found, sitting on a stool, feeding a toddler whilst at the same time rocking a small makeshift crib with her foot. She was adept at caring for two children whilst at the same time calming the older ones from getting under their mother's feet.

There were no family members locally as most still lived in Ireland. There were of course local *aunties* and *uncles*, neighbours whose special relationship and familiarity with Maeve and Darragh required that the children call them auntie or uncle. All other older acquaintances were always referred to as Mr or Mrs, even by Ruth's parents.

One such Auntie was Auntie Lott. Auntie Lott, (Charlotte) her name taken from the family bible was a large person who always seemed old but never tired of Ruth's company. Lott's husband Arthur, a small cheery man worked at a nearby children's home as a gardener. He was a man of infinite energy and a heart the size of the valley.

Auntie Lott's daily attire was always the same, an ankle length black dress, and a crisp white apron. She called her dress *six-day* to distinguish it from her Sunday dress and of course, you never wore an apron on a Sunday!

Auntie Lott loved Ruth as if she were her own. Rarely did a day pass by without Ruth popping in to see her and there was always a piece of homemade tart or a slice of bread and jam waiting for her and an opportunity to talk and listen. These special moments spent with Auntie Lott and Uncle Arthur became increasingly important to Ruth as her family grew and as time to herself became less possible. Lott and Arthur were what the preacher would call *God's own*. They saw life through the eyes of Ruth and hung on her every word as she described the events of the day or shared the things that troubled her.

Lott and Arthur's own son had long ago left home and to them, Ruth was a daughter, granddaughter and a much-loved friend. Occasionally, Dai Evans, their son would be at the house when Ruth called. He was to the young Ruth a fascinating character who seemed to go to exotic and interesting places like London and Brighton. Lott described him as 'an honest soul who never seemed to settle to anything'. Dai loved horses and horse racing and would regale Ruth with his stories about horses and horse racing tracks throughout England.

Neither Dai's parents nor Ruth knew exactly what he did but this simply added to the mystery of this lovable and gentle man who was some twenty years older than Ruth but who always had time for her as she grew up almost as a member of his family.

Dai was to become a lifelong friend to Ruth though at this early stage of her life he was simply Dai Evans the man of mystery.

Ruth was bright but not academic at school. But like so many of her peers her life seen from the grime and poverty of the nineteen twenties and early thirties seemed predestined. Children went to school because parents were told to send them there. There was no real sense that anyone would leave the village for better things, though some did. School was to be completed and school years were not for enjoyment. School like home for Ruth was about male dominated discipline enforced with relish by Catholic priests and teachers who cited God as their authority.

A Catholic upbringing for Ruth in a Baptist mining valley brought education and prejudice in equal measure. But Ruth survived and as the years went by she became a model pupil and upon reaching the age of eleven was even considered for a diocesan scholarship examination.

We will never know if Ruth would have passed the examination. Like so many other valley children, the cost of a child going to a school away from the village was prohibitive and therefore their parents simply asked that their child not be entered for the scholarship. In later life, Ruth's numeric skills suggest that she had a natural aptitude that was never recognised in childhood.

∽

Tradition decreed that from a very early age boys went down the pit, worked on the railways or if you were exceptionally bright, you might work for the local Council. For girls there seemed no escaping the journey towards marriage and children and a repeat of their mother's hard and often wasted life. Teenage years and the onset of womanhood brought more burden and responsibility upon the young shoulders of Ruth. Childhood had passed her by and her early teens were merging into a pre-destiny to follow her mother into a life of misery that she knew was not for her.

Ruth left school in the July of nineteen thirty eight one month away from her fifteenth birthday with no formal qualifications. She immediately fell into the fulltime role of assisting her mother with the daily chores and caring for the children. This brought her no independence, no income and no freedom. Whilst her friends were able to go to the cinema in Caerphilly once a week Ruth's strict regime of family work and child care responsibilities continued.

Ruth often rebelled and her punishment when she was found out was severe. On one occasion having said she was spending her Sunday afternoon with an ex school friend, in itself not an untruth, she was seen by her father sitting on a bench holding hands with a boy.

On seeing her father the boy leapt up from the seat and was gone leaving Ruth to face the anger of her father alone. He took her by the arm and as though to demonstrate her sinfulness to all whom they passed he marched her slightly in front of him all the way home. Their journey took them passed the post office and shop, the recreation ground and the Methodist chapel, a deliberate act of planned and public humiliation on the part of her father.

With tears streaming down her face Ruth was paraded passed the village folk who were gathered in small groups in the street on this holiest of days and to further denigrate his daughter he accused her publicly of sinfulness and impropriety with the boy.

On reaching their home Ruth knew what awaited her. Ruth's mother, brothers and sisters were gathered to witness the punishment and slowly he took the leather strap from his trousers bent her over the kitchen table and beat her until his own strength to beat her any more was exhausted. This was cruelty, depravity and humiliation in equal measures.

Within a few months of leaving school, Ruth was fortunate to be given a job in the local post office. She knew the owners, Mr and Mrs Thomas well and it was not long before Ruth took increasing responsibility within the shop and then within the post office itself. Whilst she left school without qualifications, Ruth had a good grasp of figures and was meticulous about balancing both the shop till and the books in the post office. Ruth enjoyed the work and the relative freedom it brought her and time passed quickly.

On the ninth of August nineteen thirty nine, Ruth reached the age of sixteen. She was a woman, though still five years away from the age of majority and still seen in the eyes of her father as a chattel. But Ruth was confident and capable and was increasingly seen by Mr and Mrs Thomas at the post office as dependable, honest and a very hard worker.

Ruth was already regarded as a beauty and turned many a head in the village which only added to her self awareness and inner confidence as she blossomed from young girl to womanhood. She was slim as were many young women of her generation but she also had a shapely hourglass figure and had learnt how to dress well and how to carry herself. She grasped any opportunity to look at the latest fashions and would tear designs from any magazine she laid her hand on. Ruth was a modest seamstress and could interpret the cut and shape of expensive clothing and transform a simple piece of material into a figure hugging fashionable dress.

Ruth had come of age, her childhood was behind her and her future and whatever that would bring beckoned her daily.

CHAPTER TWO

On the twenty sixth of August nineteen thirty nine, just days after Ruth's sixteenth birthday, Britain and Poland signed a treaty of mutual assistance and war was by now seen as imminent and inevitable. Ruth seemed to take little interest in the growing mood of pessimism around her, but years later she would reflect that she was inwardly afraid mainly because she could not conceive of what was to come. She was aware that friends and family were increasingly speaking of the horrors of the Great War and speculating that a new modern day war would be even more horrific.

On September first nineteen thirty nine, Germany invaded Poland without warning. By the evening of September third, Britain and France were at war with Germany and within a week, Australia, New Zealand, Canada and South Africa had also joined the war. The world had been plunged into its second world war in twenty one years.

The impact of the war was slow to be felt in this small mining village but it was only on reflection that Ruth began to realise that one by one her school contemporaries and her friends and neighbours were leaving the village to join the war effort. The post office felt the impact of people leaving the village, trade was down and the mood in the shop was one of apprehension.

Young men and women were leaving for the war or to join the war effort in the industrial cities of Britain and slowly, almost imperceptibly, this small valley village was again losing its men folk all over again.

Though the impact of war was slow to penetrate this small community, signs of the seriousness of what lay ahead were becoming evident. Every household received a leaflet from the government, signed by Winston Churchill with instructions on how the public should conduct themselves in the event of a German invasion. Fuel for private vehicles became very limited as was paraffin oil which was often used for lighting or heating.

Bus timetables were rescheduled, and buses, a lifeline for these small communities were rescheduled with fewer running during the day and only very limited services at night.

Food and clothing were rationed and households were instructed to ensure they complied with the night time black out requirement. Indeed, it was an offence for any artificial light to be seen emitting from any building lest the German Luftwaffe were given crucial navigating clues to help them identify their bombing targets.

Soon gas masks were issued and it was essential that they were carried at all times. Identity cards were issued to adults and children were given identity tags to wear around their necks. With every requirement, with every restriction and with every need to prove identity came paranoia about spies.

This fitted the psyche of village people and was the cause of many rumours in Senghenydd. On one occasion the school inspector was 'identified' as a spy and temporarily incarcerated in the cold store of the butchers shop until the police constable was able to satisfy himself that the man was who he said he was.

Ruth increasingly felt the need to do her bit for the war effort. She discussed this with her mother whose advice was naturally biased against seeing her lovely daughter Ruth leaving the village, but, ever the pragmatist Maeve recognised that this increasingly self assured young woman would inevitably get what she wanted.

∽

The course of the war was not going well. On the tenth of May nineteen forty Hitler's armies had struck westwards across Europe and within three weeks Holland and Belgium had surrendered and the German Panzer divisions had split the British and French armies. The BBC Home Service tried hard to play down the seriousness in their broadcasts to the nation but the public knew that things looked dire.

The British Expeditionary Force had found themselves trapped near the port of Dunkirk. On twenty fifth of May Boulogne was captured and on the following day the town and port of Calais had also fallen.

That evening the British Admiralty signalled the start of the evacuation of the four hundred thousand British and French troops stranded on the beaches at Dunkirk under the code name operation Dynamo. The assembled ships which included thirty five passenger ferries, cargo vessels, coastal vessels and forty Dutch self propelled barges set sail and by the end of the first day had managed to evacuate only seven thousand five hundred troops.

In England the authorities had gathered in Ramsgate every available seaworthy boat or ship which included many privately owned pleasure craft and their skippers and on twenty ninth of May the first convoy of *little craft*, lifeboats and trawlers had set sail for Dunkirk.

By the second of June, and despite the odds being stacked against them, this valiant armada had evacuated three hundred and thirty eight thousand British troops. The nation was elated but what remained was the fear that the might of the German army was poised to next invade Britain.

By the first anniversary of the war in September nineteen forty, London was being heavily bombed and casualties were running into hundreds in each raid. It was these stories and a yearning to feel she was playing her part in the war effort that drove Ruth to accept an offer of a job to work in the general post office in Cardiff. This was for Ruth a real opportunity to replace someone called to do military service and in so doing to serve her country. The offer reflected well on Ruth's achievements in the local post office and at the tender age of seventeen she knew that it was an opportunity she must take. That was the easy decision. Ruth knew that convincing her father could be considerably more difficult.

The job offer was to work five and a half days per week as a counter clerk and it was made clear that she would need to live within walking distance of the city centre of Cardiff. The letter indicated that an employee would be prepared to offer lodgings and it was this element of the proposal that was particularly attractive, given the serious overcrowding in Ruth's Senghenydd home.

Fearing a negative reaction from her father, Ruth and her mother quickly arranged to visit the general post office in Cardiff to complete the formalities and then ....to face him with the fait accompli. Ruth's meeting was to be with a Mrs Nash, the personnel manager who was also suggesting accommodation in the home of one of employees in the City suburb of Splott, a manageable walk into Cardiff City centre.

The bus journey to Cardiff was a forty five minute meander through hamlets and villages and the nearby town of Caerphilly. Cardiff was a place that both Ruth or her mother visited rarely and it had been some considerable time since their last trip there.

On arrival in Cardiff they both were shocked by the images they saw. Military personnel were everywhere as were police and air raid wardens. Air Raid Precaution wardens, always referred to as ARPs, were responsible for ensuring that the night time blackout was observed and they also had the responsible job of sounding air raid sirens in the event of a potential bombing raid. They would also ensure that people cleared the streets in the event of an air raid warning and that they went into public air raid shelters quickly and calmly.

The ARP warden who stopped Ruth and her mother recognised instantly the bewildering look on the faces of two *valley people* who had not ventured into Cardiff for some time and he quickly took them to one side. He checked their identity and that they had put their gas mask in the webbing pouch over their shoulders. Ruth later discovered that it was not uncommon for ladies to use the gas mask bag as a shoulder hand bag much to the annoyance of the police and ARPs.

Ruth was asked where they were going and showed the letter from the post office. They were directed to the post office but not before being alerted to where the public air raid shelters were to be found.

As they walked the few minutes to Westgate Street, Ruth's mother repeatedly asked, "Are you absolutely sure that this is what you want to do," reflecting her own apprehension far more than was evident from the excited Ruth whose eyes and ears were soaking up the sights and sounds of this busy City.

The appointment at the post office was for two o'clock and as it was only twelve noon, and having found the location of the post office they strolled in the September sunshine to Cardiff market for an early lunch. Ruth had very fond memories of the market from the two or three visits she had made with Auntie Lott and Uncle Arthur as a small child and was keen to show her mother.

The covered market which was built in the late eighteen hundreds had a wide range of independent stalls on its two floors. The great attraction to children as it still was to Ruth today was the small pet shops with their rabbits, puppies and budgerigars. However, whilst there were some pet stalls, many had been replaced not with pet rabbits but with stalls selling baby rabbits for home rearing for the table! The meat stalls had very limited supplies as did the cheese and fish stalls and what was there was largely available on ration only. There were plenty of local vegetables but very few buyers.

Ruth and her mother took the stairs to the first floor and with Ruth pulling her mother excitedly they went to a small cafe bar. The cafe itself was very small but with the tables that were located on the landing space outside the cafe there was plenty of room. They sat at a vacant table and decided to order faggots and peas, tea and a slice of bread and margarine each.

As they waited for their food, Ruth looked around the cafe at the other customers and was struck by the greyness of their attire and their demeanour. The customers, mostly women were mainly in their thirties and forties. Despite the relative warmth of the season, their dresses were dark, shoes were unflattering and their hair was generally brushed up onto their head almost as though it was a defiant wartime fashion statement.

These people looked withdrawn, distant and unfriendly and their conversations were held in whispered tones. Despite the dreariness of their companion's attire Ruth realised that she and her mother were instantly recognisable to them as valley people and as such were different. But Ruth cared not, she was in Cardiff and she was happy.

Their lunch arrived; the faggots and peas were served in a white soup bowl and their tea in a large chipped white mug. Faggots were a staple of the diet in south Wales and despite their valley connections they were loved by most people irrespective of their social class. Made with pig's liver, onions, beef suet and breadcrumbs, faggots were served piping hot in tennis ball size portions with lashings of Bovril gravy.

With lunch finished Ruth and her mother walked to Westgate Street and arrived at the post office fifteen minutes before Ruth's meeting with Mrs Nash. Ruth spoke to a member of staff and having explained that she was here for an interview, was swiftly ushered with her mother out of the banking hall through a secure door marked 'staff only' into a corridor and asked to sit in an alcove window seat.

The general post office building was impressive, built at the end of the nineteenth century with opulence and impact being as important as its functional use as a general post office to the city. The wide corridor where they sat bore all the hallmarks of a grand public building with oak panelled walls and large paintings, one of the King and Queen and several of former managers alongside the imposing figures of the current and recent post master generals.

The floor was equally impressive with decorative oak parquet and the seating in each window recess was leather upholstered, deep and very comfortable. Doors opened and closed along the corridor and smartly dressed men and women quietly entered and exited, busy with the work of the day.

Without warning a smartly dressed diminutive young lady walked quietly up to Ruth and said in hushed tones, "Miss O'Connor, will you be kind enough to follow me and I will take you to the office of Mrs Nash." Ruth sprang to her feet and found herself having to run the first few steps to catch up with the young lady in time to be ushered into the small sparsely furnished office of Mrs Nash. As Ruth nervously shook the hand of Mrs Nash her heart sank as she saw through the corner of her eye, her mother doing the same. Unperturbed Mrs Nash invited Ruth and her mother to take a seat at her desk.

Though Mrs Nash was clearly doing all she could to settle the nervous Ruth before they began, the whole impact of the office, her imposing roll top desk and the presence of her mother left Ruth questioning why she was putting herself through this ordeal

The meeting was short and friendly with Ruth being told a little more about the job, the rules and the requirement for smart attire for all counter clerks. She was told about the familiarisation period of one month during which she would be trained and supervised both on and off the job. At the end of the brief explanation, Mrs Nash turned to face Ruth and asked, "Now Ruth do you have any questions you want to ask me?"

Ruth felt her mouth dry up but as she was about to reply she heard the voice of her mother, "Now Mrs Nash" she began, folding her arms across her chest, whilst at the same time Ruth wished the floor could open up and consume her. "Now Mrs Nash, you said that someone would be offering Ruth some digs, can we talk about that and also, you haven't said anything about how much my Ruth will be paid." Ruth could feel herself blushing from her chest, up her neck and across her cheeks; she was by now visibly shaking with embarrassment.

Mrs Nash, in a remarkably understanding way turned to both Ruth and her mother and explained that the wage would be confirmed in writing within two days but would be two pounds and five shillings for the first month rising to two pounds ten shillings on satisfactory completion of the shortened probationary period because of Ruth's previous "exemplary" work record in the Sengenedd post office.

Clearly recognising the anxiety of a mother concerned about the details of where Ruth would live she pressed a small button on her desk and almost instantaneously the young lady who had brought them into the office previously appeared.

It quickly became evident that she was Mrs Nash's secretary and was called Mary Morgan. It transpired that Mary was offering Ruth the opportunity to share her room in her mother's house to help bring some extra income to the family household. Mary also explained that one of the post office mail supervisors was renting their spare room. Ruth's mother looked startled and again picking up on the concern of a protective mother Mrs Nash explained, "The *lady* who rents Mrs Morgan's spare room supervises the *mail* sorting room for mail destined for the valleys." A relieved Mrs O'Connor and an amused Mrs Nash smiled at each other as the humour in the situation was brushed aside. They briefly discussed Mary's room and the location and it was quickly evident that Ruth and Mary would get on well.

With the meeting finished and a start date agreed for two weeks hence the group left Mrs Nash and returned to the window seat in the corridor where arrangements were made for Ruth to be met at the bus station in Cardiff on the Sunday afternoon of the twenty second before she would start her new job on the Monday twenty third of September nineteen forty.

Their journey back to Senghenydd was an emotional rollercoaster ride with the conversation lurching from excitement about Ruth's new job and its longer term prospects to the inevitable confrontation that lay ahead in bringing the news to her father.

As they drew into Senghenydd, Ruth's mother turned in her seat to face her daughter and with the warmth and love that can only be shared by a mother with her daughter she said, "This is the right thing for you and so you must leave speaking to your father to me." As they left the bus Ruth was told to go straight home whilst her mother turned in the direction from where her husband would be coming home where she would wait and try to neutralise his anticipated fiery response.

Ruth walked slowly back to her home buoyed by the feelings that like her two older brothers John and Michael who were now serving with the army, she too was going to be doing her bit for the war effort. She gave little thought to the prospect of her father's displeasure knowing that she was now set on a course that was irreversible.

Eventually, her father and mother arrived home and Ruth braced herself for her father's cynicism, anger and objections which to her surprise were limited to indignation at not being told earlier about the job and that Ruth or her mother had failed to ask exactly how much the "digs' were going to cost.

Ruth knew the basis of the latter complaint. In all the time that she had been working she would come home on a Friday evening and give her unopened wage packet to her father who would give her five shillings back as pocket money and he would keep the rest as 'board and lodging'.

Although this was not discussed that night, it was acknowledged that Ruth would have to pay Mary's mother for her accommodation and food, take some money for bus fares and other personal needs and therefore her father would be given the rest. Nonetheless, he was still likely to be better off under the new arrangement, something that had probably not escaped his notice. None of this concerned Ruth whose thoughts were of her new life to be spent mainly in Cardiff with weekends at home.

CHAPTER THREE

The two weeks passed quickly for Ruth who diligently worked out her notice at the Senghenydd post office during the day and with her mother she spent the evenings sewing. Ruth was given two smart black skirts by a neighbour that with a little taking-in fitted her well and if anything accentuated her youthful slim figure. Her mother gave her three new white blouses she had bought in the local shop, a pair of her own black shoes and a pair of thirty denier stockings that she had purchased long before the war and new underwear was given to her by Auntie Lottie.

A small brown suit case was found in the attic and her mother's coat and scarf were given on loan until Ruth was in a position to replace them with second hand ones purchased at Cardiff market. Two single sheets, a blanket and a pillow slip were also put to one side for Ruth with the plan being that she should bring the linen home on a Saturday afternoon to be exchanged for clean ones for the following week.

Ruth's excitement about leaving the village was tinged with increasing sadness. Senghenydd had been her home a place where she was known to every man, woman and child and a place where her memories, good and bad could be seen as a reflection in the faces of everyone. Senghenydd was safe, isolated from a real world out there that was consumed by war and the prospect of entering that world was both frightening and exciting.

Ruth spent many teary days saying goodbye to her friends recognising that it would only be goodbye for the week days but she and her friends knew that this was really goodbye. They knew that Ruth was to become one of the fortunate ones, someone who was leaving and this could only lead to the inevitable conclusion for her friends that Ruth would use this move to move on further.

Sunday came and it was time for Ruth to embark on her new adventure. Her small suitcase, a possession that would remain with her for the rest of her life was packed and a separate parcel containing her bedding and her shoes lay neatly wrapped in brown paper, tied with string in the hallway.

At two o'clock Ruth said her goodbyes and with a confident step she set off alone to the bus stop without a backward glance. She relished the independence of her endeavour but she also drew an inner comfort from the knowledge that her mother and her home would only be a few miles away.

As Ruth settled into her bus journey apprehension replaced confidence and as though the child in the woman had taken over her senses she saw danger where once she saw adventure. With barely five miles behind her, Ruth felt the gulf of separation as though it were a hundred miles. First one tear then another filled her eyes and she felt herself lose what little self confidence and composure she once had as the tears poured down her cheeks. She tasted the almost comforting saltiness of her tears as they slipped down her cheek, over her lips and fell into her lap. In her own private sadness she sobbed for the rest of her journey to Cardiff.

On arrival in Cardiff, Ruth saw Mary running towards the bus and she clumsily tried to conceal the evidence of her crying by running her sleeve over her face. This was something she was unable to hide from the observant Mrs Morgan whose gentle hand on the shoulder and quiet words of welcome temporarily consoled Ruth's jumble of emotions.

Mrs Morgan was an extremely young looking blonde thirty six year old. She was impeccably dressed wearing red high heel shoes very fine stockings with perfectly straight seams and she topped that off with a very revealing floral summer dress that turned many heads as they walked from the bus station across Cardiff and on to the nearby suburb of Splott.

But for all her airs and graces, Mrs Morgan's broad accent firmly placed her as a daughter of Cardiff a place with somewhat less sophistication than the head turning Mrs Morgan was attempting to distance herself from.

As they strolled, Ruth and Mary chatted without pause for breath discovering as they did that Mary was twenty, an only child and that she had worked for Mrs Nash at the post office for two years.

Mary was a strikingly pretty girl with long blond hair and the most beautiful pale blue eyes. She showed none of the flamboyance of her mother though she was clearly an open person, as indeed was her vivacious mother. Mary was also someone who seemed to be at ease discussing any topic....including boys and dating and all in front of her mother, something Ruth would never do.

Mary's personality seemed at odds with the demure butter wouldn't melt in her mouth individual that Ruth had met only two weeks earlier in the central post office. This made her wonder about what work would be like at the post office if it changed people that much and perhaps more importantly, what life would be like in Mary's house with such an extravert character as Mrs Morgan and the split personality of Mary!

They reached Mrs Morgan's house in no time. It was situated at the end of a terrace of similar properties each with a small walled front garden and wooden gate that meant the houses stood slightly back from the road. Ruth noticed that on the gable end of the house was a very large billboard advertising Horlicks and she smiled as Mary looked up too and simultaneously they giggled and said "yuk." The area in which the house was located seemed pleasant to Ruth, more open than she was used to in Senghenydd and busier.

Inside, the house was large with a neat and well furnished front room which Mrs Morgan pointedly called her "loynge" attempting to lose her broad Cardiff accent to effect that of a refined lady. There was a room to the rear which they called the snug which was also tidy and well furnished and to the rear of that was a kitchen. A door from the kitchen led to the small yard area and garden, an outside toilet, a washing shed and an air raid shelter hugged the rear wall.

Upstairs brought its surprises too, there were two large bedrooms and a single room that was used by the post office mail supervisor someone called Edna Gray. It seemed that Edna worked permanent nights and when she was not on shift she went back to the valley village of Ystrad Mynach and stayed there with her elderly mother.

The room Ruth was to share with Mary was a nice size with two single beds against the walls and two wardrobes that were placed in such a way that they caused there to be some semblance of privacy between the two beds. In the corner of the room was a wash basin, a luxury that Ruth had never seen before and the wooden floor was covered by a series of small expensive looking oriental rugs. The window overlooked the main street and it was possible to see in the distance the cranes of Cardiff docks. Mary explained that the pub on the far corner, of the road, The Stevedores Arms was popular with the dock workers as it was the first of many on their walk back to the city and to their homes.

Ruth quickly unpacked and settled herself down on the bed as she listened intently to Mary outlining the strict rules that governed staff who worked in the general post office. Ruth was comfortable with the need for smartness and the need for hierarchical respect and saw sense in the rules about checking and double checking the identities of people who were from outside the Cardiff area who used the post office, these were post office rules and Ruth was both acquainted with them and a stickler for their enforcement

It surprised Ruth that this person who oozed deference in the office as though it was natural to her upbringing was so dismissive of it outside the office. Indeed, Ruth pondered that for all the fact that she was a valley girl she believed she had far more complementary standards to those expected by her new employer than did Mary. Mary then moved to explain the strict rules that governed life at home.

Ruth was not prepared for what Mary was to explain and the fact that it was couched in such a matter of fact way. Mary started by saying, "My Dad left my Mam about ten years ago and if he ever shows his cheating face around here again, neither of us would welcome him back." She went on to say that her mother worked as a weighbridge clerk in the docks from eight o'clock to five o'clock Monday to Friday a job she had done for more than ten years. Then came the bombshell, "My Mam likes to entertain her men friends some nights so we have to be in our room by ten o'clock, especially on Friday" she said. Now Ruth might be from the valleys, and she might be seen to be unsophisticated and unworldly but it took her no time whatsoever to put two and two together and end up with rather more questions than answers.

Ruth quickly settled into the routine of work and far from finding the post office rules overbearing she embraced them. The routine and the rules complemented the sets of values she had grown up with and she found that she was soon identified as a model worker. Ruth revelled in the increasing responsibility she was given over time and yet she never invited any attention and nor was she regarded as in any way being pushy.

The routine at her new home in Splott was rather less predictable. But, over time Ruth built a deep friendship with Mary who was increasingly like a big sister to her, though their age difference was hardly noticeable. It was also the case that despite Mrs Morgan's, or perhaps because of Mrs Morgan's eccentricity and open, transparent attitude to life and relationships, Ruth enjoyed her company too and her thoroughly outrageous lifestyle.

Ruth also settled into the routine of travelling home early on Saturday afternoon and returning to Cardiff on the last bus from Senghenydd on a Sunday afternoon. She had also befriended the children who lived next door to her in Splott where she would spend many happy hours.

These children, Megan a beautiful and bright nine year old and Reece an equally beautiful but impish six year old enjoyed Ruth's company and would look forward to evenings when she would stay with them whilst their mother was working. Ruth would read to the children but what they enjoyed the most were her own stories. These were sometimes of her own creation but many were about the characters and the comings and goings in the village of Senghenydd, many learnt at the knee of Auntie Lott or Uncle Arthur. Ruth's ease with children was often spoken about and she would blush when mothers remarked that one day she would make a wonderful mother herself.

Despite her responsible job in Cardiff and her continued contribution to the family income Ruth remained a child in the eyes of her father whose strict Victorian rules and attitudes saw him interrogate Ruth each weekend about what she was doing outside work and who she was seeing in Cardiff. If only he knew the liberating and exciting world she occupied from Monday to Saturday he would surely bring it to a halt.

As the Christmas of nineteen forty fast approached, the post office did what it could to bring the festive season into the otherwise austere world of Cardiff more than a year into an increasingly bloody war both on the battle fields of Europe and in the major cities of the United Kingdom. Even Cardiff had experienced bombing but not nearly on the scale of places like London, Birmingham, Liverpool and Swansea.

There was little appetite for Christmas festivity amongst staff and customers who daily would bring stories into the post office of family members or loved ones dying in far off lands or in the blitz that was wreaking havoc and death here at home. Nonetheless, the staff decided to bring some joy to the banking hall and over the two weeks leading up to Christmas they made daisy chain decorations and with little more than a few sheets of crepe paper, Ruth and her work colleagues managed to festoon their counters with festive trimmings.

A Christmas tree was placed in the entrance hall and staff managed to dress it with what few baubles and tinsel could be found. The place looked bright and cheery for customers many of whom hurriedly sought to beat the British Forces deadline date for parcels to be sent to family members on the front line overseas. As Christmas week approached staff exchanged small Christmas gifts and managers took the extra time to personally thank staff for their dedication and commitment over the year.

At Ruth's Splott home Mrs Morgan decided that as a Christmas treat, Mary and Ruth deserved a night out with her at the Merchant Navy Officers Club in the dock area, a regular and favoured haunt of hers for many years. And so with only two days to go before Christmas the three ladies, dressed in their finest set off into the blackout with torches in hand to visit Cardiff docks and into Mrs Morgan's nocturnal world.

As they settled into the smoke filled club, Ruth was awe struck to find that this was a world filled with handsome young officers dressed in their magnificent uniforms all clearly with an eye for the ladies. She could overhear their stories of exotic places on the other side of the world and their encounters when being escorted through the dangerous shipping lanes by the Royal Navy.

The club was filled with the blue grey haze of cigarette smoke and the strong smell of beer and spirits and in the dimmed light Ruth could see a smattering of ladies who Mary described in a nonchalant manner as, "liberal minded" who wanted a "good time with these brave young fellas." Ruth scanned the large bar area and observed dozens of uniformed men all who seemed incapable of any kind of coherent conversation in the company of the bevy of beautiful young ladies.

With hardly a moment's thought for Mary and Ruth, Mrs Morgan slipped away with someone who was later identified as the captain to "inspect his ship" only to return an hour or so later looking almost as chirpy as the captain.

Mary and Ruth struck up the occasional conversation with those young men who tried to enter their company but Mary was adept at seeing them off with a whisper in their ear that resulted in the strangest look at both of them before they went on their way.

Ruth and Mary were much more preoccupied by the comings and goings of the ladies and their officer friends. Ruth pressed Mary about her mother: "You have mentioned your mother's men friends" she said, "But tell me more" giggled Ruth anxious not to leave this place without a feel for why Mrs Morgan loved it so much. And in that matter of fact way that Ruth had become accustomed to and valued, Mary simply said, "she has a lot of men friends who always want to see her when they are in port and what she gets up to is up to her." Mary paused and ended by saying, "I wouldn't want that kind of life or those kinds of relationships but Mam has had to do whatever was necessary to have the life she wanted" She went on, "My Gran was the same and so we just don't talk about it."

As Ruth and Mary sat drinking their lemonade they talked a lot about men and relationships and concluded that men only want one thing and neither of them was inclined to give it to them. Whilst not being at all interested by the constant attention of the men in the bar, they were both fascinated by the way that some of the women seemed to move from one man to another leaving Mary to simply say, "They're going to be exhausted by the time they get home tonight."

Ruth travelled home to Senghenydd on the afternoon of Christmas Eve carrying gifts for her family bought from the few shillings she had managed to save over the past few weeks. She also carried a bag containing a selection of rationed items given to her by Mrs Morgan crammed with some of the gifts given to her by her men friends.

The bag contained a bar of chocolate, twenty American cigarettes, a Cuban cigar, two pairs of stockings, Dutch cheese, a salami sausage, six eggs, and half a pound of bacon and half a pound of butter. As Mrs Morgan gave the parcel to Ruth she said, "This is for you and your Mam and Dad from me for being such a good girl." And with a glint in her eye she whispered, "And there are to be no question asked"! Ruth felt slightly uncomfortable about carrying what were clearly black market goods but knew that her Mother would be thrilled, as indeed she was.

Christmas was an enjoyable time, as it gave Ruth an opportunity to be with her family and to see friends who she had not seen for some months since starting work in Cardiff. She called in to see Auntie Lott and Uncle Arthur and was delighted to see that Dai was home. Ruth had grown up in the company of Dai and she loved his stories of where he had been and what he was doing.

All too soon Ruth was back into Cardiff to work the few days between Christmas and New Year as part of a skeleton staff. It was decided that as New Year's Day fell on the Wednesday, and Ruth would have to be back in the post office on the Thursday, she should stay in Cardiff rather than go home to Senghenydd.

Having worked through to six o'clock on New Year's Eve Ruth took some persuading by Mary that they should stay up until midnight but they did. She loved the sense of naughtiness and the feeling that this is what adults do. Not surprisingly, Mrs Morgan was at the Merchant Navy Officers Club and so at a few minutes to midnight Ruth and Mary ran out into the darkened street to join neighbours and passersby in cheering in the New Year much to the annoyance of the ARP who reminded everyone that there was a war on and that they should observe the blackout.

Despite earlier apprehension Ruth was overjoyed to be able to say that she had seen in the year of nineteen forty one a New Year of hope for everyone. How short that celebration would be and how rapidly the tears of happiness would be replaced by tears of grief and despair.

CHAPTER FOUR

It was the second of January and having worked all day
Ruth and Mary, wearily walked arm in arm on their
short stroll from the post office to Splott in the cold
evening air of winter. They were a matter of a minute or
two from their home at about six thirty when the air raid
sirens wailed their eerie tone across the city. First one
could be heard then another, then more. Ruth looked to
Mary and in an instance they knew to run the few yards
home. On entering from the rear gate they rushed
immediately to their air raid shelter at the bottom of the
garden.

Mary dashed into the house and collected the paraffin
lamp that was always kept by the back door. She also
grabbed the blankets that were kept in the same place
and a loaf of bread from the kitchen. Mary had hardly
reached the shelter when the sound of bombs exploding
could be heard in the general direction of Grangetown
and Adamsdown. They could by now hear the crack,
crack, crack of the anti aircraft guns as searchlights
combed the night sky for German aircraft.

The girls grabbed each other as the sound of more
explosions could be heard and they knew instinctively
that this was going to be bad. They closed the door of the
shelter and threw themselves to the floor as explosion
after explosion could be heard nearby. Still more
terrifying blasts could be heard as the relentless

explosion of bombs shook the ground. In tears and screaming the girls grabbed each other and shook with fear.

They had spent many nights in the shelter in the past and had experienced the fear of bombing before, but nothing they had been through was as intense as this. As more bombs rained down upon Cardiff and the docks area, it became clear that the shards of light they could see piercing the holes in the door were not just searchlights but they were also the flames from intense fires burning some distance away. The bombing continued for some time before it abruptly ended.

After about ten minutes of silence they heard the sounds of neighbours shouting and screaming. Not waiting for the *all clear* they stumbled out of the shelter and stood awe struck by what they saw. There were fires raging across the whole horizon in the direction of Whitchurch, Canton and Adamsdown all areas of Cardiff close to Splott and very near to Cardiff docks. Before long people were relaying stories that Llandaff Cathederal was alight and that Llandaff Village had also been hit.

As the few minutes passed by it became clear to Ruth that she could not stand there and do nothing. She quickly asked a few of the neighbours if they were willing to go to Adamsdown to see if they could help. Mary and three other women were instant volunteers and within minutes those who could not go were offering blankets, sheets for bandages and thermos flasks of hot tea.

Ruth and her group of ladies ran as quickly as they could in the general direction of the flames and as they came closer the full horror of what they had heard and seen from a distance confronted them. They saw the full impact that the bombings had visited upon these streets and homes. Houses were alight, many were mere heaps of rubble still more had the whole front blown out and family possessions were eerily visible in the bedrooms that were now torn apart.

There were many injured and frightened people in the street, some walking aimlessly in circles still dazed by the sheer ferocity and devastation of the bombing others were too injured to move, others were clearly dead. Ruth saw a police officer and explained that she and other volunteers were here to help. They were immediately dispatched to the corner of a street where a temporary refuge centre was being established to help cope with the many confused, frightened and very distressed women and children who were in deep shock.

Ruth soon realised that unless these good people were wrapped up warm, very quickly many could perish on this bitter cold night. As Ruth organised her band of helpers to assist this group, she was drawn towards a makeshift medical area a few yards away that was acting as a holding location for people who needed hospital treatment and who would need to wait until an ambulance arrived to transport them. Men were clearing rubble from the streets to provide access to ambulances and the fire engines. It was already evident that in the absence of ambulances, any available vehicle was being commandeered to rush these dreadfully injured people to the care of doctors and nurses in the nearby hospital.

Ruth recognised one of the people giving assistance as a customer from the post office and knew that he was a local family doctor. She asked if there was any help she could give and, looking deep into Ruth's eyes, he explained that many here would die before they reached hospital, and that all she and others could do was to make them comfortable before their inevitable demise. He warned that what she would see would be shocking and distressing and asked her to be certain before she offered her help.

Ruth was drawn to a woman whose injuries were repulsively shocking, she was very badly burnt and it was clear that she had face and head injuries. The woman was laying on the pavement, dust and rubble around her. Ruth knew she was going to die alone if she didn't face the horror and bring some care and comfort quickly.

Ruth knelt beside this poor wreck of humanity and slowly moved her burnt head into her own lap and gently placed the woman's hand in hers. In the flickering light of the fires Ruth looked into the face of this young woman and, as her mother would do for her when she was in pain, she gently stroked her face and quietly sang the only hymn that came into her head which was the twenty third Psalm: As she sung these poignant words so others knelt beside the two of them and joined Ruth:

The Lord's my Shepherd, I'll not want.
He makes me down to lie
In pastures green; He leadeth me
The quiet waters by.

My soul He doth restore again;
And me to walk doth make
Within the paths of righteousness,
Even for His own Name's sake.

Yea, though I walk in death's dark vale,
Yet will I fear none ill;
For Thou art with me; and Thy rod
And staff me comfort still.

My table Thou hast furnished
In presence of my foes;
My head Thou dost with oil anoint,
And my cup overflows.

Goodness and mercy all my life
Shall surely follow me;
And in God's house forevermore
My dwelling place shall be.

There they stayed until, sometime later the doctor came over to Ruth and with an experienced compassion he gently closed the woman's eyes and softly said to Ruth, "This night I have seen the very worst and the very best that mankind can do one to another." He looked back at Ruth and said, "Your kindness and your compassion has meant that these victims of war didn't face their maker without firstly looking into the eyes of kindness, you are a brave young soul and I will not forget what you have done here tonight." With that the kind doctor moved on. Ruth moved from one person to another, some who would not survive and others that simply needed a caring word to see them through this terrible, terrible night.

Some hours later Ruth met with her friends and they slowly and in silence walked back to their homes each with their own mental pictures of what they had seen. It was many more hours before the full extent of what had happened began to unfold as it became clear that dozens of people had been killed and many more were injured. People who were running from the general direction of the fires brought with them terrible tales of destruction and death. Neighbours were calling out to passersby to ask if they had seen their loved ones. Then suddenly Mary realised that there was no sign of her mother.

It was by now gone ten o'clock and Mary was becoming increasingly concerned. One neighbour said they had seen Mrs Morgan in Grangetown and another said she was definitely at the docks. The confusion was soon resolved when a dishevelled smoke covered Mrs Morgan was brought to the house by a police constable declaring her to be the heroine of the hour for personally dragging several people from a burning house in Grangetown, returning several times before she was satisfied that all the residents had been evacuated.

The all clear siren did not sound in the Cardiff area until just before five o'clock in the morning and perhaps it was only then that this small group of people realised the real danger they had put themselves in to try to help the dead and the dying. The following days were to reveal that more than one hundred and sixty people perished and several hundred more were seriously injured many with hideous burns.

The scars from what Ruth had seen were deep. Whilst the sense of duty in Ruth saw her return to work the following day, she became increasingly frightened by the prospect of further bombing raids. She shared none of her deep anxiety with her mother though it was clear that her mother and father were worried about the impact this incident had on Ruth and the prospect of further bombing raids on Cardiff which was an important strategic port for munitions for the war and food for the nation.

It was not long before Cardiff once again was the target of the Luftwaffe. On the tenth of January further air raids shook Cardiff and this continued through February and into March. Perhaps it was the bombing raids of twelfth of March that sealed Ruth's fate with her parents. Once again these raids took many lives and became the major talking point in the valleys as they absorbed news that not only Cardiff but the relatively nearby centres of Swansea, Bridgend and Newport were also the target of these and other bombing raids in recent times.

The talk in the valleys was of these towns resembling the London blitz which was an exaggeration in terms of scale but none the less valid for the devastation caused to civic buildings, peoples' homes and the disruption to public services.

CHAPTER FIVE

It was by now the summer of nineteen forty one and it was increasingly clear that Britain needed more aircraft and that even more women would be required to replace men in the factories to produce them. Ruth and her parents were by now in full agreement that every day Ruth worked in Cardiff, she needlessly put her young life at risk and that if she really wanted to do her bit for the war effort she could do it in another and safer way.

The decision that Ruth should be moved to Blackpool was brought about because her cousin Moira lived there and she had suggested that Ruth live with her and take a job in the aircraft factory at Squires Gate aerodrome where she worked.

Moira was the daughter of Ruth's uncle Fred, her father's brother. Moira and her husband Jack moved to Blackpool in the early nineteen thirties when Jack became a bus driver for the Blackpool Corporation. Moira was thirty nine and married Jack who was fifteen years her senior when she was just twenty two. Because they had no children they were fortunate to be able to rent a small terraced house in a pleasant leafy street about two minutes walk from Blackpool sea front.

Arrangements were reached for Ruth to go to Blackpool and it was with great sadness that Ruth said goodbye to her friends and colleagues at work. Ruth was already regarded as something of a hero in the post office but there was considerable regard for her decision to move to Blackpool to work in a factory. Her bosses regarded the move as not surprising but also a great loss to the post office.

But Ruth's saddest goodbyes were for her dear friend Mary and her enigmatic, flamboyant and deeply lovable mother, Mrs Morgan. Having said goodbye to Mrs Morgan in the house, Mary took Ruth to the door. She drew Ruth close to her and held her as though this might be the last time they ever met. Mary squeezed Ruth's hand and said in whispered tones, "You have always loved me and have never questioned why I'm different to other girls and I love you for this." With that she dashed back into the house in floods of tears. Ruth mused what Mary might have meant by her comments but simply put it down to the emotions of the moment.

Ruth had only met Jack and Moira once and that was some years ago when they paid a visit to Senghenydd, and so it was with some apprehension that she boarded the train in Cardiff with the promise that they would meet her several hours later in Blackpool.

The parting from her mother on that late September day, only a month after her eighteenth birthday was a painfully sad moment for the young Ruth. Her mother was by now her closest friend and confidant and had seen her through the devastating experiences of the bombings in Cardiff and what she had seen.

Ruth had already said a tearful goodbye to her brothers and sisters before boarding the bus with her mother to take the journey from Senghenydd to Cardiff. Her father's parting comments were as always short, calculated and on this occasion insightful: "Don't enter this village again if you disgrace yourself, don't bring shame on this family, and don't ask for my help if you do – you'll be on your own......"

As Ruth said goodbye to her mother on the platform of Cardiff railway station, she cried uncontrollably. Today, with so many young men saying tearful goodbyes to their families Ruth felt as though she too was destined for far off shores... perhaps never to return.

The train journey out of Wales to the north of England in carriages filled with young men moving to regiments and air fields throughout the country failed to make an historic impact upon Ruth, whose thoughts were of her new life in Blackpool and her family now miles away in Wales. What did make an impact though, was the way in which these, for the most part young men, were looking at her.

It became clear to the young Ruth that she was the topic of conversation amongst those sitting in the cramped compartment with her and those crowding the narrow corridor outside. For Ruth, this was an exciting but slightly uncomfortable experience as she became aware that her every move and gesture was being observed and commented upon by these noisy and excited young men around her. She crossed her legs and they noticed, if she ran her slim fingers through her long black hair their eyes would followed. There was no movement or gesture that was not noticed and commented upon in whispers.

Ruth began to see herself in a quite different light; if she could captivate these young strangers with the very slightest movements of her body she knew that her own sense of her attractiveness was confirmed. She spent the next few hours brazenly teasing these young men and she loved it. Two or three of these self conscious young men attempted to strike up a conversation with her but their blushes and the teasing of their friends limited the discourse to pleasantries such as the weather and their respective destinations.

Ruth reached Preston railway station where she needed to change trains for Blackpool tired and emotional. Suddenly a wave of anxiety and panic washed over her as she left the carriage and realised she was alone in a completely strange place needing to rely entirely upon her own decisions. She had no perception of time except that it was already late afternoon, she was hot thirsty and hungry and by now she needed to find a lavatory. She searched desperately for the station clock and for signs for the toilet. The platform was crowded; people pushed to leave the platform and jostled with others looking to board departing trains. Ruth's senses were bombarded by the noise from the people who surrounded her and from the smell and taste of steam and fumes emitted from the many trains entering and leaving this busy station.

A soft voice from behind her penetrated her consciousness as she began to realise that the calls of "are you all reet luve" were directed towards her. The voice with its strong Lancashire brogue was that of a lively woman in uniform. "Yer lost luve aren't you and the way yer dancing says yer bustin for a wee." The woman a chirpy slightly rotund sixty odd year old had a WRVS band around her arm and was busily directing soldiers to transport trains on various platforms with the ease and charm of a dear friend or family member.

The woman took Ruth to a ladies lavatory that was by now crowded and as Ruth entered the queue the lady pointed her to the platform where the Blackpool train was due to depart from. However, Ruth was advised that there would be a bus taking her from Preston to Blackpool because Blackpool Central station was closed.

It was only later that Ruth realised that the reason for its closure was that only a few weeks earlier on the twenty seventh of August, whilst on a training flight two aircraft had crashed in mid air only a few hundred yards from the thousands of holiday makers who had been enjoying the summer sunshine and 'free air show'. One of the aircraft a twin-engine Blackburn Botha operated by Coastal Command crashed through the roof of the entrance hall of the Central Station, showering aviation fuel over the platforms which started a massive fire. The other aircraft involved in the tragic accident was an RAF Defiant. Over the course of that day and the coming weeks, sixteen people would die from that accident, more than would die in all the enemy air raids on Blackpool and the Fylde Coast during the entire war!

On arrival in Blackpool, Ruth eagerly sought out a friendly if unfamiliar face on the platform which she might connect with that somewhat distant memory of her cousin Moira who was to meet her. For Moira, Ruth was an easily recognisable figure in the crowd. She was dressed in a short slightly shabby coat over a smart floral summer dress drawn tightly in the middle and wearing old but clean simple flat shoes that had seen many summers and crisp, white ankle socks.

Ruth looked tired as she walked from the platform carrying her small brown suit case with its reinforced corners which had seen little or no wear, a dainty little white hand bag and a brown package tied with string. She looked like a character from Dickens, a sad even pitiful sight with a little girl lost face and a vulnerability which belied her age and her own growing sense of confidence and independence.

Moira was emotional as she ran quickly to rescue this sad and lonely young woman. She reached Ruth and without a word said she threw her arms around her and kissed her sad tear moistened face. Ruth was the first to speak as she handed the brown paper parcel to her cousin and told her with that distinctive valley accent that it was a gift of Welsh cakes from "Mam." As Moira took the parcel and again drew Ruth into her arms Ruth reflected that this must be a good woman. She felt love and she felt safe.

Their journey from the crowded station to her new home took her quickly from the busy terraced side streets with their gaily painted guest houses displaying 'vacancy' or 'rooms to let' and 'no children' signs in the windows to the open promenade and Ruth's first ever view of the sea. Moira pointed out that whilst the warmth of the summer breeze was pleasant, the winter would bring bitter cold and penetrating south westerly winds that could blow you off your feet. Ruth pleaded with her cousin to be allowed to cross to the seaward side of the promenade and as they did she had her first view of the vast expanse of flat beach that in happier times would have been filled with even more holiday makers from the cities of Scotland and the north of England.

Ruth was taken to a smart tree lined side street with semi-detached red bricked houses and was ushered through a small wooden gate to the front door of twenty three Apple Tree Crescent. She was whisked into the house and immediately shown up the stairs and into a small bedroom. Moira stood at the door to the room and said, "Ruth this is your room." Ruth looked into the simple room and without warning broke down into uncontrollable floods of tears: she was inconsolable. Moira had never seen such sobbing, Ruth could not be consoled no matter how much Moira tried. Her whole body shook and as each convulsion of sobbing eased it was followed by an equally powerful further eruption.

Initially Moira thought that Ruth didn't like the room or perhaps she didn't like her, but she quickly began to realise that this small room, a room they had otherwise called the box room, would for Ruth be the first private sleeping space she had occupied in her eighteen years. Moira held Ruth tightly and slowly pointed out the tiny wardrobe with its full length mirror and the small but matching dressing table with an oval mirror, and the hand crocheted centre piece and the several glass jars and dishes.

Moira, as much to break the sequence of sobbing joked that whilst the room was not large enough to swing a cat she had better not try it with Rosie the family pet. With that a large black cat strolled into the room and with a graceful leap dropped onto the bed and lay down stretching and purring, and gently nuzzling Ruth to stroke her. Ruth immediately sat on the bed and stroked the much spoilt overweight cat and turning to face Moira said, "Do I really have this room to myself?"

Assured that the room was hers Ruth quickly set about unpacking and familiarising herself with the house. Upstairs there were two bedrooms a bathroom and the box room which was to be hers. She never really discovered why she had not been offered the second bedroom which was considerably larger than her room especially as Ruth was to discover that her cousin never entertained house guests and certainly never took in occasional lodgers. However Ruth liked the intimacy of her room and its window out onto the street.

As the house was positioned on the corner of the crescent she had a slightly obscured view to the left where there was a small shop towards the end of the road. To the right, between the roofs and trees she could just see Blackpool Tower as a silhouette against the evening skyline and could faintly hear the sound of the trams as they clattered along the sea front. There were no street lights and the nearby houses emitted no light because of the blackout but she could see children being chased by parents to come in from their play.

The family bathroom was small with oblong white tiles to about half way up the wall, and had a small bath sink and toilet. Ruth looked around the room and thought this was sheer luxury and quickly washed her face, brushed her hair and dashed down stairs to join Moira and her husband Jack, who had by now returned from work for supper. Downstairs there was a small hallway a front room for special occasions and the 'back room' which led onto the scullery.

The three of them sat down at the small kitchen table and ate a simple evening meal during which Moira talked excitedly about plans for the following day when Ruth would go with her to meet the foreman at the factory where she worked. She explained that the factory made parts for aircraft that were assembled locally for the war effort. Ruth was told that there was a job for her but she would need to demonstrate to the foreman that she could do simple measurements of small parts to confirm they were made to the exacting requirements of the manufacturing specifications.

Moira explained that the development of the aircraft industry in Blackpool dated back to the government's re-armament drive prior to the war when, in nineteen thirty six they announced a five-year program of constructing 'shadow' factories to boost the output of aircraft and aircraft engines .

Jack, who until now had remained fairly quiet, explained, "Although these factories were established by the government they are operated by large companies and have been established across the country, mainly in areas less vulnerable to potential air attack." Ruth listened intently enthralled by the closeness that she was getting to the real workings of the support effort for the war. Jack continued, "The Ministry of Aircraft Production 'shadow' aircraft factory at Squires Gate Aerodrome, here in Blackpool, together with a satellite assembly line at Stanley Park Aerodrome is managed by the Vickers-Armstrong company who will be your employer."

Moira explained that Vickers employed thousands of people many of them women and that they were building Wellington bombers. As always, when speaking of such things, Moira ended by lowering her voice and repeating the government's mantra of *keep it under your hat* and *careless talk costs lives*. Much of this went completely over Ruth's head as a mixture of tiredness, excitement and some trepidation led her to ask if she could go to bed.

Ruth slept well but was nonetheless shocked to be woken and told the time was five o'clock and that they needed to be out of the house by a quarter to six. Moira gave Ruth a dark blue overall and light blue shirt to wear and told her to put her hair into a head scarf which must enclose all her hair. When she eventually emerged for breakfast it was clear that Ruth had never seen hair drawn into a headscarf in the way Lancashire ladies have done for years.

With a little help from Moira, Ruth eventually was able to master the wrap and knot and she felt rather good that she had been able to transform herself into a factory girl. What a contrast this was to the neat attire she was expected to wear in the post office and how liberating it felt to wear the dungarees rather than a skirt.

On arrival at the factory, Moira took Ruth to the clocking on station which was located just inside the factory gates, alongside the security office and showed her where her card could be found if she was employed and how to drop the card into the machine and clock on. 'Clocking on' was loathed by all workers at the factory. It was seen as a cynical way in which bosses could cut wages for what were seen as minor infringements such as being a minute or two late for work. Workers at the factory were astute and when the supervisor was not stood by the clocking on station they would clock on their friends who they knew would be late.

Ruth was quickly taken through the noisy factory area past rows of whistling lathes up some stairs that led into the foreman's office. His office had a commanding view over the factory floor and Ruth couldn't help noticing the blaring sound of music being played over the Tanoy speaker system. The noise and industry of this place only served to amplify the extreme contrast to the silence she had been used to working in during her short time in the Cardiff post office.

Moira introduced Ruth to the foreman and was quickly dismissed to get on with her work. The foreman, a short balding man eventually swivelled around from a large drawing board and without getting off his raised chair he slowly inspected Ruth from head to toe. Throughout the inspection not a word was spoken until eventually he signalled for her to come to the table. There he picked up a small aluminium machine part and pointed to a drawing. Over the course of the next hour, he showed Ruth how to read measurements from the drawing and using a precision micrometer to check that the machine part conformed within prescribed tolerances shown in the drawing.

Once this was over, the foreman confirmed that Ruth could be employed and would be working in a shift group of thirty, mainly women on a three shift, five day rota of six in the morning to two o'clock in the afternoon, two o'clock to ten in the evening and ten in the evening to six in the morning. Each shift would be for a period of two weeks but always working with the same people.

Ruth was taken aback; she never thought that she would ever work night shifts. However, she was pleased to be able to do her bit and also pleased that at eighteen years of age, she was to be taking on what was clearly an important task in the assembly of aircraft. She reflected back to Moira that the foreman had said it was only because of her developed numeracy skills and her ruthless commitment to accuracy that she was being given this job and that she should realise that many of the people she would be working with were innumerate and made many silly mistakes.

CHAPTER SIX

Ruth quickly settled into the work at the factory and the confidence placed in her by the foreman was clearly not misplaced. She had not realised until the end of the first week when she received her wage packet that her position was officially that of 'trainee machine parts inspector'. Ruth established herself as a tactful and personable individual within the shift and struck up several new friendships. She also realised that many of the small, irritating measurement errors she was detecting were both costly and time consuming and set back production.

Ruth suggested to her foreman that far too many of the machinists where having problems translating measurements from the drawings often because they could not visualise the part they were making. Based in part on her recommendation, the shift foreman established a routine whereby at the start of each shift, each machine would be calibrated for the machine parts that were to be made and where a part required several different sizes to be machined, rather than transferring a measurement from a drawing to a machine setting the machinist would have one completed part placed alongside the machine that could be used as a template reference. This simple adjustment saved thousands of hours and reduced wastage to a minimum. It also did a great deal for the self confidence of the people on the lathes and further endeared Ruth to the work group.

What Ruth didn't adjust to nearly as well was the three shift pattern. The six to two and the two to ten shift were fine and indeed they offered Ruth the opportunity to spend time in Blackpool often at less crowded times. However the ten to six shifts took Ruth many nights to adjust to. She would find it difficult to get to sleep in the day time and by the time she had done so, she invariably found it was time to get up for work. Equally, she found that readjustment to picking up the following six to two shift very difficult. But having worked the shift pattern for some months, like others she settled into a routine.

Another routine for Ruth was to write once each week to her brother Michael who was by now serving in the Royal Army Medical Corps in Singapore and to her mother back in Senghenydd. These letters were important links for Ruth back to Michael who she loved dearly and to her family in south Wales. The letters from Michael were infrequent and had the nature of never flowing from one to the other because letters frequently were lost or delayed and so each letter had a familiar tone: From Ruth, they spoke of happy things and happy times and from Michael, they moved from his love of the army, a boyhood ambition, to a man concerned for the direction of the war, concerns that were always in coded, guarded language but sufficient for Ruth to note that he was afraid.

Her last letter from Michael had a dark and sad tone to it with Michael speaking of his concern about the Japanese potential to move south, through Malaya to Singapore. His words were considered and deep as he spoke of his love of life and his fears that the war was coming his way. That latest letter ended in the saddest of ways. He wrote: '*I am young but have seen many things in my life. I have known love in abundance from my family and especially from you my dear sister Ruth. I have seen the dawn in exotic places and I have experienced the beauty of this wonderful country and its hard working people. Ruth this may be the place where my war ends but if it is, you should know that I am happy for so many of the things I have seen*'. His letter closed with the following line: '*I miss the valleys of my beautiful Wales and the song of its people, I miss the sparrow and the black bird but I am a happy man, and if I should die here in this far off land, tell Mam ..... I saw swallows in February*'. Ruth wept as she read the letter knowing that his fears for the ambitions of the Japanese forces were well founded.

The letters to her mother also followed the same familiar structure: Ruth would start by answering the questions raised by her mother in the previous letter, questions that were beginning to have a familiar ring to them. Her mother could ask the same question in so many different ways and Ruth could herself answer them with the same opaqueness.

The questions would start simply enough, 'Are you eating enough, are you sleeping enough and how's the weather been?' Inevitably they would move to the vague: 'Are you able to get out much?' or 'What are your friends like?' and 'Have you met anyone nice this week?' They both knew that the central theme of the questions were the same, "Are you going out with a boy?", or 'Do you have a boy friend?' and if so 'What is he like?' The word game continued for months with neither party saying exactly what they thought.

The next part of the letters from Ruth's mother was taking on an increasingly open and adult theme as her mother opened up to Ruth about her father's moods, drunkenness and ill behaviour both in the home and at his place of work. Ruth would politely offer sympathy but recognised that in part these letters were cathartic and as such required no response.

Then a letter came in early December in which her mother confided that her father had been sacked by the colliery for his fighting at work and his ill tempered behaviour. The fights, of which this was only one of many, were always about the same thing, why he was not fighting on the front line as many other Irish men who had come to Wales had gone on to do for the British crown to which so many still felt loyalty, and why Ireland had remained steadfastly neutral. This fight however was one too many and as a result, Ruth's mother was confiding in Ruth that she felt the prospects of him getting work in Wales, or anywhere in England were poor. She went on to say that she feared that before many days passed they would be thrown out of their tied cottage. The strict rules set by the colliery company who owned the house were that you can live in it for as long as you are employed by the colliery.

The following two weeks of letters in the run up to Christmas revealed that a date had been set for the family to move out of the house. Without any job or prospects of getting one her mother wrote: '*It is increasingly likely that we will have to move back to County Roscommon in Ireland where the Arigna Coal Mine is eagerly looking for workers with experience of working in very narrow seams*'. Ruth knew that her father had this experience but she also knew of the dangers of working in such seams.

Ruth quickly wrote back to her mother and arranged that she would telephone Mrs Thomas at the Senghenydd post office at a pre arranged time so that they could speak. On the morning of Christmas Eve as arranged, Ruth went to Blackpool post office and made the telephone call to her mother. The conversation was short and emotionally charged as Ruth absorbed the news that her whole family; her mother father, brothers and sisters would indeed be moving to Ireland in one week's time.

Her mother begged Ruth not to succumb to the demands from her father that she must move back to Ireland with them. She explained that at best they would move into appallingly small tied accommodation and that the pay would be poor for her father given the circumstances of his dismissal and the requirement that he demonstrated good character or he would lose this job too. Her mother explained that Ruth should continue her job and make a success of herself but that she should at least promise to keep up the letters to her once they settle into Ireland.

Ruth rang her mother one more time to make final arrangements to meet her and the family at the ferry terminal in Heysham. Heysham was one of the few ports still running a regular service to Belfast whereas services to Dublin from England or Wales were curtailed or unreliable. Heysham was also convenient for Ruth as it was a very short distance up the coast from Blackpool.

Ruth arrived at the rail terminal in Heysham with little time to spare before her parents arrived to board the Duke of Lancaster which would take them to Belfast via the Isle of Man. The terminal was busy mainly with other Irish people either returning home or visiting loved ones in their mother country.

In the few moments Ruth was able to have alone with her mother, she confided in her that she had indeed met a man who she liked. Ruth explained that it was an acquaintance more than a boy friend and was complicated by the fact that this man, Edward Carmichael was with Sarah Prentice a girl who Ruth had met on a few occasions at Blackpool Pleasure Beach, Ice Drome.

Ruth tried to explain to her mother her feelings for someone who in truth she had only met a few times and had only spoken to twice and even then always in the company of Sarah. Ruth hurriedly explained that she knew nothing about Edward but that she was very attracted to him and that she saw some signs that he was also attracted to her.

Ruth's mother listened to the increasingly excitable Ruth and saw instantly that this was no mere acquaintance and nor was it a relationship that would ever be straight forward or easy. She counselled Ruth: "Go slowly, and be careful not to lose the friendship of Sarah by getting between her and someone who she is clearly in a relationship with." Their conversation continued until the arrival of her father and her brothers and sisters to say goodbye.

Ruth kissed her father on the cheek but few words were spoken. Perhaps he knew already that Ruth was aware of the circumstances of their hasty retreat from Wales. Or perhaps he realised that this composed, dispassionate young girl was now a woman and that she, like most women could see through him and through his feeble attempts to put a gloss on their move as being a move back to their homeland and "friendly people." Ruth kissed her siblings saying to each in whispered tones to "look after your mother and your mother will look after you."

Ruth's final farewell was to her mother. As she walked into her mother arms she felt the strangeness of the role reversal of a daughter gently comforting her mother. Tears were reserved for another day when each would reflect the chasm that would now separate the two of them. They clung to each other until they felt the vice like grip of her father's hands tearing them apart. And still they did not cry. Ruth felt a terrible sense of foreboding that however saddened she felt today it would be as nothing compared to what she would experience in the years to come.

Ruth saw in her mother's eyes a reflection of her own fears. As she turned towards the ferry Ruth's mother looked back and saw the long shadow her daughter's image cast in the evening sunlight and with a final smile she slipped into the darkness of the ferry terminal and out of Ruth's life.

Chapter Seven

Nineteen forty two started with the worst possible news. Ruth's mother wrote to her explaining that the army had written to say that on the fifteenth of February, Singapore had been overrun by the Japanese and that their son Michael was either a prisoner of war or missing presumed dead.

Ruth had been keeping up with what news there was from Singapore and was already aware that things were not good. By the time her mother's letter arrived towards the end of February, there were already stories that at the Alexandra Military Hospital in Singapore, Japanese soldiers had brutally murdered the patients they found there.

Ruth knew that Michael had been based there but this was in a much earlier letter and she hoped that he had moved on. Earlier stories of the battle of Jitra in Malaya in the December spoke of captured and wounded allied soldiers being killed where they lay. There was even a story that some captured Australian troops were doused with petrol and burned to death.

Ruth refused to concede that Michael might be dead, preferring to hold out the hope that he would eventually get a letter home to say he was well. Nonetheless, Ruth could not stop herself from looking to the skies as he might in Singapore to see if she too could see 'swallows in February'.

Throughout the year of nineteen forty two Ruth threw herself into the routine of work with a renewed vigour. She saw herself as needing to build a life for herself rather than simply doing a wartime job. This would entail being good at what she was doing and she determined that she would also live life to the full. She spent the spring and summer months in her routine of work shifts and wove around them hours spent with friends either on the beach or dancing.

Ruth also renewed an old friendship when Mary Morgan came to Blackpool for three days with her mother. They arrived on the Friday afternoon and arranged to stay at a small guest house just off the promenade. It was agreed that Ruth would meet Mrs Morgan and Mary on the Friday evening after they had eaten supper and show them a little of Blackpool.

It was not long before they were seated in the Tower Ballroom surrounded by servicemen eager to dance with all three of them. Mrs Morgan was more than happy to oblige leaving Ruth and Mary time to talk.

Ruth noticed that Mary was more insular less easy to talk to than previously but put this down to the time they had spent apart. They reminisced about the night of the bombing in Cardiff and this seemed to change Mary's mood as slowly they regained the intimacy they had enjoyed previously. Much of their talk was about old work colleagues at the post office and a couple of sad stories of husbands who had been killed in the line of service. Neither of them was particularly enjoying the ballroom and they agreed with Mrs Morgan that they would leave her there and return to the guest house.

As they walked arm in arm along the sea front Mary noticed a sign saying 'Palmist, have your fortune told here'. They giggled and eventually agreed that it would be fun to 'look into the future'. They went into a darkened area immediately inside the main doorway to where a man sat protectively at a small table. Seeing the girls approach he said that it would cost a six pence each to see *the gypsy* which they paid.

They were then ushered into the dimly lit area where the gypsy was sitting at a round table. As she looked up she beckoned them to sit and rather alarmingly her first words to the girls were, "I know that this is the first you have seen of each other for a very long while and I know that you both have much on your minds." Ruth and Mary looked at each other with surprise wondering how she could know this.

The gypsy then turned to Ruth and took her right hand in hers. She pondered this for some time, occasionally running a finger over her palm but mostly looking deep into Ruth's eyes. This was unnerving and Ruth was beginning to wonder if this had been a good idea. The gypsy then turned to Mary and again took her hand in hers. On this occasion, her concentration was much more focussed upon her palm with the occasional glance into her face.

Eventually, as the gypsy turned, she lifted her head and still holding Mary's hand said, "You must share your secret with only those you trust, and you know there will be some that will want to damn you. You are destined to know a kind of love that will always be questioned. You will live long but yours will be a barren journey through life. You will sing, and laughter will come to you eventually but you will also weep many tears." These words disturbed Mary who knew instantly what the gypsy was saying but she simply giggled and looked towards Ruth whose eyes were wide open with anticipation of what the gypsy would say to her.

The gypsy turned slowly to Ruth, but this time with a troubled face. "The gypsy speaks to many people but you are different" she said. "In your life you will have the blessing of many children but you will endure lifelong sadness." In hushed tones and with a great sense of foreboding she said, "Your name is Ruth ... and I can see the life you have yet to live. I warn you now that you will go through life seeing children in your shadow." She rose and gently touched Ruth's face with the back of her fingers before she said, "Ruth, you will walk many paths in your life but before the sun sets every day, you will see those children in your shadow."

Trembling, Ruth and Mary left the booth and ran nervously giggling out onto the sea front. But Ruth stopped abruptly asking Mary, "What did she mean by saying to me you will walk many paths in your life but before the sun sets every day you will see those children in your shadow?"

As Ruth asked the question so she could see that Mary was deeply upset. "It's only a bit of fun" Ruth said but Mary clearly saw it differently. They walked over to the seaward side of the promenade and down onto the beach where they dropped onto the soft dry sand. Mary turned to Ruth and said, "The gypsy said that I should share my secret and I want to share it with you. You are my best friend and the only person I can share this with."

Mary began slowly to tell Ruth that from the age of about twelve she knew that she was different from other girls and by the time she had reached the age of about sixteen she knew that she could not have any sort of physical relationship with boys. She said that she had managed to fool most people into believing that she had boyfriends but asked Ruth to consider how often she had seen her with a boy.

Mary went on to say that on occasions she would be in the company of girls when one of them would look at her in a certain way that made her tingle inside. At this point, Ruth began to fidget uncomfortably and picking up on this Mary said, "Ruth I'm not trying to tell you that I fancy you. You are my best friend, but there are occasions when I meet other girls that, well yes, I do fancy them."

Mary continued by explaining that Ruth was the only person in the world to know her secret with the exception of someone she met some months ago. She excitedly described a slightly older woman who shared common interests with her and someone that she felt an emotional attachment to and that this was a shared feeling.

Ruth felt out of her depth but offered Mary the assurance she needed that she neither shunned her because of her emerging sexuality and neither did it have any bearing on their relationship. Ruth could see that for Mary this was an important step in her life particularly as she regarded Ruth as her dearest friend. They rose to their feet and resumed their journey back to the guest house, arm in arm as usual.

Meanwhile, Mrs Morgan spent more time away from their guest house than in it. It transpired that on their first night, Mrs Morgan had spent the whole evening in the company of a rather dashing American officer who, though careful not to say too much was part of an advanced group who were setting up facilities for for American airmen who would transition through

Blackpool for flight training. Mrs Morgan was smitten and spent the whole of her time in Blackpool being 'entertained' by her mystery man

Neither Mary or Ruth met the man but on the few occasions when their paths crossed at the guest house, Mrs Morgan spoke only of 'Colonel Arthur Brockenbeck' who was fondly referred to by his United States Air Force flying nickname, Colonel *Hawkeye* Brockenbeck.

The three day holiday was all too soon over but Mary and Ruth resolved to continue their letter writing to each other with the hope that they might meet up again very soon. As they embraced before Mary and Mrs Morgan departed Mary whispered into Ruth's ear, "I love you as my best friend and I hope you find your Mr Right very soon."

CHAPTER EIGHT

Ruth spent the entire night of her nineteenth birthday with a party of friends on the beach chatting and singing wartime songs and occasionally dodging the police who were not in the least bit impressed by their high jinks.

Having fun was the intention of the many thousands of young people who like her worked in the factories around Blackpool. And having fun would not be difficult in Blackpool a town that seemed immune from the war with very few air raid warnings and even fewer actual bombings, indeed throughout the whole of the war only two bombs fell on Blackpool. It was discovered many years later that Blackpool was spared the Luftwaffe's bombings because Hitler wanted it as his personal playground after the war where he dreamed of his troops goose-stepping down the Golden Mile and unfurling the Swastika on top of Blackpool Tower

As the autumn gave way to winter the vibrancy of life in this seaside town was retained especially as it was home to thousands of military personnel here to do their basic flying training but also to make the most of the night life. Over the course of the war, almost three quarters of a million airmen would be given their initial training at the Winter Gardens by day whilst not interfering with the thirst for entertainment in this historic building by night.

Blackpool was also home to thousands of London based civil servants posted to this northern resort to continue their Whitehall work outside the by now blitzed London. The blackout was observed as strictly in Blackpool as it was anywhere else in Britain and rationing bit as deeply here as it did elsewhere. However, the only thing that wasn't rationed was entertainment. The night life was extensive; during the season there were shows on at all the major theatres and ballroom dancing took place in the Tower Ball Room, the Winter Gardens and in many of the larger hotels.

Ruth enjoyed dancing and would often go with friends from work to the Winter Gardens. She had no particular boy friend though she would occasionally see the same person more than once. Like many young, attractive girls in Blackpool the prospect of establishing any really meaningful relationship with young men was remote given that most people of her own age were simply in Blackpool for their basic training before being moved on to their regiments or squadrons. But for all of that, life was fun and Ruth was building life skills both at work and in her social life.

Ruth continued to go to the Blackpool Ice Drome and began to meet Sarah there at least twice per month. Sarah was the same age as Ruth, slim and very attractive. During one of their intimate conversations, Ruth learnt that Sarah was previously a trainee seamstress having worked from age fifteen to eighteen in a large department store in Preston which explained why, whenever they met, she was always exceptionally well dressed. Sarah went on to explain that she had recently begun to work for the English Electric factory on Strand Road in Preston a company that everyone locally knew as Dick Kerr's who were building Handley Page Hampden aircraft and the Halifax bombers.

Ruth liked Sarah but she was never sure if the feelings were returned. She had aloofness about her personality and she seemed uneasy in company; unable to hold a conversation especially when several others were in their company. Sarah liked to be noticed and had mannerisms that resembled those of a peacock, always needing to be seen, always strutting and always repairing her makeup to ensure she looked her best. She flirted and was skilled at getting the attention she seemed to crave. Nonetheless, in Sarah's less self centred moments she did have time for Ruth and there was always the prospect that Sarah would bring her friend Edward, who Ruth really rather cared for.

Ruth occasionally broached the subject of Edward and discovered from Sarah that their relationship had been going on for more than a year, beginning when Edward had been working at Dick Kerr's in Preston.

Ruth was curious about why Edward, a twenty two year old fit and healthy looking man was not serving on the front line. Sarah explained that all she knew about Edward was that he had served in the Merchant Navy as a wireless operator on the SS Malakand between April and September nineteen forty. The Malakand was a ship most people here in the north of England would remember at the time as the one that blew up in Liverpool docks.

On the worst night of the Liverpool Blitz, on the third of May nineteen forty one, the S.S. Malakand, loaded with over one thousand tons of shells and bombs, was destroyed. It was thought that a deflated barrage balloon fell onto her deck and burst into flames. Despite all attempts to put out the fire, the Malakand had to be abandoned. The resulting explosions from the ship completely destroyed the dock and it was said that parts of the ship were thrown up to two and a half miles away.

Sarah went on to explain to Ruth that Edward returned to his parents' home in Blackpool having left the ship and had since then worked at the Vickers Armstrong factory as an engineer working on the Wellington bombers. This intrigued Ruth because when she had in passing mentioned to Edward that she worked at Vickers, he had never once remarked upon the coincidence.

Sarah's final comments struck a chord with Ruth when she described Edward as a man of mystery, always guarded, never saying more than he needed particularly on the subject of his work and especially what he did outside work. Over the following weeks, Ruth continued her conversations with Sarah and probed to see if her relationship with Edward was one that might lead to marriage.

On most of the occasions when Ruth and Sarah met, Edward would be present and Ruth's fascination with 'are they aren't they' a couple continued. Ruth noticed that on the face of it they seemed close, they would kiss and make small talk and gave all the outward signs that they were in love. But Ruth also noticed that when Sarah was not present Edward paid considerable attention to her, flirting and often getting rather closer to her than she thought appropriate to someone that seemed on the verge of marriage.

On one occasion when Edward was not present, Sarah explained to Ruth that it seemed inevitable that Edward and she should marry. She said that they were deeply in love and had even discussed when a marriage should take place. Sarah explained that she was a Catholic and Edward was a Protestant and that unless Edward was prepared to convert to the Catholic faith there would be no marriage.

It seemed that Sarah was not simply a Catholic but a devout Catholic and could see no prospect for their relationship going further if Edward did not soon indicate his willingness to convert. Although Ruth too was Catholic she could not quite comprehend why one's faith should get in the way of true love.

Ruth was never quite sure after her conversations about Edward whether Sarah saw her as a friend or a possible rival. She therefore tried to arrange to see Sarah only when Edward was not present on the pretence that 'three's a crowd'. This cemented their relationship as friends and avoided the potential for embarrassment.

It still however remained that Ruth was intrigued by Edward, his flirtatious nature concealed in an overly secretive aloof personality. This did not stop Ruth from trying to find out where Edward worked on the Vickers site in part to satisfy her curiosity about what he did there that was so important and to also be in a position to engineer a chance meeting if she felt so inclined.

Ruth was not going to need to engineer such a meeting as without warning in the early February of nineteen forty three she was summoned to the senior foreman's office and there wearing a three-quarter length white inspector's coat and looking somewhat superior was Edward Carmichael. Neither acknowledged that they knew each other which was perhaps fortuitous when Ruth's foreman explained, "Mr Carmichael needs a trainee inspector in the aircraft assembly section and I have put forward your name as a very suitable candidate for Mr Carmichael."

Ruth's instinct was to grab this possible promotion with both hands, after all she had determined in her own plans that she would drive herself to achieve her full potential in this job and start to build a career for herself. But deep in the back of her consciousness there was an alarm bell tolling a warning to her that such a move could not have come about without strings being pulled. Was Edward playing games with her emotions as well as her job? Ruth agreed to go over to the assembly area right away with Edward and decide if she felt confident about taking on this new role.

Their walk to the assembly site took about fifteen minutes during which time Edward paid considerable attention to Ruth asking how she was enjoying her work and remarking that he had not seen her with Sarah in some months. They talked about everything except the new job and Sarah. Nonetheless, Ruth rather enjoyed the intimacy of a conversation with a man who had remembered their previous conversations and seemed to be showing genuine interest in her.

Eventually, Ruth mentioned that she would be seeing Sarah on Friday evening and questioned if he would be there. She knew very well that her arrangement with Sarah was that they would meet only when she was not seeing Edward but she was curious to hear what Edward would say. He paused before answering and then with a hang dog look on his face he said that he and Sarah had rowed and things looked bad between them. Ruth didn't press him any further on the matter and quickly changed the subject back to work.

They arrived in a massive aircraft hanger and Ruth was stopped in her tracks by the sight she saw before her. There, in an almost fully assembled state was a Wellington Bomber and behind that were others each apparently on the verge of completion. On the fuselage and the wings of the aircraft and on the floor space below it were dozens of men and women testing or assembling essential elements of an aircraft that would be used in Britain's defence of its nation and to prosecute the war deep inside Nazi territory.

The trainee inspector role, grand as the title might seem was one of many similar roles deployed in the testing of the components and then the assembly of those components onto cockpit panels for installation by others into the aircraft. Ruth's role was to be in the instruments section where each of the vital aircraft operational, navigation and radio instruments were tested before being released for installation on the aircraft. Ruth was told she would work for the team of instrument inspectors and would initially be supervised to test and calibrate instruments in a room euphemistically called *the cockpit*.

The people in the room were an even mixture of older men and younger women who seemed genuinely welcoming towards Ruth, each explaining what they did and each encouraging her to accept the post. There was an added attraction, with the exception of the rarest of occasions the job was five and a half days per week starting at eight o'clock and finishing at five. It was also a *white coat* job which meant that Ruth would be able to set aside the less than flattering dungarees and head scarf and would be able to wear a skirt or dress again.

As Ruth moved around the 'cockpit' she established that Edward was the inspector for all radio equipment and worked with a small team in an adjacent room. Little more was known about their work or Edward. Once again Ruth detected the air of uncertainty and mystery about Edward that was coming from his work colleagues. None seemed to know him but all knew of him and with some sense of respect they acknowledged his position and his expertise. None of this explained why what he did could not be done by an older person or indeed by a woman!

Ruth accepted the job and was told to report to the cockpit on the following Monday morning. This meant that the agreed Friday evening meeting with Sarah would take on a special air of importance, as it did.

The arrangement was that Ruth and Sarah would meet outside the Tower Ballroom where they had agreed to spend the evening dancing. They settled down in a corner of the ballroom that was quiet, once they had skilfully warded off the attention of several Polish Airmen who were part of the massive contingent based here in Blackpool for RAF training,

Ruth soon moved on to the subject of Edward. She chose to open their conversation by mentioning that she would be starting a new job on Monday in a section that was nearby to where Edward worked. Ruth excitedly talked about the end of shift working and the few extra shillings she would have in her purse each week.

She then asked Sarah about how she and Edward were getting on and to Ruth's surprise Sarah began crying. She said nothing and after a moment Sarah said she was going to the lavatory to repair her makeup and could they go somewhere a little quieter when she returned. Sarah returned once again transformed into the glamorous, composed woman of old. Her makeup was impeccable and there was not a trace of the tear stained face save for the swollen eyes that no makeup could repair.

They left the Tower and walked in the moonlight along the promenade. This late February evening was cool but pleasant and apart from the occasional group passing by and the clanking sound of the trams they were alone on the vast expanse of the Golden Mile. After a while of walking arm in arm they stopped at a brightly coloured cafe stall where they bought a cup of tea and sat in the dark on a bench looking out over the beach and listened to the calm melodic sound of the incoming tide.

Eventually Sarah broke the silence and explained that she and Edward had met the previous week and that the subject of their proposed marriage had once again been discussed. Sarah explained that by now it was clear that both of them wanted to get married, they loved each other deeply and that the only stumbling block was whether Edward would convert to the Catholic faith in order that they could have the Catholic wedding and the Catholic life after that wedding which was so important to Sarah.

Sarah stumbled over her words as she explained that Edward had given her an ultimatum. Sarah could hardy form the words as she explained, "He was sharp with me and said that I should put aside my foolish notion that he would ever convert to Catholicism or there would be no marriage." Ruth asked what Sarah's response had been and in sombre tone she said that she had told Edward there was no way that their relationship could go any further if he was not prepared to make this sacrifice for her.

At that point Sarah turned to Ruth and asked, "You are Catholic; if Edward were to ask you to marry him you would do the same wouldn't you?" Ruth took a moment to reply, pondering as she did the prospect of Edward ever asking for her hand in marriage. She also knew that her response would be an immediate no strings attached "yes."

Setting aside her foolish day dreams Ruth suggested to Sarah that there were as always two sides to the issue and that Sarah should consider whether she was prepared to lose the only man she had ever loved for the sake of her faith. In a zealot like response Sarah retorted, "To forsake my faith is inconceivable and I would rather go to my grave a single and celibate woman than give up my faith for this or any man who would ask me to do so." Ruth knew that unless there was a massive change of heart on Edward's part Sarah's position was firm and final.

As Sarah and Ruth went their separate ways home Ruth reflected upon the 'coincidence' of the meeting with Edward earlier in the week and whether she should draw any inference from it. There was no doubt in her mind that she was attracted to Edward though she knew so little about him.

Ruth also reflected upon Sarah's comment as they went their separate ways. When Ruth asked if Sarah would meet her to go ice skating in two weeks time Sarah was clear and very decided in saying, "I shan't be going out at all. I have agreed with my mother that for the time being I will stay around Preston until I have completely banished Edward from my mind." Ruth took this to also mean that she didn't want to see her either. Was this an invitation for her to see Edward; was this Sarah's way of saying 'the coast is clear for you', or was it her way of saying that she wanted to sever all ties with Edward and those associated with him?

CHAPTER NINE

Ruth reported for work at the 'cockpit' and quickly settled into the routine of this important work. The demand for Wellington Bombers was so great that the whole factory was operating at maximum production and so there was little time for fanciful thoughts of Edward though she did see him occasionally as he walked past the cockpit.

She wondered whether Edward had forgotten that she now worked there or whether he simply didn't mix work and pleasure. This latter point was soon to be dismissed when Edward came purposefully into the cockpit one afternoon and asked if she would like to go out for the day with him in his father's car this weekend. Ruth inwardly blushed as she found the word "yes" leave her lips with rather more haste than perhaps she should have, considering her conversation with Sarah had only been two weeks previous.

Arrangements were made to meet by the bus station in Blackpool at nine o'clock in the morning and with that Edward was gone. As Ruth looked around she was aware that her work colleagues were smiling and one whispered quietly that Edward had been asking after her for days. Ruth blushed with embarrassment but she was also flushed with excitement about the prospect of spending some time with Edward alone.

Ruth returned home and confided in Moira that Edward and Sarah had ended their relationship and that Edward had now asked her to spend the day with him on Saturday. Moira listened and observed Ruth, detecting in her the signs of a woman that was besotted and though there were pieces of advice she was keen to give to Ruth, she felt this was neither the time nor the place to do it. Her husband was due into the house very soon and she was keen that any discussion about Edward and any advice she was going to give to Ruth should be when they were not likely to be disturbed.

That opportunity came when later in the evening Moira knocked gently on Ruth's bedroom door and asked if she could have a chat. Ruth was clearly as excited now as she was earlier but was nonetheless receptive to a woman to woman conversation that she anticipated would be supportive.

Moira sat in the small chair at the bottom of the bed whilst Ruth lay, face down on the bed with her head cupped in her hands. Moira asked what Ruth knew of Edward and was particular to ask if Sarah had imparted any information about him that would throw a light on his character and his intentions. Ruth failed to pick up on the nuances of the line of questioning and went on to excitedly outline all she knew of Edward with a particular emphasis upon the mystery man persona she had built up in her own mind about him.

Moira was polite and listened intently before asking Ruth if she felt that Edward was a man of sincerity and whether he was possibly looking for Ruth to temporarily fill the void created by his parting with Sarah. Ruth either didn't pick up on the line of the questioning or decided to side step the real issue at the heart of Moira's question. Moira decided that the only course of action was to be direct and straight with Ruth.

She started by pointing out to Ruth that she was an extremely attractive young woman with an allure of innocence that was so often what men were looking for. Not content with a foray into the subject of men's intentions towards young attractive women, Moira continued; "In my experience, a man that's on the rebound from a woman who is not giving him what he wants, and clearly Sarah isn't, will often look for some innocent young thing like you to have his wicked way with." Ruth immediately jumped to the defence of Edward exaggerating her flimsy knowledge of him by portraying him as a man of great honour who if anything was treating her almost as a sister or best friend.

Moira closed the conversation by asking if her mother had explained not just the facts of life but the ways in which she could protect herself if Edward came on to her. Ruth was extremely embarrassed, as neither had her mother or anyone talked about intimate things like that and she was certainly not going to engage in that talk now, if for no other reason than to save herself the embarrassment of having to admit she frankly knew nothing about relationships and even less about how to tame an amorous man.

Moira realised that she was making no headway and as she rose from her chair she stroked Ruth's beautiful black hair and said, "I have been where you are today and I've made mistakes that embarrass me even now, so please feel that no matter what happens in the future you can always talk to me." Ruth raised her head and said, "I'm sure I love him Moira and I will be careful but this is the first time in my life that I have felt like this about anyone."

Ruth took some time to reflect upon her feelings and the advice she was receiving but she could only visualise one thing in her mind and that was the time she would be spending with Edward on Saturday. She tried to rationalise her own feelings about Edward with the advice she was getting from Moira. But by the time she picked up a pen to continue her letter to her mother, Moira's advice had been consigned to the back of her mind and as though to ensure she received no further advice on the subject, she didn't even mention the matter of Edward in the letter she had begun writing to her mother.

Instead, she took up the thread of her mother's letter to her which reflected a less than easy transition to their new life in Arigna, Ireland. Her mother had explained in her letter that the Arigna Valley was a luscious green and beautiful haven and not in any way the kind of bleak and dusty place one associates with coal mining. She explained that whilst her father had tried to prepare himself for a return to work in this old and hazardous mine he had clearly chosen to block from his memory the incredibly challenging working conditions which after all these years left him questioning if he had the agility and physique to deal with the extremely narrow seams.

Ruth had been pleased to hear that whilst the cottage given to her parents by the colliery was small it was manageable. As Ruth closed her letter she simply wrote, 'I'm doing well at work and Moira is looking after me so don't have any worries for me'. This was a sentence that, upon reflection, her mother would be bound to see through.

The week passed slowly but when Saturday came it was a cold crisp end of February day during which Ruth was looking forward to seeing a little of the local countryside ....as well as spending time with Edward. Her preparations for the day included making a picnic of crab paste sandwiches, two small pork pies, some cheese and a small bar of chocolate, a real luxury in ration weary Britain given to her by Moira who also provided a flask of tea and a bottle of homemade lemonade.

All of this was carefully packed in a small hamper which seemed incongruous given the season as Ruth walked in the crisp morning sunshine to Blackpool bus station to meet with Edward. Not content with this image of summer at the end of February, Ruth decided that she would wear her pretty white summer dress under her winter coat so that when they were together she would look at her best. The fact that the dress was also somewhat revealing and had the benefit of showing off her youthful figure was regarded by Ruth as purely incidental!

Edward arrived on time and off they drove in his father's Austin eight car. This beautiful two door dark blue car with highly polished black wheel arches and leather seats was purchased by his father in nineteen thirty nine just before the start of the war. Edward jokingly warned Ruth, "The car doors which open to the rear are often referred to as suicide doors because if they are opened, very slightly even at low speed, they have a tendency to swing open violently taking you with them."

Edward was proud to be able to drive such a nice car and as they swept along the generally deserted roads he explained that this was a pre requisition car. Such cars he explained "beat the July nineteen forty regulation whereby the British Government had taken over stocks of all new cars and banned their purchase by private individuals, except under special circumstances." Ruth nodded in all the right places as Edward continued his story explaining that getting petrol for cars was very difficult as it was strictly rationed.

Edward opened up a little, explaining that he and his father were able to get extra petrol because they both would use the car for their work; Edward as a Special Constable in the Lancashire Constabulary in the Fleetwood and Blackpool area and his father as an officer in the Home Guard. Ruth found this an interesting revelation about Edward that she was unaware of and this made her feel that the concerns expressed by Moira were unfounded as surely a policeman would be honourable and decent.

Their day together was to be spent travelling the short distance to Lytham St Annes, just along the coast from Blackpool where Edward said he had a surprise for Ruth. Lytham St Anne's to the people in Blackpool was regarded as the sophisticated part of the North West Lancashire coastline, perhaps better known for its peaceful parks and beautiful gardens. Ruth was particularly impressed by the old half-timbered houses that were in such sharp contrast to the gaily painted guest houses in the terraced side streets of Blackpool. It was also immediately obvious to Ruth that Lytham was such a quiet peaceful place with its quiet promenade and lovely sandy beach.

At first, Ruth was shy and apprehensive and felt a little clumsy in Edward's company, being careful, perhaps too careful not to give the wrong impression. By contrast, Edward had the air of a sophisticated man, he carried himself with confidence despite his small stature and he was clearly at ease in the company of a woman.

Edward was well dressed wearing a smart three-quarter length raincoat under which was a well tailored blue blazer a white shirt and at the neck he wore a light blue cravat. The ensemble was finished off with a neatly pressed pair of grey flannel trousers a pair of black and white correspondent shoes a trilby hat worn jauntily at a very slight angle to his left and brown leather gloves. Ruth had last seen such a well dressed person when she worked in the post office in Cardiff, but somehow Edward's attire seemed out of place and slightly contrived. Edward was clean shaven apart from a thin moustache which was painstakingly groomed.

After a couple of hours in each other's company they became very much more at ease. They had at least one common interest that being their work but it was not long before they set that subject aside and they were soon laughing and joking in the way that young lovers might. Being courted was an entirely new experience for Ruth who had only experienced the close company of young men she had grown up with or the flirtatious couple of hours with someone she would meet at a dance before each went their own separate ways.

Ruth felt grown up and although she knew she was inexperienced she felt as though she was giving back to Edward the companionship and interest he was showing towards her. Inexperienced as she was she knew that the two of them were not as comfortable as they should be and she knew that this was because neither was showing the true extent of their feelings, or at least she wasn't.

As they arrived in Lytham St Annes, Edward carefully parked the car and in a gallant gesture came around to Ruth's side of the car and opened the door. As she stepped out of the car, in a moment of sheer emotional pleasure and a calculated move to break the ice she drew Edward to her and gently kissed him on the cheek, lingering sufficiently for him to understand that she was happy in his company and that they should both try to relax a little. This did break the ice and it was not long before they were walking hand in hand drawn close to each other. They walked along the promenade and eventually came to Fairhaven Lake where Edward insisted that they should hire a small sailing boat.

As Ruth looked on ever so slightly worried at the prospect of sitting in a small boat on this bright but chilly day, Edward said, "This is your surprise, I love to sail and ever since I was a small boy I have been coming here with my parents and I wanted to share with you the joy of sailing." It took real courage and great fortitude for Ruth to smile and show an appreciation for this gesture whilst inside she was terrified.

With the boat booked, Edward stepped into the dingy and after setting the sail and adjusting various ropes and the tiller he held his hand out to Ruth to help her into the boat. It was clear from Edward's face that Ruth had been unable to keep up the pretence that this would be exciting. The look of sheer terror must have been as evident to Edward as it was to the onlookers who were by now huddled in small groups observing this solo craft taking to the lake on this chilly winter's day.

Not daunted, and having settled Ruth into the boat he gently slipped away from the shore and with great skill smoothly manoeuvred the boat around the lake. Ruth set aside her earlier fears as she began to feel safe and somewhat more at ease. There was her hero skilfully tacking and weaving his way around what is a relatively small lake with skill and some degree of pride. That was until there was a sudden and sustained breeze which required rapid adjustments to the sails and an urgent requirement for the centre board to be fully lowered. And therein lay the problem: with Edward mastering the helm and Ruth unable to put the required downward pressure on the centre board to fully lower it Edward was less in control than was the wind.

Before long it became clear that their intended destination, the point where they had hired the boat was less likely to be the point that they hit land. Looming in their sights was the children's play pool which was cordoned off by a set of floating markers. As the dingy mounted and crossed the floats and came gently to rest against the shore line Ruth found herself unable to contain her laughter any longer and as they disembarked their small craft both could by now see the funny side of their alarming experience and fell into each other's arms laughing and thoroughly enjoying the humour of the moment.

It was at this moment that Edward kissed Ruth with a passion that she had never experienced before. He clearly had done this before and Ruth allowed herself to be taken along with the sheer pleasure and intimacy of the moment. After a while and with the air becoming ever cooler, they returned to the car and settled into the picnic lunch Ruth had carefully prepared. The car had no heater so as they ate their sandwiches they wrapped themselves in two warm blankets and watched the gathering clouds that were darkening the south western sky. As they chatted and drank their hot tea so the windows of the car steamed up isolating them from the passersby, the weather and the cold, adding to the privacy of the moment.

They remained in Lytham St Annes until the late afternoon. But as the skies darkened further with the prospect of a winter storm and the early dusk swiftly transformed the daylight into darkness, Edward announced that they must set off to Blackpool so that they were home before six o'clock. Ruth pressed him and asked if they couldn't go somewhere in Blackpool for a couple of hours, anxious not to end what had been a wonderful day. Edward was adamant that they must get back now and after being pressed further he snapped, "There is a war on and I have my duties to do." Ruth was rather taken aback by Edward's abruptness and immediately put the remains of their picnic back into the small hamper, folded the blanket over her knee and sat back as Edward drove off heading back to Blackpool.

They said little on their journey back to Blackpool but Ruth was disturbed by Edward's impetuous outburst which resembled a child who would have what he wants or throw the toys out of the pram. On their arrival into Blackpool Edward stopped at the top of Apple Tree Crescent and switched off the engine. As Edward was doing this Ruth concerned herself with how Edward should know where she lived as she was sure she had never divulged this to him at any time. Moreover, she had never shared her address with Sarah, always relying on friends or friends of friends to make arrangements when they should meet.

Ruth's curiosity could not be contained as she asked Edward, "How on earth did you know where I live?" "It was not difficult" he said, "I know what bus you get from Vickers to your home each night and I know that you get off at the same stop as Gloria, the rest was easy and now you have just said you live in Apple Tree Crescent." It was by now almost six o'clock and knowing Edward's eagerness to get on his way Ruth thanked him for the day and kissed him goodbye. As she did Edward asked if Ruth would like to go ice skating in two weeks time but in the mean time could he take her to the Tower Ballroom the next night. Ruth took this as a positive sign that he really did like her and wanted to take the relationship forward. As they parted they made their arrangements to meet and Ruth gave Edward one final long and lasting kiss.

The night out at the Tower Ball Room was followed by two other dates in the same week. Each meeting served to confirm their growing friendship as they both became more at ease with each other. Ruth could also sense that Edward was very attracted to her physically. She would notice him looking closely at her and she knew that he often watched her shapely figure as she walked towards him. Innocently, Ruth was flattered rather than cautious about Edward's reaction so soon in their relationship.

The days went by quickly as Ruth spent her time with Edward, whilst she continued seeing her other friends. Ruth was anxious not to lose touch with her friends so she spent most evenings in their company. All were curious to hear how Ruth's dates with Edward had gone and each probed to get the most intimate details of their day and their evenings together.

During their conversation Ruth asked if any of them had seen Sarah and one of them said she was seeing her the following night and would Ruth like to join them. Ruth quickly agreed as she was keen to gauge Sarah's reaction to the news that Edward and she had started courting. She was soon to find that out, when the following evening they met at the ice rink.

On the group's arrival Sarah rushed over to Ruth, embraced her and said, "I know you are going out with Edward and I'm pleased for you Ruth. As you know, Edward and I are finished so it doesn't matter to me and it shouldn't affect our friendship." The gesture felt contrived and it was soon evident why, when Ruth saw Edward only a few feet away with a group of young men and it was obvious that he had seen her and Sarah too.

Sarah, having achieved what she appeared to have set out to do, smugly moved over to where Edward was by now seated. She broke into their company kissed Edward on the cheek, whispered something into his ear and in a slow haughty manner she returned to Ruth's group. Clearly there were games being played and Ruth felt distinctly uncomfortable.

As the evening wore on, the inevitable happened and Ruth found herself isolated at one end of the ice rink very close to Edward. Edward, evidently pleased to see her, threw his arms around her, drew her towards him and kissed her. Ruth enjoyed the embrace but pressed Edward to know what Sarah was up to. "Oh Ruth" he said, "You have so much to learn ...she's jealous of you and she knows that you and I are having a good time and frankly, she wishes she were in your place." Ruth thought this a plausible but rather arrogant perspective but let it go.

It was to be another week before Ruth and Edward had planned to meet up again and so it was a surprise, as they skated back towards their group of friends when Edward asked if she would like to come to his home on Sunday for lunch where she could meet his parents and his two aunts who would also be there. This seemed to Ruth to be a rather impulsive offer and as they walked off the rink, Ruth checked that Edward's mother would be happy with his arrangement and she also asked if it was not a little sudden in their relationship for her to be meeting his parents. Edward responded by drawing her close to him and saying, "Well you know I love you and I think you love me so let's see what my family say."

That evening Ruth lay awake thinking of the two statements Edward had made; the presumption that she loved him and the statement that he loved her coupled with the suggestion that she should in some way now be meeting his family at this early stage in their courtship. Ruth repeatedly asked herself if she was in love with Edward. She pondered this for a while before convincing herself that despite some, perhaps many, reservations yes she did love him. Therefore, logically it followed that there was every reason why Edward should want to invite her to meet his family.

Ruth discussed the week's events and revelations with Moira the following night and not surprisingly, Moira was concerned by the haste and the implications of moving this quickly when Ruth knew so little about Edward. Moira counselled Ruth to use the time with Edward's family to learn more about them and Edward and to form a more considered view about the pace of their relationship once she had a perspective on him and his family.

Chapter Ten

The Sunday arrived and as Ruth looked at her diary all she could see was Sunday eighth of March *lunch with Edward's family*. Ruth had bathed that morning and following the war time regulation she had used less than four inches of only tepid water. Bathing more than once in ten days was regarded as wasteful and so Ruth was more used to standing at the sink and washing herself down with a damp flannel each day. She had made a smart new dress for the lunch meeting, being careful to avoid the frivolity of fashion which was so denounced by older people as unbecoming in war time Britain.

Rationing was tough on women where all that was deemed necessary in a year was one pair of shoes, six pairs of stockings, eight ounces of wool or two yards of fabric, one silk dress, two or three pairs of knickers, two or three brassieres or a girdle, and six hankies. Ruth had been known like many other women to paint her legs with gravy browning to imitate stocking which were expensive and hard to replace. However, today was the day to wear the stockings given to her by Auntie Lottie and to wear her best shoes. Moira had helped wash and brush Ruth's long black hair to make it look its best, which it did.

The arrangement was that Ruth should call at Edward's house at twelve o'clock which she did. The door was opened by a tall man who introduced himself as Edward's father, Sam. He was a smart slim looking man who was dressed in a grey suit and wore what was clearly a regimental tie. Ruth had not been brought up with such formality in the home and felt herself immediately disarmed. Mr Carmichael, as he clearly expected to be called ushered Ruth into the house and through into a small living room where she was then introduced to Ellen, Edward's mother and his two Aunts, Matilda and Dorothy.

Ruth felt a flush rising up her neck and she also felt her knees knocking as it became clear that for the time being at least there was no sign of Edward. Ruth was politely asked to sit in the only chair in the room whilst the rest of the gathering sat on two small sofas. Ruth sat and looked out at the penetrating eyes of the Carmichael's who would not have been out of place as characters at the Spanish inquisition.

With the pleasantries such as they were, out of the way, Ellen asked, "So how long have you known our dear Edward?" When Ruth politely replied that she had known him for some months Aunt Matilda seized upon the opportunity to say, "Ah yes you met our dear Edward through Sarah ....we love Sarah and....well, my dear I cannot understand why she and Edward didn't reconcile their differences and get on and marry." Ruth had never encountered anyone with the poise and composure of this tiny woman and had not expected that the two delicate subjects of marriage and Sarah would enter the conversation at all and certainly not quite so early in their meeting.

Ruth acknowledged that she was well aware of the circumstances that led to Edward and Sarah breaking up their relationship but felt she had to politely but firmly point out that it was not until after they had split up that she accepted Edward's invitation to date.

The questioning continued, Aunt Dorothy, asked, "I understand that you are from Wales and that your parents are Irish, what a quaint combination of two very poor Celtic nations ... what was it like growing up in a poor mining area?" Ruth, ever the innocent drifted back to her strong valley accent and proudly proclaimed the tremendous merits of growing up in a mining community where no one had much but what they had they shared.

When she had passionately reflected her love of Wales and its people Aunt Matilda spluttered as though the coal dust of the valleys had caught in her throat and declared in a disparaging voice, "Oh how charming it is to hear the simple tones of Ruth's Welsh lilt though I was expecting to hear some of your parents more earthy Irish brogue penetrate your accent."

The questioning and innuendo was relentless. When there was a momentary pause Ruth took the opportunity to ask if the assembled company knew where Edward was. Sam grasped the moment to speak and said "Oh he's in his wireless shack....." and with that the assembled company glared at him as though he had broken wind. "I mean he is playing with some old radio, I'll go and get him."

The conversation moved from questioning Ruth to the three women speaking about her as though she were not in the room. At length, Edward arrived and sat on the arm of Ruth's chair. Other than acknowledging her with a quiet hello and welcome, and without showing any affection towards Ruth, Edward immediately fell under the protective spell of these matriarchs.

Edward's demeanour was almost childlike as each vied with the other to stroke the ego of their beloved boy. As their darling only child, Edward seemed to be the centre of both their attention and their comments, and their nauseating sycophantic comments continued throughout lunch. It seemed that all Ruth could hear were uttering's of pride for Edward; his school achievements, his engineering skills, his contribution whilst in the Merchant Navy and his vital input to the work at Vickers. To Ruth, the only thing they had not mentioned was Edward the walking talking potty trained infant prodigy!

In an attempt to enter the Edward fan club Ruth took a momentary break in the conversation to ask Edward to tell her a little about his work as a Special Constable. The room went silent as each turned to the other until eventually Edward said "In war time it is improper and dangerous to idly talk about the work of any such body" and that was the matter closed. Once again, Ruth found that any attempt to penetrate the real Edward and his work was simply closed down as no go territory.

When the lunch was finished Edward's mother announced that she had made an apple pie from cooking apples stored from last autumn. Edward was dispatched to the kitchen in a well rehearsed routine to make the custard to a chorus of "Oh Edward makes wonderful custard." By the time lunch was over with and Ruth was about to depart it seemed to her that the only story that had not been told about Edward was his ability to feed the five thousand and walk on water!

With polite thanks to everyone, Ruth and Edward left the house with Edward walking her to the bus stop. Ruth waited until she could not be heard before asking in her strongest Welsh, Valley accent, "What the hell was all that about...they clearly had decided before I arrived that a valley girl was not good enough for their precious Edward." Edward was dismissive saying that the family only wanted the best for him. He went on to say that there was no doubt that they were very fond of Sarah but that they would also grow fond of her too. Ruth was furious but saw the problem as entirely that of his parents and Aunts. As they strolled to the bus stop they set aside the challenges of the lunch and agreed to meet again the following weekend.

Ruth and Edward continued to date most weeks throughout March and April spending time in the company of their friends and also going out alone to the cinema and dancing. In the middle of May, with the days growing longer Edward asked if Ruth would like to take a trip out with him on the following Saturday evening to visit the Trough of Bowland to see the sun setting over Morecambe bay. Ruth was delighted and immediately agreed. She saw the offer to get out into the countryside and into the hills as a welcome opportunity to remind herself of her Welsh hills and valleys.

Edward picked Ruth up at about seven o'clock and they chatted as they left Blackpool and headed towards the Pennine hills in the distance. Edward continued his drive up to the narrow winding Trough of Bowland road, across the bleak open moorland between Lancaster and Abbeystead. Ruth lay back in the car seat and soaked up the sheer beauty of the barren hillside which on that late spring evening was by now catching the rays from the setting sun.

Eventually, they reached a stone tower set alongside the road which Edward explained was called Jubilee

Tower. The small square Tower, built to commemorate Queen Victoria's diamond jubilee was located on this spot because of its commanding views across Morecambe Bay and Blackpool with some saying that on a good day you can even see to the Isle of Man.

Edward confided that this was one of his favourite places on earth, a place his father would bring him as a child and somewhere that for him encapsulated his beloved Lancashire. Ruth was touched by the way that Edward spoke in a voice that betrayed a genuine emotion as he described the many trips he had taken here as a child. As Edward talked at length about his love for the countryside and people of Lancashire Ruth was drawn into the intimate relationship he and his family had for these moors and the place and county he passionately called home.

Edward parked the car as the sun was lowering in the western sky. He stepped out of the car, opened the passenger door and gently took Ruth's hand and walked her across the road to the tower where they climbed the few steps to the top. The view was breathtaking as the colour infused light from the sinking sun skipped across the water of Morecambe bay casting a long band of light that seemed to point directly at them. There they remained until the last sign of the sun had faded below the horizon. In all the time they had been there they had not seen another vehicle or another person. They were totally alone and free to embrace and share their love for each other without interference or embarrassment.

❧

Perhaps it was the occasion or perhaps they had reached the point in their relationship when they were ready to give themselves to each other but that night on that moorland they made love.

They remained there until about nine thirty when Edward suggested that they must leave and with little said they stepped back into the car and set off down the hill to return to Blackpool. Ruth's memories of the passionate moments of their love making were fading as the stark reality of the possible consequences began to trouble her mind. She found herself constantly seeking reassurance from Edward: "You do love me don't you" to which he readily answered "Yes."

On their journey back to Ruth's house they arranged to meet again in three weeks time. Edward explained that he could not see her sooner because he had commitments to his Special Constable work every night for three weeks. Edward drew the car to a stop at the entrance to Apple Tree Crescent and with a brief kiss and a hug they said goodnight and Ruth walked the few yards home.

Ruth was tormented throughout the night as she tried to put out of her mind the wrath and damnation of her God that kept her from sleep chastising her for what she had done that night and the demons that were saying she surely would be pregnant.

Night after night those demons would torment her; she felt guilt, revulsion and terrible fear. This was not helped by her nightly glances at her diary that showed she was firstly days and then a week overdue for her period.

Ruth was not eating and had begun to look drawn and tired, sufficiently so that it was being commented upon at work and probed nightly by Moira. Eventually, the night came when she was to meet Edward and when they met she fell tearfully into his arms. Edward tried unsuccessfully to establish why she was so upset never once making the simplest connection that three weeks earlier she had lost her virginity to him or that she might need reassurance from him that their relationship was at least stronger as a result.

At Edward's suggestion Ruth left early and went home arranging to meet mid week to go to the Winter Garden's dancing. The following morning, a Saturday, Moira heard Ruth crying in her bedroom and having knocked on her door a few times she entered the room and sat alongside Ruth who was laying in bed, her head buried in the pillow. Moira turned Ruth's head towards her and said, "You're pregnant aren't you?" Ruth tried to say she wasn't but all she could say was, "I don't know."

Moira swiftly but with compassionate and sensitivity gathered Ruth up, got her dressed and immediately took her to see her own family doctor whose house was but four doors away. His wife answered the door and seeing the distress on Ruth's face and the anguish on Moira's she asked them to come into her own sitting room rather than the main waiting room until such time as her husband could see Ruth.

After what seemed like hours but were only a few minutes Dr Carr, a young looking man with a kindly face came into the room and asked Ruth to go with him. He suggested to Moira that she should wait in the sitting room and that his wife should chaperone Ruth.

Ruth was relieved that she would not have to go through an examination in front of Moira and nor would she have to speak in front of her cousin of what had gone on that night three weeks ago in.

Ruth sat down in a comfortable chair alongside the doctor at his desk with Mrs Carr sitting close to her.

"Now tell me what's so bad that would make a pretty young thing like you so unhappy" he said. Ruth began to cry and with that Mrs Carr put a hand on hers and said "Do you think you're pregnant sweetheart, is that the problem?" Ruth nodded and in that instance she knew, even before the inevitable examination, she knew that she was pregnant. Dr Carr examined her and took a urine sample but confirmed that in his mind she was indeed pregnant. He explained that with the wonders of science he would be able to confirm if she was pregnant from the urine sample.

At that point Ruth was taken back to Mrs Carr's sitting room and Moira went into the surgery to speak with the doctor. He explained that he believed she was pregnant and that her urine sample would be sent to the hospital for testing. He explained to the attentive Moira who was trying to understand how he would know from a urine test if Ruth was pregnant that the hospital would use a 'frog'. He went on to explain to the dumbstruck Moira that the urine of a woman who was thought to be pregnant could be injected into the dorsal lymph sac of the female African Clawed Frog; if the woman was pregnant the female frog would ovulate within eight to ten hours.

Both the science and the simplified explanation of how the science worked went completely over Moira's head. What she was reassured about and extremely grateful for was the indication that if she called back to the house on Sunday morning before Church, he would have the test result. Moira went back to the sitting room and settled the fee for the consultation and the test which in total came to half a guinea.

They left the house and Ruth asked if they might walk to the park where they could talk undisturbed. They sat for about an hour and pondered the consequences of any confirmation that she was pregnant. Ruth, in a rather more composed state than was Moira by this time made it quite clear that she would not even countenance the thought of an abortion. Although she was not a 'practicing' Catholic she held to the strong belief that abortion was the taking of life. This moved Moira to the obvious next question whether Ruth felt that Edward would do the decent thing and marry her. Ruth was not sure, she knew that Edward was amenable to marriage with Sarah but, based on the experience of her one meeting with Edward's family it seemed that they might well be the arbiters of whether Edward should marry her rather than Edward.

Their conversation then moved on to option three that being to have the child, if indeed she was pregnant and then to go on to have the child adopted. This brought out in Ruth a passion that was to live with her all her life. She explained that to her putting up your child for adoption was sinful, an abdication of responsibility and as unacceptable as abortion.

The logical elimination of these options led them to the final one which was that if Edward didn't marry Ruth, how she would bring a child up on her own. In this regard, Moira made it quite clear that the option of remaining in her house after the child was born was entirely out of the question as her husband was not fond of children to the point of never even letting neighbours children come into the house even with their mother. Moreover, Moira reminded Ruth that the landlord had made it clear that there were to be no children living in his house. By the time they left the park, Ruth was less visibly upset but the turmoil continued in her head. They agreed to say nothing to anyone at least until Dr Carr had reported his findings tomorrow.

If it is impossible to go a whole night without sleep, Ruth broke the rule. She tossed and turned imagining how she might tell Edward and what his reaction would be. She entered the dark prospect of a conversation with Edward's mother and even worse the five foot Attila the Hun masquerading as Aunt Matilda. The dark forces of the night gave way to the dawn and Ruth lay in her bed a further two hours until she was sure that Jack had left the house.

Ruth rose and went to the bathroom to wash. She stood before the full length mirror looking at her perfectly flat stomach trying to see if there were any signs that a new life was forming to change her shape, but there were none. It was agreed that Ruth should go to Dr Carr's house alone and knowing that he always went to the nine o'clock mass in the Catholic Church she called at the house at eight thirty.

Mrs Carr opened the door and took Ruth through to the waiting room where she sat alone deep in thought and prepared for the anticipated news that she was pregnant. Dr Carr eventually called her into his office and confirmed that which she knew already, that she was indeed pregnant.

The relief of knowing brought some comfort to the young Ruth's mind as she walked the few steps to Moira's house. Moira saw the news written across Ruth's face as she entered the house slipped up the stairs to lie on her bed where she remained for the whole of the day.

Sleep returned to Ruth though the prospect of what lay ahead in the coming days when she would have to confront Edward tormented and frightened her.

CHAPTER ELEVEN

Ruth returned to her work on the Monday passing off any comments that she was looking unwell as nothing more than a summer cold. She saw Edward pass the cockpit windows several times that day and the next but resisted the urge to go and see him, waiting until their planned meeting later in the week.

Ruth was conscious of anyone whose momentary glance could be construed as being able to detect her massive secret. Although she had several close friends at work she did not succumb to the temptation to confide in any of them. Ruth continued to feel a massive sense of guilt, a guilt that would wash over her without warning and leave her feeling cold and clammy. She felt sure that the world would condemn her once it was known that she had engaged in sex with a man before marriage.

Though the nineteen forties were supposed to be liberating times for women who in many ways were the backbone of the home economy and the war effort, the Victorian values and influence remained. Young women were regarded as promiscuous simply for being seen to walk hand in hand with a boy and if they were seen by the older generation of women to kiss in public they were branded brazen and loose. Those girls who did become pregnant out of wedlock were seen to bring shame on their families. Therefore, it was not at all uncommon for such girls to be packed off to an auntie some miles away until the child was born following which they could return with a contrived story of going to assist a sick relative or being taken away from the reminders of war.

Very few girls braved the challenge of being a single parent partly because they couldn't afford to but also because they would be shunned and ostracised by any community they went into. Rooms were hard enough to rent by mothers whose husbands were on the front line or had been widowed by wartime death, but there would be no room for a mother and her bastard baby. The only accepted course of action if the father was not known or if he was unwilling to face up to his responsibilities and marry the girl, was for a young mother to return to her family or to have her child adopted which Ruth had completely ruled out, or for the child to be taken into care. Many children were already in care, housed in children's homes which were often run by the church.

For Ruth, the prospect of anyone taking her child from her was completely out of the question though she had not yet followed through the implications if Edward rejected her, and that she would at some time have to leave the place she called home with Moira. These were huge issues for the young Ruth to be wrestling with but she felt her fate, whatever it was would at least be sealed once she had spoken to Edward.

Their arrangement had been to meet outside the Winter Gardens but Ruth slipped a note to Edward suggesting that they meet at the Cottage fish and chip shop in Blackpool for tea before going on to the Winter Gardens. Though a little off the beaten track, this was a favourite place to meet and somewhere they had visited on many occasions. Edward agreed and they met as planned at six o'clock.

When Edward arrived he was chirpy and very talkative and it was not until their meal had been served to them that he stopped to take a breath. Ruth waited until she could wait no more and whispered in Edward's ear, "Edward, we need to talk I have something to tell you." Edward continued his supper only nodding to acknowledge that he had heard what she said. By now the cafe was quiet and with the staff nowhere to be seen, Ruth again said, "Edward we need to talk." With that Edward looked at her and said, "What is it, what's so urgent?" Being unable to say what she needed to say in any other way she turned to Edward and said, "I'm pregnant."

There was a moment of silence before Edward firstly looked around to be sure that no one was listening and then said, "What do you mean you're pregnant, how do you know?" Ruth explained that she had seen the doctor and that the tests he had carried out confirmed that she was pregnant. A further moment of silence passed before Edward said, "And am I the father?"

There was no containing Ruth's fury. She stepped up from the table and dragged Edward outside the cafe and without pausing for breath she launched a tirade upon Edward, the like of which he had never been subject to before: "How dare you, you who have knowingly taken my virginity accuse me of being with another man." She went on, "For once in your life face up to the implications of your actions in the same way that I will have to do by at least acknowledging that this is your baby."

Edward waited and eventually, in a soft tone said to Ruth, "It was unthinking of me to say that, of course it's my baby and we will get through this together." Now that was the sort of scenario that Ruth had not rehearsed and she was completely taken aback. Moreover, Edward continued, "You know that I love you and what we must now consider is what we do from here." These were the kind of reassuring words that Ruth needed to hear. What she didn't need to hear was what came next.

Edward, with a sense of manly purpose rose to his full five foot seven and said, "Right let's get the bus over to my house and discuss this with my parents who will of course be angry but will help us to decide what we should do now." Again Ruth felt angry and though by now she was being rushed along the road to the nearest bus stop, she felt compelled to again raise her voice to Edward. "Can't you do anything in your life without having your parents decide for you? What would you like to do? What do you think I would like us to do? Don't you think we should answer some of those questions before we tell your parents?"

There was no stopping Ruth who hardly stopped for breath before she continued. "Isn't this a time when you and I should be going to them and telling them what we think is right for us and the baby?" Edward was visibly taken aback and on reflection so was Ruth. She wondered as they continued their journey to the bus stop where was this stridency and determination was coming from.

They moved to an area just before the bus stop and sat on a wall. Edward turned to Ruth and explained that since he was a child, an only child, his life had been mapped out for him by his parents and his aunts. He explained, "They pushed me to achieve at school, they managed to get me into Blackpool Technical Collage and when I had finished there they managed to get me into

Radio School before pulling more strings to get me into the Merchant Navy, considered at that time to be the safest of services during war time."

Edward continued what was beginning to sound like a long overdue reflective moment by explaining that it was again strings that were pulled that led to him being saved from other military services. He paused and said, "I will explain more about what else I do some other time but suffice to say that I am not the coward or the conscientious objector some people think I am. I do my bit and I do it well." Ruth chose not to probe any of what she had just heard as tantalising and intriguing as the temptation was. Instead, she returned to the vexing theme of what they wanted for their future and their child.

Taking the bull by the horn, Ruth asked boldly and bravely, "Are you going to ask me to marry you?" Edward, who clearly had not reached that point in his thinking spluttered and said, "Well why not. If my parents agree, then would you marry me?" Tirade number three was about to explode when Edward sensing that Ruth was again about to erupt, interrupted and said, "That came out wrongly" he said. "I would be honoured if you will agree to marry me and if you do, then we should go immediately to my parents and tell them the news." Ruth, taking this as a serious offer of marriage said "Yes."

They boarded the bus and set off to see Edward's parents. As they did so, Ruth reflected upon the enormity of what Edward had just asked but also considered the prospect of whether she should at this stage be telling her parents, firstly that she was pregnant and then that she was to be married. The thought of telling her mother that she was pregnant out of wedlock was, for Ruth simply not worth contemplating at this juncture.

Before long they had arrived in Garden Walk where Edward lived. Edward opened the door and shouted in "Hello it's me and I have Ruth with me." The first person to emerge from the sitting room was the dreaded Aunt Matilda, to be followed by Ellen and Sam. There was a look on their faces that immediately suggested to Ruth that this was a family that was unused to people just dropping in.

Ruth reflected how dissimilar this was to her Welsh upbringing where it was quite normal, indeed it was expected that you would simply knock on the door shout your name and walk into a house that was familiar to you bringing with you anyone that was in your company. The Carmichael household was clearly not that familiar and based upon the glaring looks from Aunt Matilda they were not likely to be nearly as welcoming.

They sat down and before the ice could be broken Edward said, "We have some news for you" and with that he turned to Ruth obviously expecting her to complete his sentence. Before another word could be spoken, Aunt Matilda, Ruth's Attila the Hun, her bête noir pointed a finger at Ruth and exclaimed, "You're pregnant aren't you?" Ruth ceased the moment and replied, "Yes I am and Edward and I want to be married."

Aunt Matilda slumped back in her chair and in a sign of resignation to what she appeared to have predicted she said, "This would never have happened with Sarah, she had standards and she would never have given herself before she was married." In a blistering attack she turned to Ruth and delivered the coup de gras; "I expected the worst from you young woman and you have not disappointed or failed to deliver."

At this point, the soft voice of Ellen was heard as she implored the family to hear the couple out and with that she turned to Edward and said, "We are where we are and we cannot turn the clock back or change what has happened, so what do you want Edward?'. He repeated what Ruth had said a moment earlier that they wanted to be married as soon as possible and that he wanted to be a good father to his child.

Aunt Matilda was by no means finished and was certainly not going to be silenced, "What proof do we have that she isn't lying, the little trollop may be playing Edward for the fool to marry him and then declare that she has lost the baby in a month or two's time." Ellen again attempted to calm the situation but Ruth was to have the last word, "Yes I may be seen as common to you because of my Welsh accent, and my poor upbringing and I may not measure up to what Sarah seemed to you, but I'm not a liar, I am pregnant and we plan to marry because we love each other." She went on, "We, that is Edward and I have made a mistake but at least we are facing up to it. Our purpose in coming straight to you was to ask for your support and blessing for our plans to marry, clearly there is no hope of that here."

Sam was distinctly uncomfortable and declared that he would slip into the kitchen and make some tea but was immediately ordered to remain where he was by Ellen who suggested that Matilda make the tea so that a calmer more rational conversation might take place between the four of them. Matilda was furious and in leaving the room to do as instructed she fired her final salvo at Ruth by again muttering in a loud voice, "She will never be the woman Sarah is and you have the evidence of that before you."

In a somewhat calmer atmosphere the conversation turned to plans for a wedding that should take place as quickly as possible before it became apparent that Ruth was expecting a baby. Sam, Ruth and Edward agreed to see the vicar at the family church and arrange for the banns of marriage to be read as soon as possible under the circumstances. It was a requirement that the banns of marriage must be called in the parish church where each person is resident. Banns needed be called on the three Sundays before the marriage, in order that any objectors to the marriage might come forward.

It was also agreed that the whole family would be discreet and make no mention of the pregnancy dealing with the sudden nature of the marriage as being 'typical of young impetuous young people in wartime, simply living for today'. There was then the matter of where Ruth and Edward should live once they were married and with some reluctance Ruth saw the sense of her moving into Edward's family home at least as a first step until an alternative might present itself.

After several hours of discussion Ruth left the house feeling that at least Ellen had warmed to her something that was confirmed when, as she was about to leave, Ellen whispered into Ruth's ear. "Now be sure to look after yourself and my grandchild." She then in an audible tone said, "Ruth, you are to be a member of this family and whilst it might take time to get to know each other, we will, and we will make this work for the best." Much nodding followed as Edward was dispatched by his patriarchal father to "carefully walk Ruth to the bus stop and see her onto the bus."

On Ruth's return home she found Moira was waiting for her anxious to know what Edward's reaction had been. She made a cup of coco and they sat in the kitchen as Ruth repeated all the news of the night. Moira was genuinely pleased and listened intently to the plans that had been formulated in the few short hours she was with Edward's parents. When Ruth had finished Moira asked when Ruth would tell her mother. Ruth was slow to respond but when she did she was adamant that for the time being at least, she didn't want her parents to know she was pregnant but under pressure from Moira she agreed to write to her Mother and tell her that she was soon to be marrying Edward.

Ruth's only hope was that her mother did not see through the words she would use in the letter and discover that she was expecting a child. That night she carefully worded a letter that was full of excitement about her forthcoming marriage in the hope that her mother would be diverted from the most obvious conclusion, that this was a marriage of convenience.

Ruth was bursting with happiness and confided to a number of friends at work that she and Edward were to be married and that they were seeing the vicar as soon as possible. Most of those she told were excited for her, some remarking that Edward was a wonderful catch. Others immediately questioned the haste and inferred that the haste may reflect urgency more than anything else. Within minutes, the whole of the cockpit was aware of the planned marriage and by the time Ruth broke for lunch her intended marriage to Edward was the talk of the factory.

As Ruth settled down to eat her sandwiches a tall pretty girl who Ruth knew to be called Victoria came and sat next to her. After a general chat about work, Victoria said, "I hear that you are going to marry Edward, congratulations." Ruth thanked her and with that Victoria began to talk to Ruth in a whisper. She explained that she was not wishing to burst her bubble but she questioned if Ruth was aware that Edward had dated most of the girls in this section. Ruth was decidedly unaware of this and attempted to conceal her embarrassment by appearing to be unmoved by the news.

Victoria explained that even when Edward was courting Sarah she was aware that he was two timing her with two people that she knew well. In a cautionary tone Victoria said that both these girls came to her a few days after Edward had taken Ruth on her first date to warn her that he was playing the field and that he was certainly two timing someone that he was supposed to be marrying. Finally, Victoria turned to Ruth and said, "Be very sure that you know what Edward is like before you tie the knot and you are trapped for ever in a marriage where he may well cheat on you."

Ruth, in an attempt to defend Edward and to suggest that she was very aware of his past, angrily said, "I know that you and the others are jealous and that you would have liked him to marry you, but it's me he has asked to marry him and that means his flirting days are over." Victoria opened her mouth to utter a final warning and stopped herself. Ruth dismissed Victoria's words as those of an envious, venomous woman and put the conversation behind her.

CHAPTER TWELVE

Having met the Vicar later that week with Edward and Sam, the wedding date was set for June twelfth, a little more than six weeks after their night of love next to Jubilee Tower. This whirl wind of plans sucked Ruth into the vortex of an experience she had long planned since her childhood to be very different to this. She felt that events rather than plans meant that the wedding was now completely out of her control. Like most young women, Ruth dreamt of a long courtship and a long engagement to plan her fairy tale wedding. This was neither.

Ruth included the date of the wedding in her letter to her mother anticipating that it would be impossible for her or any member of the family in Ireland to be able to attend. Ruth's greatest fear was that her mother would see this as a shotgun wedding and make her views known on the day if she did attend. She also knew that if her father were able to afford to attend, the day would certainly not pass without him feeling the need to punch someone, anyone to mark his displeasure.

Ruth met with Edward's family outside their church on the first Sunday that the Banns were to be called. Not surprisingly, Aunt Matilda and Aunt Dorothy were both there. Ruth could only imagine that their presence was akin to knitting alongside the gallows!

Edward's family were clearly well known by parishioners attending the church with many passing the time of day with them or stopping to have a few words as they walked up the pathway to the main entrance of the church. The Carmichael's entered the church in what seemed like seniority order, with Sam, being followed by Aunt Matilda then by Ellen, followed by Aunt Dorothy then Edward, and finally Ruth. They went to an empty pew, clearly the one the family had been using for many years and a place that other parishioners would never use at the nine o'clock service. As they sat in the pew, Ruth was conscious that people nearby were whispering to each other clearly noticing the new appendage to the Carmichael Sunday line-up.

Ruth had not been much of a church goer since she was in her early teens but she could see that this Church of England service was not too far removed from the typical Catholic service she had attended all those years ago with the very helpful exception that the service was in English and not Latin. However, her thoughts were drawn to the threats of hell and damnation, preached by her Catholic priest in Wales as the punishment for any of his brethren that might be seen to cross the threshold of a Protestant church.

The Sunday service eventually moved to the point where the vicar gave his parish notices: The sad death of Sergeant Morrison, killed in action; the demise of Mrs Postlethwait at the age of sixty nine and finally the illness of Mildred Evans. Parishioners were asked to pray for them all.

Then came the formal reading of the Banns: "*I Publish the Banns of Marriage between Mr Edward Carmichael of this Parish and Miss Ruth Dervla*

*O'Connor also of this parish. If any of you know cause,
or just impediment, why these two persons should not be
joined together in holy Matrimony, you are to declare it.
This is the first time of asking."*

As each of the solemn words were read, so heads in
the congregation began to turn as it registered slowly for
some, rapidly for others that Edward was to be marrying
someone not known to them in what could only be
described as 'haste' in this hallowed place. More was to
come, as the parishioners rose to leave the church at the
end of the service they looked over towards the
Carmichael pew and their gaze followed Ruth and the
Carmichael's until they were outside.

The usual ritual that slows down the rapid departure
of parishioners from the church, the shaking of the
vicar's hand gave time to the more inquisitive in the
queue to take a good long look at the person of Ruth
O'Connor. Ruth had deliberately worn a modest high
neck dress but one that fitted her slim body sufficiently
that for those who sought to detect the merest hint of a
swelling stomach there was much disappointment. As
the party reached the vicar and shook hands, he
whispered that he would be looking forward to seeing
Ruth again next week.

With the ordeal over, Ruth and Edward walked hand
in hand to his parent's home. There they finalised the
arrangements for the wedding. It was agreed that the
witnesses would be Sam and Matilda for the
Carmichael's and Ruth was asked who would be the
witness for her family. Ruth faced a terrible dilemma.
She dearly wanted to have members of her family present
at the wedding but feared that if any attended it would
not be long before her secret was revealed and that was

something she simply could not face at this time. Deep down, Ruth was hoping that once the wedding was over with she could announce to her family that she had become pregnant on their wedding night and then hope that the mathematics of the date of birth added up and fitted her story.

Ruth had been dreading this question as she had no idea if any member of her family from Ireland would attend and so in desperation she acknowledged that it was likely to be her cousin Moira and her husband Jack, if he could get the day off work. Aunt Matilda looking down her nose remarked "I thought you Welsh and Irish had more family than you can count, surely you're not telling us that your only family at the wedding will be a factory girl and a bus driver." These comments were intended to undermine Ruth's confidence which they did and no matter how many times Edward would ask her to ignore the comments she found they increasingly cut deeper.

It was finally agreed that in these austere times the Carmichael's would provide a finger buffet at the house after the wedding. It was also acknowledged that it would not be reasonable to expect the bride's side of the family to pay. With the arrangements finally over Ruth asked if she could see the room that she and Edward would be sharing in less than four weeks time. Edward, rather than his parents or the dreaded Aunt Matilda was immediately reluctant saying that the room was not tidy and suggesting that she view the room the following Sunday. Ruth was irritated but sanguine realising that she must not let small things bother her especially when Aunt Matilda could be relied upon for bigger ones.

When Ruth and Edward walked to the bus stop, Edward excused his reluctance to show Ruth his room by saying that he had several old radio parts in the bedroom that made it look cluttered and he wanted to make the room look special and at its best before she saw it. Suspicious of his remarks, Ruth seized upon the issue of his radios pointing out the collective family silence when his father had previously suggested that Edward was in his radio shack. Ruth also reminded Edward of his own comments that he would explain to Ruth more about what else he did for his country. She reminded him of his emotional comments about not being the coward or the conscientious objector some people though he was.

Again Edward tried to brush off these comments but eventually, Ruth confronted him, "If we are about to be married there should be no secrets between us, so tell me, why is it that you are not in military service and what is all this about radios" she asked making clear to Edward that she expected answers. Edward was clearly uncomfortable with Ruth's tough line of questions and so Ruth pressed harder, "Are you some sort of spy, is that what you are" she asked. Again Edward dodged the question by saying, "I do my bit for my country and that's it."

In an aloof and patronising manner, Edward went on to tell Ruth that she should not meddle in things that didn't concern her. His closing remark sent a chill down her spine, "If you are to be my wife you are going to have to change your ways and get rid of that independent streak that is so unbecoming in women." Ruth was about to respond when she could see that there was no point at least for the time being.

Edward's comments were concerning though. Ruth who was determined to make her point looked at Edward and cuttingly remarked, "I don't see myself as a feminist or a suffragette however, you and many others like you need to understand that the world is changing. Women are doing jobs previously only done by men, they have proved themselves on the land, in the factories and are even flying aircraft on delivery to the RAF, so don't patronise me and pat me on the head as you would a child" she said, making it clear that this conversation was not over.

Women no longer expected to be treated as a chattel, a servant to their husband or to be expected to stay at home and look after the home and children. They expected more and felt they had earned the right to do so. In Edward, Ruth detected the same values she saw in her own father and what she saw she didn't like. They agreed to put their differences aside but Ruth knew that they would return to them again.

The following Sunday Ruth underwent the same rituals as the previous week when the Banns were called at the parish church for the second time. However, on this occasion the brethren had the benefit of a whole week to gossip and compare notes and were now more fully 'informed' than the previous week. The final Banns were called the following Sunday leaving just six days before the wedding. On this occasion when Ruth returned to Edward's home she was eventually invited to look at the bedroom that would become her marital home in less than a week.

The room was a generous size dominated by the double bed that had hastily been moved in from the spare bedroom. There was a wash hand basin in the corner and two small but adequate wardrobes. The bedroom overlooked the rear garden which had been divided into a very large vegetable area, possibly taking more than half the garden which was immaculately tended with signs of peas, beans and potatoes growing alongside fruit cages and at least a dozen apple trees.

To the right was a beautiful flower border filled with summer colours. Finally, at the bottom of the garden was a large wooden hut, from which wires led to a tall mast with an aerial. It was obvious from what little Ruth knew about radios that the large horizontal aerial had been lowered from its operating position that would normally be much higher. In an attempt to show little regard for what was going on but to demonstrate that she knew a little about these things Ruth said, "Why didn't you tell me that you were a radio amateur or radio ham or whatever you call yourselves?"

Edward took his time to respond and simply said, "That's right I'm a radio ham and that's the radio shack Dad was talking about." Ruth left the conversation at that and during this rarest of times alone with Edward they cuddled up together on the bed and talked about the plans for the next weekend.

Edward announced that his father had agreed that following the wedding, they could borrow his car on Saturday and Sunday. Like an excited child, Edward announced, "I plan to drive my new bride to Morecambe where we will stay at the Battery Hotel for the night." Ruth was surprised and delighted as she had not even considered that they would be able to go away for a honeymoon.

They eventually left the room when, after being there for about an hour, Sam threw open the bedroom door and walked in declaring, "This is no place for a single woman to be especially on the Sabbath irrespective of your current condition." Once again Ruth detected the Victorian standards of a male dominated household.

Ruth returned to Moira's home where they enjoyed a long overdue chat whilst Moira made the final adjustments to her own wedding dress which they had successfully managed to alter to fit Ruth. All was by now ready for the wedding largely because the arrangements were very much in the hands of the Carmichael family.

Ruth went to her bedroom where she opened the letter she had received the previous day with an Irish post mark. She dreaded opening the letter because whatever it said she knew that it would bring upset. The letter began with a quick update on what was happening with the family and a vivid account of the poverty they were reduced to. This acted as the precursor to the simple message that said, '*Even if the wedding had been arranged with less haste, it would be impossible for any of the family to be able to afford to leave Ireland to go to England*'. The final paragraph contained the sentence Ruth had been dreading; "*You cannot fool your mother with your claims to be so in love that you need to marry immediately. Your father swallowed it, in fact he was even happy for you, but I'm your mother and I know that you are hiding something from me. If you can't tell me then for sure you can't tell the Lord himself and so Ruth you will have to live with what you are doing or what you have done*'. Her comments cut deep.

CHAPTER THIRTEEN

Ruth's wedding day was every bit the fairy tale she had so dreamt of as a young child growing up in Wales. She slipped into her wedding dress for the final time as she prepared to leave for the church and took a moment to look at herself in the mirror. Her hair was combed into soft curls that fell to her shoulders reminiscent of the styles of the beautiful starlets of the screen that so influenced the aspirations of young women of the day.

Her dress, or to be precise Moira's dress was adjusted to fit so tight around the waist that it would lay bare any assertion that she was pregnant. Indeed, Ruth herself had begun to forget that she was pregnant as she looked at herself in the dress. This stunning dress which had been made out of nine yards of white brocade with waterfall pleats and a fishtail train brought back so many memories for Moira who was reliving her own wedding day through the excitement of Ruth. There were tiny heart-shaped buttons around the neck line of the dress and on the elegant long sleeves. Her matching veil was held with a pearl tiara and finally, Ruth would carry a large bouquet of white lilies, and an enormous decorative horseshoe and key.

Jack had hired a car for the day to take Ruth to the church and beamed with pride as he ushered her to the rear seat. As Ruth had decided against brides maids because of the cost it was agreed that Moira would act as her lady in waiting and she joined Ruth in the car constantly remembering her own wedding so many years ago.

The short drive from Ruth's home to the church was filled with mixed emotions. Ruth was saddened as she thought that it should be her father driving the car and planning to give her away, instead it was to be Jack. She quietly shed a tear as she reflected that it should be her family, her mother and her brothers and sisters that should witness the happy occasion but they would not.

This was to be a very one sided wedding but Ruth was determined that it would not spoil her happy day. As they reached the church, Jack swiftly ran around to the rear of the car and helped Ruth and Moira out and waited for them to adjust the veil and train before the slow walk to the church door. As Ruth arrived at the door and prepared herself for the ordeal of the walk down the aisle, out of the darkened doorway stepped Mary and Mrs Morgan.

Ruth was beside herself with joy breaking free from the arm of the man who was to give her away to embrace Mary before, welcoming Mrs Morgan in a somewhat more restrained manner. Mrs Morgan lived up to her reputation and wore a figure hugging dress with a deeply plunging neckline that was destined to turn heads. Moira wiped the tears from Ruth's face as Mary continued to cling to Ruth with tears streaming down her face. "We love you Ruth O'Connor and you will always be a part of our family", shouted Mrs Morgan whose cleavage had entertained Jack during this short interlude before the main event.

Ruth slowly walked down the aisle and as she did she saw Edward waiting for her at the altar respendent in formal morning coat and sporting a white carnation. As they reached the alter Edward handed his top hat and gloves to his best man and stepped forward to take Ruth's hand from Jack. The moment of Ruth's dreams had arrived, she was to be married to the man she loved.

Ruth was to remember little about the wedding service as waves of emotion filled her mind. She remembered the 'I do' bit, but who wouldn't and was told that she repeated the marriage vows without error or too much emotion in her voice. She recalled being sure that her now fading Welsh accent returned to leave no one unaware of her proud Welsh origins with their roots deep in the soil of the Valleys.

Photographs were taken outside the church, not by a professional photographer but by a friend of Edward's who seemed upon reflection to feature Mrs Morgan in just about every set piece family grouping! And as the bride and groom left the church for the reception in time honoured custom Ruth was greeted by a chimney sweep, dressed also in top hat and tails but his face was darkened by the soot of his trade and carrying a Sweep's brush. He stepped forward and with great charm gently kissed Ruth on the cheek to the evident delight of the wedding guests and those passing by the church who had stopped to see the bride.

The custom of chimney sweeps attending weddings dates back to the time when a London Chimney Sweep saved the life of King George the second. It is said that the Sweep had been the only person brave enough to step forward when the King's coach and horses bolted. The Sweep rushed to the monarch's aid and pulled up the horses. The King was said to be so pleased that he proclaimed by Royal Decree that all Chimney Sweeps were bearers of good luck and must therefore be treated with respect.

Due in part to the unexpected company of Mary and Mrs Morgan, the reception buffet turned into a happy cheery affair and even Aunt Matilda seemed subdued but that may have been the two glasses of Harvey's Bristol Cream sherry she had consumed upon arrival. The buffet wedding breakfast had the hallmarks of one-upmanship all over it. The vol-au-vents brought class as did the wide range of canapés and as though to complete the statement there wasn't a sausage roll in sight.

In the early afternoon, Mary and Mrs Morgan announced that they had to leave to catch their train back to Cardiff. In an instant Jack gallantly leapt to his feet, to the annoyance of Moira who had been observing his obsession with Mrs Morgan's anatomy with growing annoyance, and he announced that he would drive them to the station in his hire car. It was also time for Ruth to change into her going away outfit and she left the room with Mary.

They went into the bedroom and Ruth slipped out of her wedding dress and into the austere brown dress that she would leave in. Mary and Ruth chatted and laughed at the more humorous sides of the day. As Ruth was about to leave the room, Mary drew her close and asked, "You are happy aren't you?' Ruth said she was and in a mild rebuke said to Mary, "This is a girl's happiest day of her life, why shouldn't I be happy?" Mary said no more except to say that this was the first time today that she had seen Ruth smile and relaxed. She remarked, "Whilst Edward seems really nice, for a man, he also seems to be stuffy and old before he is young. Mary finished by saying, "And be careful Ruth he still has an eye for the ladies." Once again a passing remark was to be dismissed by Ruth only perhaps to be recalled in months to come.

Ruth and Edward's journey from Blackpool to Morecambe, a journey that would take a little more than an hour was filled with happy reflections on their great day. Even Edward commented that he had not seen his family so relaxed and at ease with people. Edward asked about Mrs Morgan and Mary and was interested to learn how they met and why they had become such good friends.

Ruth recalled for Edward the happy and the tragic time she had spent in their company in Cardiff a story that was to occupy much of their journey. When Ruth had finished her story, Edward with some feeling said, "In your short life you have seen and done things that I'm not so sure I could handle in the way you have. You've seen the dying and have seen death, you have felt the full force of the blitz and yet you still seem to have retained your youthful innocence, I don't know how you did it." He went on to say that in his war he had so far seen nothing like what Ruth had seen. He also remarked that he could see how close Ruth was to both Mary and her mother and commented that he didn't really have friends with whom he had ever built such a friendship.

Ruth took the opportunity to ask Edward how many girl friends he had been out with if he found it difficult to make friends. In an instance he said, "Just two and you are the second." Ruth knew this was not true but chose to approach the question a different way. "Come on" she said, "Surely, with so many lovely ladies to choose from at Vickers, surely you have dated one or two." Edward's demeanour changed; he slowed the car down and then stopped. He was visibly angry when he turned to Ruth and said, "What's this all about, don't you believe me? You shouldn't believe the tittle tattle you hear at work especially from that tart Victoria."

That final comment intrigued Ruth because it seemed to give some credence to Victoria's cautionary warnings about Edwards's roving eye. Here was Ruth on her wedding day at the start of what had the makings of her first real row with Edward but she felt compelled to challenge what he had said, and oh, how she did! Ruth came straight to the point, "I'm not in the least bit interested in how many girls you've dated, and I'm turning a blind eye on how many you may have slept with, but it's the talk of Vickers that you have dated many girls there, including Victoria, so why lie to me, especially today of all days?"

Edward banged the steering wheel and retorted, "I've told you I haven't been out with any of them especially Victoria who is a known trouble maker." Like a lamb to the slaughter came the cri de Coeur from Ruth. "I know that you were seeing these girls, including Victoria the one you call a tart, whilst at the same time you were also seeing Sarah but that's your past. What I need to know is, are you going to two time me and continue to see Sarah?" The angry man in Edward suddenly became the pouting child as he implored Ruth to believe him that it was all over between him and Sarah and that whoever was spreading vicious rumours about him were doing so out of jealousy. The row was over and Ruth found herself retreating to the position of becoming increasingly unsure about Edward but giving him the benefit of the doubt, at least for today.

Their one night honeymoon attained the status it was intended as they 'consummated' their marriage that night. However, if yesterday Ruth was the 'virgin bride' today she was the seven weeks pregnant woman as she spent the morning before their departure back to Blackpool with her head over the sink experiencing what was to become the beginning of a period of eight weeks of morning sickness.

They journeyed slowly back to Ruth's new home stopping occasionally for Ruth to take some air discovering that without warning she had also become car sick. On arrival back in Blackpool Ruth spent the rest of the day and night in bed before settling into the domestic pattern of marriage.

Each day, Edward and Ruth would leave the house together to travel to work and at the end of the day they would arrive home together. During the day Ruth was careful whilst at work to conceal her pregnancy which for Ruth was difficult given that she could be sick at the very sign of food or, strangely by the smell of some of the protective sleeving used to harness instrument wires.

Concealing her pregnancy was becoming difficult and at about the three month mark she decided to announce to her friends that she had just had confirmed that she was pregnant. This allowed herself to be visibly absent from her work bench on her frequent trips to the lavatory. The rouse seemed to work but Ruth realised that it might become more difficult to conceal later in her pregnancy particularly when she would be attempting to truncate nine months down to seven or so.

Life in the Carmichael house was already beginning to show the strains of two married women vying for the attention of Edward something that Edward revelled in but which was beginning to irritate Ruth. As a relatively new bride she wanted to cook and wash for Edward but found these tasks remained exclusively Ellen's. Pointedly, Ellen would select all of Edwards washing from the laundry basket and whilst he was at work she would wash and iron them and place his things neatly folded on their bed. If in the evening Edward should ask for a snack, the by now more nimble Ellen would leap to his request and make a sandwich or a cup of tea. His every need other than those reserved exclusively for a wife was met by Ellen. This resulted in Ruth spending her evenings washing and ironing her own clothes and therefore having less time with Edward.

Ruth established her own routine of spending every Monday evening after work in the company of Moira. They would have tea and chat about work, the Carmichael's and of course the progress of her pregnancy and the war. Her weekly visits also provided Ruth with the time to read her letters and to reply. Ruth continued to use Moira's home as her correspondence address to maintain the ever more complex ties with her family and friends.

Ruth would start by writing to her mother, careful to maintain an air of excitement about her new marriage, careful not to disclose any hint of her advancing pregnancy. Occasionally, Ruth would slip a ten shilling note into the envelope knowing that this would be used by her mother for her own use. Ruth's mother, as Ruth herself would do in later years had a number of teapots in which she would keep money. One would be for the rent, one for the milkman and one for the doctor but money that was her own would always be kept in her knickers drawer 'for a rainy day'.

Ruth would write each week to Mary whose letters were becoming increasingly dark as she confided more of her own challenges with her sexuality. In a recent letter Mary disclosed that she had taken a trip to London with her 'friend' and had her eyes opened to the large number of bars and salons that were frequented by women like her, women who openly spoken of themselves as lesbians.

Mary explained that she was taken to the Gateways club in London where she had a wonderful time meeting openly with and being able to share feelings and emotions with women who felt like her. Mary had explained that the club was also fascinating for the range of different people from all social classes who were there, which included women serving in the military as well as women of high status who lived in London. Mary revealed in her letter that she was clearly drawn to the freedoms that London had to offer women, even during wartime.

Ruth's final letter was always reserved for Auntie Lott and Uncle Arthur in Senghenydd. Lott's letters were always chatty and gave revealing accounts of life in the village, and the comings and goings of the many people who were familiar names to Ruth. Lott would always include in her letter news about Dai her son who by now had been married for about five years though from the snippets Ruth could piece together from the letters the marriage seemed to be in serious trouble.

It was difficult for Ruth to maintain the pretence with Lott, of not being married and of the fact that she was expecting a child as she was one of the few people in her life that she had always felt she could confide in. Ruth felt she was betraying that childhood friendship by being secretive but as each letter writing week passed it became harder for Ruth to untangle the web of deceit she was weaving with her mother, Mary and Lott.

Edward's evenings became a predictable routine. He would eat his evening meal and once it was dark he would retire to the radio shack. He could spend the entire evening there and on many occasions he would not go to bed until the early hours of the morning.

On the occasions that Ruth would try to show an interest in Edward's Radio Ham activities she would be dismissed and only once did she ever enter into the whistling, crackling world of the 'Shack' with its oscillating sounds, mainly of Morse code coming from an unremarkable looking radio set on the bench. There were meters which meant nothing to Ruth and there were some that did but putting the whole lot together, Ruth could not see what could be so captivating to keep him there for so many hours each night. When Ruth once asked Ellen how she tolerated Edward's nocturnal hobby she simply shrugged it off and no more was said.

What was slowly becoming obvious to Ruth was that Edward the Special Constable had not yet surfaced and feeling a little playful one evening when they were in their bedroom she said to Edward, "I haven't seen you in your police uniform yet so why don't you put it on for me, you know I like a man in uniform." Edward became defensive and tried to change the subject. With that, Ruth went to Edward's wardrobe, opened it and looked inside to try and find the elusive Special Constable uniform. Edward leapt to his feet and angrily said, "You won't find it there" and stormed out of the room.

Ruth was intrigued; so if the uniform wasn't there, where was it? She was not prepared to let it rest and followed Edward from the bedroom where she found him in the kitchen with his mother. "Where does Edward keep his Special Constable's uniform" Ruth asked to the visible annoyance of Edward. Ellen turned to her and snapped, "The problem with you is that you interfere too much, just leave it alone and let Edward get on with his life." Clearly the tension of two women in this house, one who seemed to know everything about Edward and the other who was trying to discover more about her new husband was simply adding to the already strained relationships.

By the time Ruth was into the third trimester of pregnancy, morning sickness was a thing of the past and she was in full bloom. Talk amongst her friends was that she seemed to blossom on her pregnancy. Thankfully for Ruth, the fact that she was still not too large seemed to be fitting the contrived story of a post marriage conception. Her plan was to work until about three weeks before she was due and then spend the time until the birth resting at home.

The strain of living with Edward's parents was becoming increasingly difficult which led to Ruth spending large amounts of time in their bedroom alone. She would listen to the wireless, read or simply sleep. Edward continued to spend hours in the radio shack at night even though it was now early winter. Ruth also began to notice that Edward was beginning to take the occasional Saturday evening out with his friends. Ruth was not consulted and on the third occasion this happened, she only discovered that he would not be home until late when she asked Ellen the whereabouts of Edward.

The following Friday Ruth announced to Edward that she would be joining him on his night out, noting that it was some time since they went out together. In the presence of his mother he dismissed her suggestion by saying, "You have responsibilities to our child and Blackpool at night is no place for a woman who is soon to have a baby." Ellen grasped the opportunity to support her son, "You are always complaining, always wanting to know this or that, never once thinking that Edward has given up a great deal for you and the least you can do is let the poor man have a night with his friends at the end of a hard week."

Ruth saw no way that she was going to defeat the combined forces of the Carmichael's and again retreated to her room. She was not at ease as she pondered who Edward was seeing and the name Sarah was never far from her mind. The fact that he was leaving with his skating boots over his shoulder only added to the turmoil in her mind that his attention might be being taken by Sarah. She became obsessed by the notion that Edward was secretly seeing Sarah and when her discreet questions to her friends at least placed Edward and Sarah in the same place at the same time, her imagination ran wild. She had no proof that Edward was cheating on her but the circumstantial evidence was mounting.

Some weeks later Ruth was awoken from her sleep at about one thirty in the morning to heavy knocking on the front door and the muffled sound of voices in the rear garden. Taking care to ensure there was no light in the bedroom, she carefully pulled back the blackout curtains and could see three people in uniform near to Edward's radio shack and by now, Sam and Ellen were at the front door. Ruth remained silent not wishing to alert anyone to the fact she was awake so that she might eves drop on otherwise guarded conversations.

Ruth opened her bedroom door slightly and could hear a police officer say that they needed to inspect the shed in the garden where they had received reports over some weeks from neighbors that there was the sound of Morse code being heard on most evenings and long into the night. Stood alongside the policeman was a person in army uniform which only served to further heighten the tension in the hallway by the front door.

Ruth heard Ellen say that Edward had been here earlier but was now working his shift in Blackpool as a Special Constable. Further questions followed before everyone moved into the rear garden and there they stayed for what seemed like hours. Eventually, the relative quiet that had descended upon the garden was shattered when Edward entered through the front door accompanied by two people in military uniform. It was hard for Ruth to understand quite what was going on until she heard the raised voice of Edward saying, "They are nosey busybodies who can frankly sling their hook." He went on, "It's nothing more than an amateur radio shack that is doing nobody any harm."

Eventually, Edward left with the assembled military and police not to return until about six o'clock as the house was stirring once again at the start of the day. Ruth confronted Edward who was looking tired and unusually unkempt. "Where the hell were you last night at one thirty in the morning when the Home Guard, the Police and the Army turned up in force to find out what you do in your shed?" Not stopping for breath she said, "You clearly were not there, were you with Sarah?" The kitchen was hushed as Sam, Ellen and Ruth waited for

Edward's response. As usual, it was Ellen who spoke for Edward, "No he was not with Sarah he was on duty at the police station in Fleetwood and before you ask more of your stupid questions, he keeps the uniform you were searching for there." Ruth saw red, "Then why didn't the local police know that, rather than banging on our door in the middle of the night?"

It was clear that the Carmichaels were once again closing ranks and Ruth found herself being stared at and being lost for words. This did not stop Ruth from confronting Edward later to ask firstly why it was that the local police seemed to know nothing about Edward being a Special Constable and why it took so long for them to find him. Edward shrugged his shoulders and said, "I'm doing nothing wrong in the radio shack otherwise they would have taken my equipment and in so far as Sarah is concerned, I haven't seen her in months." Ruth knew this was not the case but simply couldn't muster the energy to argue any more.

CHAPTER FOURTEEN

Christmas nineteen forty three was a subdued family affair in the Carmichael house celebrated by attending church on Christmas morning with Aunt Matilda and Aunt Dorothy before returning to the house for Christmas presents and lunch. The impact of the war meant that the Christmas presents were small simple tokens. Ruth had purchased a scarf for Aunt Matilda, a set of handkerchiefs for Aunt Dorothy, socks for Sam some Eau de Cologne for Ellen and for Edward she bought a rather modern pair of pajamas to replace the ones that resembled those her father would have worn. In return Edward bought Ruth a book by Nicholson Eastman entitled *Expectant Motherhood*.

Ruth waited in anticipation of what other gifts might come her way from the family. Ellen broke the silence and said, "We have decided that we will not be frivolous and buy you presents now, instead we will buy baby clothes once you have had the baby, just in case there are any problems!" Ruth was not surprised even on this holiest of days that the family should be so cruel as to even suggest that there may yet be problems with her otherwise uneventful pregnancy.

Christmas lunch was pleasant if not restrained with Ellen serving a very small chicken that Aunt Matilda had brought and the vegetables were a collection of what was in season from each of their gardens including the seasonal Brussels sprout. To follow there were small mince pies and apple pie.

Boxing Day spent with Moira and Jack was anything but a dull affair. An invitation was extended for Edward to attend which caused him to have to choose between Ruth's only family in the area or a visit to Aunt Matilda, not surprisingly he declined Moira and Jack.

Though the food was simple and modest the company and the laughter were hearty. Ruth received a large pair of knickers and a nursing bra from Moira and a full length winter coat from Jack. Though the coat was second hand it was a very welcome gift and when she wore it in her one person fashion show with the knickers tucked over the front of her skirt and her battleship size bra worn over the winter jumper she was wearing she felt suddenly at ease for the first time in months.

Ruth presented Jack with a small garden trowel which she knew would replace the one that broke months ago and for Moira a small bar of Fry's five boy chocolate depicting a boy's face, in five different stages, changing from crying to smiling and then happy. Ruth had purchased the chocolate in the summer from a friend at work who needed extra cash and was selling treasured items. She also gave Moira a scarf she had lovingly knitted over months. The love that went into the scarf was explained when she revealed that a dear friend at work, Chris Pearce, was a wonderful knitter and she would help Ruth at lunch times through the autumn and early winter to knit what for Chris would have taken a few hours. The scarf consumed the wool from a knitted jumper that Auntie Lott had given her when she was in her early teens and had been a treasured possession even though she had long since grown out of it.

With Christmas over and the subdued celebrations of the New Year of nineteen forty four behind them the date when Ruth would temporarily stop work had arrived. It was Friday the eleventh of February and should be a matter of days before Ruth's baby was due. She was pleased that she had managed to go so late into the pregnancy before having to take time away from work as it served to continue the deception that she had become pregnant on her honeymoon. However, Ruth's diary revealed what many others would show, that it was only thirty five weeks since her wedding and she now hoped that her baby would play its part and delay arrival for at least a couple more weeks.

Ruth was by now very large with her pregnancy and despite the large maternity dresses she was wearing it was clear that she was either carrying a large baby or twins or further along in the pregnancy than Ruth would have people believe. The other date in Ruth's diary was the actual date she became pregnant and that was the second of May which made her forty weeks pregnant on the sixth of February which was only a couple of days away so she was very likely to have her baby at any moment.

Aunt Dorothy, who was a trained midwife but currently a matron in a hospital in Preston was to deliver Ruth's child at home, and like most matters that affected Ruth, she played no part in this decision and had to stand idly by as the plans for her own confinement were in the hands of others. Even the date Ruth should stop working was decided by Aunt Dorothy who had also done her calculations and had also decided that now was the time for her to temporarily leave work and stay at home where she would deliver the child.

Aunt Dorothy was predestined to be a matron, unlike her sister Aunt Matilda she was five feet eight inches tall, of large build and she oozed authority. Requests emanating from Aunt Dorothy had the status of orders and when Ruth had occasionally been examined by her during the pregnancy she could see that Aunt Dorothy was entirely detached and would have no nonsense, treating her with a dispassion that came from years of ensuring that it was the matron that was important in health care not the doctor, and certainly not the patients. Indeed, Aunt Dorothy was at pains to constantly point out that pregnancy was not an illness and that women knew what they were getting into when they embarked upon their journey towards motherhood and if they claimed they did not, then it was certainly not her role to teach them.

Ruth spent the following days trying to spend as much time as possible either in her room or with Moira. It was in her quiet moments at the writing desk that Ruth would shed the occasional tear as she wrote letters to her mother, not once revealing her pregnancy. What was emerging for those who would read Ruth's letters was that she was not a happy newlywed. This may have acted as a fortunate subterfuge for Ruth, as it seemed to divert her mother from the underlying sense of fear and foreboding that she was about to give birth and bring a child into an already unhappy marriage.

All of this did not escape the constant motherly attention of Moira who was concerned that Ruth was close to becoming ill through the pain of worry and the underlying suspicion that Edward was seeing Sarah again. This was not helped by Edward's complete detachment from Ruth hardly seeing her except for meals at the house and with him spending increasing time either in the radio shack or in his duties as a Special Constable. Ruth had developed a fixation that his duties as a Special Constable were code for him spending time with Sarah. She spoke to Moira on several occasions that she had a sense of foreboding that the Carmichaels would one day make life so unbearable for her that she would be forced to leave.

On the eighteenth of February Ruth went into labour at about three o'clock in the morning and as usual Edward was nowhere to be found. Aunt Dorothy, an experienced clinical practitioner stirred only to pass a message through Ellen that she was not to be disturbed again until the contractions were regular and established.

Ruth bore the fear and pain of labour alone until about nine thirty in the morning when her cries for help were heard by the rest of the household. Throughout the ordeal of the night she muffled her screams and wiped her own tears from her face, she bore this whole confinement alone and in tears. The cry for help was responded to and with that there was a flurry of activity as firstly, Ellen came into the room and then Aunt Dorothy to inspect the stage of her labour. At length, Edward appeared which served as the point when the valve that had been containing Ruth's pain and anger released and Ruth screamed at him to leave and not to come back until the baby was born. That moment was very near and as calm returned to the room Ruth was skilfully and by now tenderly coaxed to bring her baby into the world.

It was at eleven thirty in the morning that Ruth gave birth to a baby girl. Its weight was six pounds ten ounces; she had a mop of black hair and a beauty rarely seen in a new born. She was perfect and as Ruth cradled the child in her arms Edward entered the room emotional and full of praise for what Ruth had achieved. Not wanting to release her baby so soon Ruth still felt an urge to see Edward with the baby in his arms. As this tiny baby rested in Edward's arms the tears fell down his cheeks, he was instantly smitten. Edward moved to Ruth's side and there they lay in a blissful sea of happiness. At that moment, Ruth felt Edwards love in a way that she had not seen for months and any fears for the safety of their marriage were soon gone.

Later that day Ruth emerged into the sitting room with her baby to find that the promise at Christmas that the Carmichaels would provide for the child was real. Baby clothes, towelling nappies and a pram were provided as well as a couple of small soft toys. Ruth was touched and was fulsome in her appreciation that they had given so much thought to the planning of these gifts. It transpired that a local shop had been on standby to provide pink or blue and Edward had rushed the packages over to the house only an hour earlier. It was at this point that her thoughts turned to her mother someone that throughout her childhood, Ruth had imagined standing at the end of her bed looking down on her as she cradled her first born.

But now Ruth was caught in the web of her own deceit. She knew at that moment that she could never tell her mother that she was now a mother too. To tell would bring scorn and shame because it would become evident that the deceit was to cover up that she had become pregnant before her marriage.

The following days for Ruth were filled with the joys of motherhood. She surprised the family with the confidence she showed in the daily routines of caring for her newborn. But they were not to know that this was something she had done several times before as she stepped in to help her mother with her newborn brothers and sisters in her own family.

On the second day the subject of what the child was to be called came up as Edward prepared to register the birth. Many suggestions came from the family, indeed they felt to Ruth more like directives than suggestions. Ruth had grown up in a home where it was the exclusive responsibility of the mother to name her children and she was therefore not going to entertain any suggestion that it should be otherwise for her own child. This thinking was alien to Edward and the family but when Ruth emerged into the sitting room and announced that the baby girl was to be named Charlotte there was complete acceptance. Of course to Ruth there was only one name for her child, a silent tribute to the lady who had given so much love to her as a child, Auntie Lott.

Charlotte had been born into an uncertain world. All hopes of an early end to the war were being foiled by the strong resistance of the Axis forces. Moral was a pendulum that swung daily based upon the snippets of heavily censored news that was broadcast by the Home Service of the BBC on the wireless and the slightly more sensational commentary from the print media.

Blackpool languished in its bubble of normality with the exception of rationing, and a chronic housing shortage which resulted in the families of Service and ex-Service men living in overcrowded conditions. The Corporation of Blackpool had been granted permission by the government to requisition empty houses but there were very few. The theatres of Blackpool thrived, and were running fourteen shows every night. They had abandoned the concept of a *season* operating for most of the war for the full fifty two weeks of the year.

After a few days Ruth embarked on the journey to Moira's home to give her the opportunity to meet Charlotte for the first time. Throughout the whole time that Ruth had been married Moira had not once been invited to the Carmichael's home and whilst this was of no concern to Moira or Ruth, they both felt that this was something of a snub to Ruth's side of the family. Moira and Jack adored the child and a routine was quickly established that they would see her once every week caring for her as Ruth sat at their desk and wrote her letters.

Two weeks after Charlotte's birth Ruth was back at work amongst friends. All were delighted to see her smiling face again in the cockpit. Ruth seemed to convince most that she had delivered a premature baby a deception that allowed her to continue the subterfuge though it should be said that the older ladies were far from convinced.

CHAPTER FIFTEEN

Ruth found the challenge of giving up her baby each day to her mother-in-law increasingly difficult. In the early months she was only seeing Charlotte for a short while in the morning often finding that by the time she returned home in the evening, Charlotte was bathed and in bed. It was only the night feeds that gave Ruth the chance to have time with Charlotte and as she progressed to sleeping for most if not the whole night, her contact grew less. Ellen was a good grandmother to Charlotte but Ruth would often notice that when Charlotte needed comforting it would be Ellen that immediately sprang to her need and over time Charlotte seemed unable to be calmed unless Ellen took over. Such was the bond between Ellen and Charlotte that Ellen the Grandmother was becoming Ellen the mother.

The tensions in the Carmichael house became less opaque with full scale rows developing between Ellen and Ruth particularly at weekends when Ruth wanted exclusive access to Charlotte. When Ruth suggested to Edward that they spend time with Charlotte it regularly resulted in Ellen and often the whole family coming along too. The only quality time that Ruth spent with Charlotte was when she went to see Moira. Ruth had taken to visiting Moira on a Saturday afternoon returning only when Charlotte was due to be put to bed for the evening.

Edward continued his nights in the radio shack and his duties as a Special Constable. Ruth was increasingly seeing Edward's nights with the Police as a euphemism for going in to Blackpool to see Sarah. Ruth continued to pick up on conversations at work that Edward was seen at the ice rink or was seen at the Tower Ballroom and when she confronted Edward it resulted in the same denial and suggestions that she was paranoid about Sarah.

Ruth was regularly invited by work colleagues and friends to go ice skating or dancing which she had always turned down. However, in the first week of July Ruth was again invited out, this time to celebrate Victoria's birthday. Ruth wanted to go because since the incident when Victoria had warned her about Edward's tendency to two time girls, she and Ruth had become good friends.

Victoria was insistent that Ruth should join them for a night out pointing out that it was Friday, and that Edward would probably be doing his Special Constable duties. Ruth waited until the Friday evening when she returned home from work to announce to Ellen that as Edward would be doing his police duties she was going out to celebrate a friend's birthday. The level of communication between Ruth and Ellen had deteriorated to such a level and had become so strained that Ellen simply tutted, remarked that any good mother should be with her child and ended the conversation.

The plan was that Ruth and her friends would meet at the Tower Ballroom at about seven thirty. A group of eight ladies from Vickers were waiting when Ruth arrived a little out of breath at about seven forty five. They spent about half an hour generally chatting before

Victoria said she was going to the lavatory and would Ruth go with her. They left the main ballroom area and when they arrived in a quieter area, Victoria took her to one side and said, "Do you really want to see what Edward does most Friday nights?" Ruth was taken aback as the last thing on her mind tonight, the first time she had been out with friends in months, was Edward.

Ruth turned to Victoria and said, "What are you talking about, he's at the police tonight." "Oh no he isn't" said Victoria, "he's sat at the far end of the ballroom and Sarah is there too." Ruth responded with a mixture of anger and surprise. It suddenly dawned on her that if Victoria was right she would have the evidence Edward had so strenuously suggested was not there, to show that he was seeing Sarah again. However, Ruth pondered whether she actually wanted to see the evidence for herself fearing the potential consequences of any confrontation, particularly with Sarah there.

Ruth turned to Victoria and coldly said, "So that's why you were so insistent that I should come out tonight, because you and the girls wanted to embarrass me and have some fun at my expense." Victoria was surprised by Ruth's reaction and assured her that she had no idea that Edward would be there pointing out that he usually goes ice skating on a Friday and that is why she had chosen to go to the Tower Ballroom.

Ruth accepted this and as they returned to their seats she glanced in the direction pointed out by Victoria. And there he was and there she was, sitting in a small group, a group which Ruth recognised. The group were happily chatting and it was clear that Edward and Sarah certainly were not ignoring each other. Ruth felt numb. She didn't know what to do, should she confront them or should she wait until Edward left the group and catch him then.

Suddenly, a wave of guilt swept over her as she started to convince herself that it was she who should not be there. The words of Ellen were ringing in Ruth's ear that a mother should be at home not out enjoying herself. Ruth had by now convinced herself that there was nothing to be gained by speaking to Edward tonight and that she should go home immediately. No pleading from Victoria could persuade her otherwise. However, as Ruth left she lingered long enough to see that whilst Edward and Sarah were evidently not a couple their body language was saying that they would like to be. Their eyes lingered upon each other as others were speaking and the occasional whisper into each other's ear served only to convince Ruth to run.

Ruth ran to the bus stop and caught the next bus home to find Ellen sitting alone in the sitting room. Ellen was surprised to see Ruth home so early and could see that she was upset. She invited Ruth to sit down and she asked her what had so upset her. Ruth thought for a moment and then throwing caution to the wind explained what she had seen. Ellen asked if Edward had seen Ruth and more particularly had she spoken to Edward. Ruth explained that she was too upset to confront him and chose to rush home instead.

Ellen paused and then said, "I will speak to Edward and I will tell him to be more attentive to you. I will not speak of what you saw this evening, best not to cause a scene, but I will ensure that he is home more." Ruth was surprised by her calm reaction but concurred that Ellen's view was probably in truth her own, that if Ellen could stop Edward from going out so much it would stop him from seeing Sarah.

Nothing could be more from the truth. Whilst it was evident that Edward did seem to be home more and that he was more attentive, Ruth was not to know that Victoria's warnings were well placed. Edward had indeed resumed seeing Sarah even before Charlotte was born and they had been seeing each other at least once per month. Edward had also managed to arrange to spend some days each month at the Dick Kerr factory in Preston as an advisor on aircraft communications and this placed him in the very department that Sarah worked in.

Edward and Sarah were meeting regularly and had discussed the folly of Edward's decision not to convert to Catholicism and go on to marry Sarah and they continued to declare their undying love for each other. Sarah's Catholic values were all that stood between Edward and Sarah having an affair but their relationship was intense and destined to go further. They had already spoken of a time in the future when it may be possible for them to marry though they acknowledged that a divorce for Edward could take some time. Their conversations were based more in the world of hope than reality with both knowing that for the time being at least theirs would need to be a clandestine relationship unless a fortuitous set of circumstances were to suddenly provide the solution that was currently eluding them.

What Ruth was also unaware of was that Sarah had been to Edward's home and had seen Charlotte on more than one occasion renewing at the same time the strong relationship she had built previously with Ellen and Sam. In those conversations it had also emerged that Sarah had been advised by her doctor that an underlying heart condition would make it dangerous for her to have children of her own as child birth would put too much of a strain on her. In all other ways Sarah was a healthy young woman.

Had Ruth known anything of what was going on it is hard to predict the likely outcome and the impact this might have had on her marriage and the course of her own life.

CHAPTER SIXTEEN

The war continued to dominate conversation in the factories, pubs and homes of Britain. After much of Europe had been occupied by the Axis powers for four years, and with public concern of a German invasion of Britain, the Allies finally launched their campaign to liberate Western Europe, codenamed Operation Overlord. The public's moral lifted with reports of massive numbers of Allied troops being landed in Europe where the RAF had already secured air supremacy. The nation's spirits were high, and guarded talk that the end might be in sight was commonplace.

It was also in the June that Ruth was to be summoned into the living room of the Carmichaels home to be told that by the end of September the family would be moving out of their home as the landlord wanted the house back. In itself this was unsurprising as Ruth was aware that the tenancy was due for renewal. What was a surprise was that the family was to move to Eastbrook Farm on the outskirts of the tiny hamlet of Whittingham set against the lower slopes of the Lancashire Pennines some twenty miles from Blackpool and about six miles from Preston.

There was no consultation with Ruth who it transpired had been kept in the dark for more than three months whilst the family had been transacting the lease for the farm. Ruth could not separate this decision from a desire on Edward's part to keep her from her friends and Blackpool though it transpired that his motives were far more Machiavellian.

The tenancy for the farm had come about because of the death of the owner, a bomber pilot who had been shot down and killed. His wife, who Sam and Ellen knew was unable to continue to manage the smallholding that had commitments to supply eggs, poultry, milk and pigs to the local community and the military forces in Blackpool.

Sam's interest in farming went back to his own childhood where he had grown up and spent over twenty years on the family's small farm on the outskirts of Pilling not very far away. He was therefore used to the farming way of life, but importantly, he saw this as a way of moving into a family business. Sam needed to pull many strings to ensure that this valuable tenancy was secured by the Carmichaels particularly as it was one of a number of prime strategic suppliers to the RAF locally. The Carmichaels seemed able to secure the transfer of the farm tenancy and the purchase of the livestock when many others who were far better qualified could and probably should have been given preference.

Ruth could only imagine what life would be like living on a remote farm, miles away from her friends, Moira and her now settled life in Lancashire. She feared the isolation and the inevitable pressure on her to spend any spare time she might have working on the farm, rather than with Charlotte. There was also the matter of how she would get to and from Blackpool. She was told that Sam would take Edward and her to Preston each day by car where they could catch buses that were especially laid on to take workers to both the Preston and Blackpool aircraft plants.

The plans seemed to Ruth to be fragile and in discussing them with Moira they alighted upon the solution that Ruth should stay once again with Moira between Monday and Friday spending the weekends with Charlotte and the family at Eastbrook Farm. Whilst this meant that Ruth would not see her precious Charlotte during the week it seemed to all concerned to be an admirable solution.

September came and Ruth and Edward managed to take a few days from their work to help with the move to Eastbrook Farm. They arrived at the end of the day when furniture and personal belongings had been delivered in the back of a truck provided by the egg packing company that would collect their eggs every two days.

They were met at the farm gate by an old man in his late sixties who introduced himself as Tom Masters, the farm hand. He was a chirpy wizened old man wearing wellington boots from a bygone age, a long coat with string tied around the middle to keep it closed from the chilling breeze and a potato sack draped around his shoulder to stop the evening rain from penetrating. "I've been here man and boy" was his greeting as he guided them to the farmhouse rather as though he were ushering royalty.

The farm itself was situated immediately alongside a single track country road that linked a number of small villages and farms. It also served as the main link to Goosnargh to the south which was where the nearest shops were located and Garstang to the west, a more substantial market town. The farm was on the road to the Bowland Forrest and the Trough of Bowland and, for Charlotte, Jubilee Tower where she was conceived. The nearest farmhouse was Bowland Moss Farm which was about half a mile away and there were small workers houses a little nearer. The farmhouse itself dated back to the eighteenth century. It had three bedrooms a large working kitchen with a wood fired stove, a small living room that overlooked the road and another room to the rear which was a boot room with a toilet and bath.

Ruth's first impression was of a dark uninviting place with low exposed beams, flaking whitewashed walls and cold flagstone floors. The bedroom that she and Edward were to share was slightly larger than she had anticipated but was also dark because of its exceptionally small window cut into the eaves of the house. The walls were papered with floral patterned wallpaper that was in good condition and the boarded wooden floor had a small carpet by the sink. There was electric lighting and power provided to the house and out buildings but as this regularly failed, there was also a backup generator.

Ruth and Edward were shown around the farm by Sam with Tom Masters close at his heel correcting any errors he was making about aspects of the farm or the stock. To the very rear of the first half acre field were rows of nesting boxes for the four hundred laying chickens and a propagation shed. As they moved towards the chicken sheds, the birds seemed to sense that as it was already getting dusk they would need to go inside where a feed would be there for them. Tom explained that if the birds were not in the hen houses by dusk it was difficult to get them in and the local foxes would undoubtedly kill some overnight.

With the birds safely in for the night their final job was to settle down the thirty six pigs. The smell as they approached the pig stalls was distinctive and lingering as Tom explained that three schools provided swill for the farm, in return for the occasional chicken. Finally Sam pointed to the nearby field and explained that there was a milking herd of thirty cows that Tom looked after seven days per week. On the edge of the other farm yard buildings were a rundown but adequate milking parlour and winter stabling.

As they turned in the fading light to return to the house, Ruth noticed the silhouette of another shed and was about to ask what that was used for when she saw the familiar amateur radio mast proudly erected alongside it. Ruth was furious as she realised that Edward must have been to the farmhouse previously to erect the aerial when he would have had the opportunity to show her the property she was to live in. When she challenged Edward, he was dismissive and firm when he said, "That shed is for my exclusive use and will be locked at all times. If you ever need to get me when I'm in there, there is a bell in the kitchen."

Ruth quickly settled into the routine of staying with Moira during the week and returning to the farm at weekends. She also enjoyed the renewed freedom of being able to come and go as she pleased. She began to reconnect with her work friends and to go out dancing and ice skating again. Whilst she met young men when she was out at night, she was quick to ensure they knew she was married and would be returning alone to her home at the end of the evening. Ruth was surprised that no one seemed to have seen Sarah around the Blackpool scene and reported sightings of Edward in the dance halls of Blackpool also dried up. Ruth took this to be a positive sign but what she didn't know was that Edward and Sarah were meeting in Preston somewhere Ruth never went.

Ruth continued her letter writing always being careful not to give a hint of the secret side of her life. This was a terrible subterfuge and was made the more difficult to manage when Ruth so wanted to confide in her mother or Mary and especially Auntie Lott. Her letters were sterile considering the constant turmoil in her life and she felt sure that those who knew her best must also know her letters were guarded and lacked the spontaneity that had so characterised her earlier letters.

In Mary's most recent letter to Ruth, she confided that her mother was about to move to Cambridgeshire to live with Colonel *Hawkeye* Brockenbeck who she had met when they visited Blackpool. Mary was concerned that her mother was planning to 'live over the broom' a common term used to suggest that an unmarried couple would live as man and wife.

Mary was no prude but she considered this to be improper and had told Mrs Morgan. Mary wrote that she would not be going to RAF Brampton in Cambridgeshire with her mother and told Ruth in the letter that she had joined the army to provide whatever help she could in the war effort. She ended her letter by saying, '*I will write to you as often as I can, my dear friend, but I hope for one thing in what I'm doing and that is to find someone to love and someone who will love me*'.

It was evident within a matter of weeks that the attempt at the good life on the farm was placing an enormous strain on the family. Sam was unable or unwilling to employ additional help and so he and Ellen were hopelessly overstretched. Ellen took on the responsibility for the poultry and with a little advice from Tom she managed to maintain the egg production but at some cost to her own health. She would work from as early as six o'clock collecting and packing eggs, cleaning the runs and managing the chicks.

Sam's natural overbearing and demanding personality had room to flourish as he drove Ellen and Tom without any regard for their health or their advancing years. On a Friday night when Ruth arrived home she would immediately be put to tasks that had failed to be done in the week mainly by Sam. Whilst Sam had nominated himself to manage the pigs they were poorly cared for and Ruth would spend much of her weekend under the command of Sam cleaning the pigsties and caring for the pigs.

The family muddled through but it was rare to find Edward or his father working. When Edward was at home on the weekend his father would give him the accounts to manage which were always done in the relative comfort of his radio shack where the sound of Morse code could always be heard whenever Edward was at home. Ruth continued to be suspicious and uncomfortable by Edward's insistence that his amateur radio hobby was indeed a hobby.

Ruth's instinct that there was somehow a link between Edward's amateur radio activities and the war was well founded but she like the rest of Britain was not to know anything of what really was going on in the back bedrooms and garden sheds of almost fifteen thousand homes across Britain.

At the outbreak of the war, the intelligence agency MI-5 rolled out its contingency plans to deal with the problems of illicit radio transmissions by creating a new body called the Radio Security Service. Their role was to intercept, locate and close down all illicit wireless radios operated by enemy agents in Britain or by people who had not been licensed under the British defence regulations to operate a radio transmitter. The newly created body needed to create a completely new organisation and because of a lack of infrastructure and expertise, the Radio Security Service turned to the amateur radio world. Under the military intelligence cover of MI-18, *Voluntary Interceptors* were recruited and trained to scan the airwaves for radio traffic from in and around Germany and the rest of Europe. It was in September nineteen forty when Edward was signed off from his engagement in the Merchant Navy that he too was secretly recruited.

Edward had been a well known amateur radio enthusiast prior to his Merchant Navy days and had distinguished himself whilst at sea for his acute skills at being able to judge the probable distance of a radio signal and an uncanny ability to recognise the 'signatures', the small traits and individual idiosyncrasies of a particular person who was sending Morse Code. Edward would know the small tell-tale Morse signature of the radio operators on any of the company's sister ships, a skill that was instantly noted and later acted upon. These were the exact skills that the Radio Security Service was looking for.

Edward was approached on leaving the Merchant Navy, asked to sign the Official Secrets Act and was then told about work that the Radio Security Service and what the Voluntary Interceptors were doing. Edward was immediately recruited. His engineering and radio skills combined made Edward ideal for work at the

Vickers factory in Blackpool as an 'essential worker' and his employment there was secured. Finally, Edward was given the cover of being a Special Constable in order that the combination of being an essential engineer at Vickers and a Special Constable might explain why he was not serving on the front line of the war.

As a Voluntary Interceptor, Edward would be allocated predetermined wavelengths to monitor and his role was to listen and log the tell tale signs and traits of broadcasters sending Morse code. These logs were sent to a 'Box' at the Radio Security Service where they were examined by discriminators. Much of the material would eventually find its way to the National Codes and Cipher Centre at Bletchley Park.

None of this was ever known by Ruth who continued to suspect any manner of reasons why Edward spent so much time in the radio shack. For Edward, this clandestine existence was both exciting and convenient.

It was now December and a bitter winter was setting in which made life difficult on the farm. The farmhouse itself was always cold with the exception of the kitchen where most of the family would gather. Christmas Day in nineteen forty four was like any other but at least the family ate well. Charlotte was by now crawling and attempting her first steps and was increasingly close and dependent upon the weary Ellen.

Ruth was tired too and on one occasion she caught sight of herself in a mirror and was shocked to see herself looking so drawn and pale. The family managed to be civil with each other over the Christmas break but it was a fragile truce. Ruth was barely spoken to civilly and comparisons with Sarah were regularly held up as being what a model daughter-in-law would act like.

Ruth had discussed with Edward the deteriorating relationship between herself and him and the open animosity shown towards her by his parents. Edward attempted to improve their relationship but could not or would not do anything to change the way his parents treated her. Ruth even contemplated leaving Eastbrook Farm and trying to set up home with Charlotte and even discussed this with Moira.

Ruth approached Edward with the suggestion that they should rent the nearby Bowland Moss farmhouse which had been empty for some time and he was outraged by the suggestion. He said that he was perfectly content staying with his parents. He simply could not see how desperately unhappy Ruth had become.

In early January nineteen forty five already depressed and looking ill Ruth was horrified to realise that she was pregnant. On this occasion she didn't need an African Clawed Frog to tell her, she knew for herself as she felt the world collapsing around her. Her only chance of escape from this unhappy marriage had hinged upon the faint hope of her finding someone to take in a mother and child... but a pregnant mother and child would now be out of the question.

CHAPTER SEVENTEEN

Ruth met the news of her pregnancy with utter despair. By now she was already six weeks pregnant and still she kept the news entirely to herself not sharing it with Edward and certainly not with Ellen. She slipped into dark reflective moods where she hated herself, despising the person she felt she had become. The impact of the deception she had created with her mother, Mary and Auntie Lott the very people she loved the most and who loved her meant that she felt she stood alone.

Ruth eventually spoke to Moira about her pregnancy and she could see on Ruth's face that the news brought her little joy. Ruth foresaw little excitement from Edward about the news and even less from Sam and Ellen. Moira insisted that Ruth should go home on the weekend and share with her husband the news of her pregnancy and not build pictures of what his reaction might be.

Moira's advice was sound but Ruth was right to be anxious. Edward was ambivalent when she told him her news almost to the point of detachment as though it was not a matter for him to get involved in. Having heard the news he turned to leave the room evidently busied by more important matters than this. Ruth stopped Edward and asked if he was pleased and taking a moment to reflect he simply said, "It doesn't matter if I'm pleased or not...you're pregnant."

It felt to Ruth that what love there might have been in their marriage was slowly draining away. But, as though he caught Ruth's mood, he slowly turned to face her and said, "I am pleased but also shocked given that we don't get much time together these days." Ruth tried to analyse the comment but settled for it being more positive than negative. They went into the kitchen together and Edward announced their news to his open mouthed parents.

Ruth's pregnancy was marked again by morning sickness and when that was over with sustained periods of deep melancholy. Ruth had grown thin and her face was gaunt. On the insistence of Moira she consulted Dr Carr and he confirmed that she was seriously under weight and that if she didn't "pull herself together" she would jeopardise the health of herself and her baby. This seemed to hit the right nerve with Ruth and armed with some tonics, iron tablets and advice to take more rest she left his house feeling rather more positive and slightly more energised. But this was the nature of her demeanour, when she was alone she would fall into deep depressions as she rebuked herself for the web of deceit she had woven. Then when someone said something nice to her, or when she had enjoyed a happy couple of hours with Charlotte her spirits would again lift. Thankfully, her duties as a weekend farmer were reduced when it was decided to sell the herd of cattle and concentrate only on poultry and pigs.

Then came the very best news of all, when on the eighth of May nineteen forty five, the BBC Home Service carried the news that a ceasefire had been signed and Britain was at last at peace. Ruth and the family sat around the wireless to hear a speech from the King and the Prime Minister. It was as though the nation had breathed a collective sigh of relief that this ghastly war was over and that loved ones would slowly return home to their families.

But the joy soon turned to tears when news came from Singapore that confirmed that Michael, Ruth's beloved brother, soul mate and friend had been killed in the massacre at the Alexandra Military Hospital in Singapore in nineteen forty two. The news from the Army said that he had been buried in the grounds along with his military colleagues and their patients who had also died on that day.

Ruth had held out the hope that Michael might have been spared the tyranny of the Japanese occupation of Singapore and so this news was a terrible shock to her. Ruth replied by letter to her mother who had broken the news by telegram. Ruth wrote of her last letter from Michael in which he had spoken so fondly of the Singapore people and she repeated Michael's own words from that letter in the hope that they might bring some comfort to her mother: '*I miss the valleys of my beautiful Wales and the song of its people, I miss the sparrow and the black bird but I am a happy man, and if I should die here in this far off land, tell Mam ..... I saw swallows in February.*'

This news hit Ruth hard but, with the encouragement of Moira she continued to gain weight and she regained some of her youthful spirit. Work continued much as before but at a reduced pace which suited Ruth as the summer months of nineteen forty five were hot and she was tiring quickly. Ruth's weekends were increasingly spent with Charlotte who seemed to have rediscovered her mother. Now eighteen months old, Charlotte was a handful for Ellen who seemed to have visibly aged. She had also mellowed a little particularly as Ruth was taking Charlotte off her hands during the weekends giving Ellen some time to herself.

As the summer heat gave way to the refreshing coolness of late September Ruth had been given time from work to have her baby which was due in just a couple of weeks. Ruth had blossomed and grown and was a picture of health. Her long black hair regained its sheen and her complexion was that of a young woman again. Ruth like many women of her time was a smoker and would enjoy nothing more than to sit on the bench in the farm yard as the evening sun set in the west and enjoy an un-tipped Senior Service cigarette. Ruth was never a drinker, unlike her father, but was encouraged by Dr Carr to take a glass of stout each evening and so Ruth was to be found on most evenings with a cigarette in one hand and her class of Mackison stout in the other. The farm dog, an ageing Border collie named Susie always accompanied her as it also marked the end of the day for her too.

The day soon came when the sisters, Aunt Matilda and Aunt Dorothy arrived to supervise the delivery of Ruth's second child. They were given the spare bedroom and until the delivery was due they would spend hours in the vegetable garden tidying up from the summer produce and preparing for the winter to come. The few apple trees that remained in what was once a commercial orchard provided an abundant crop for the family. These were sold at the farm gate to passersby and were also sold through the local market.

On the morning of fifteenth of October, Ruth went into labour and some six hours later had given birth to a baby girl. The thoughtless, haughty consensus amongst the Aunts and Ellen was that the child was a throwback to Ruth's Irish ancestry because of her shock of red hair and the small cherub nose that in their view "didn't have the strong Anglo Saxon features of the Carmichael line." Her child was nonetheless, claimed by all, including Edward to be a beauty something that Charlotte found unconvincing pointing out the wrinkly skin!

Once again, following the tradition of her own mother Ruth announced the baby was to be called Maria Clare. The tutting was clearly audible to Ruth but she simply reconfirmed the name and that was it. Maria was a petite child with fair complexion and the early signs of freckles across her cheeks. She was a contented child from birth, rarely crying and always attentive to the world around her. But Maria would fight for the attention of her father and the family who continued to lavish their love on Charlotte who was by now enchanting and entertaining to the family.

The days that followed Maria's birth saw Ruth's mood change rapidly and alarmingly. She became depressed again and cried without any apparent reason. What was more worrying was that her depressive state made it impossible for her to continue to breast feed her baby. Aunt Dorothy saw similarities to some of the mothers she dealt with in her maternity wing at the hospital recognising the symptoms of what she called 'the blues' or a state of deep depression. She was unimpressed declaring that Ruth should "pull herself together."

Medical advances were yet to recognise that a combination of her unhappy marriage, her loss of individual identity and the recognition of the trap she was in were all combining forces that amounted to what we now call post natal depression. The ignorance of the times cannot be excused for the disgraceful way in which Ruth was to be treated in the coming weeks.

Firstly, she was taken to a doctor who referred her to a Psychiatrist at the nearby Mental hospital known locally as 'The Asylum'. The Psychiatrist had the same attitude to Ruth's malaise that Aunt Dorothy displayed, that "the girl should pull herself together." After two further weeks and no improvement, Ruth attended the hospital again when the same Psychiatrist, under some pressure from Edward and Aunt Dorothy to get on with some sort of in-patient treatment, admitted her to the asylum having diagnosed that she had Schizophrenia.

Ruth stayed in that awful place for five months with its wide range of patients whose lives had been put on hold whilst medical science discovered that for people like Ruth, time and gentle cognitive therapy were what was required not to be locked up as mad. Indeed many of the patients in that place for people that failed to conform to society's strict conventions might well have considered if it was the system and its doctors that were mad and not the patients.

During her time in the asylum, Edward initially visited every week but that soon drifted to every two weeks. Ruth's pleas to see Charlotte and later to see her new baby were dismissed as being inappropriate. She asked if she could write a letter and only after she had been there for many weeks was she able to convince a nurse that she was sane but sad. That nurse posted the letter to Moira who was beside herself with worry. She knew that Ruth had delivered her baby and that she was extremely tired from a quickly scribbled letter written by

Ruth the day after the birth. Moira was therefore relieved but distressed to find that she was in the asylum.

Moira quickly made plans to visit the hospital and after some difficulty she made the journey to the hospital and was shown to a visitor's room where she met a worn down, very nearly institutionalised Ruth. Ruth came to life over the course of the hour Moira was there, so much so that Moira insisted upon seeing a doctor. The hand of fate was on Ruth's shoulder that day as Moira confided in a young, newly qualified consultant psychiatrist and opened the book on Ruth's troubled life. Many unanswered questions led the doctor to concur that the best therapy for Ruth was to be slowly reintegrated with her family. Moira and the doctor were convinced but it took a further four weeks before Edward was persuaded to bring Charlotte to see her mother which he did one Sunday afternoon.

For Charlotte, this must have been a shocking experience. Simply approaching this imposing Victorian building from the main driveway sent a chill up the spine. Built in the early eighteen seventies, this structure had the responsibility to keep people in, to keep those in society that were seen as mad or strange, or different away from the ordered life of the Victorian era. The site had its own infectious diseases sanatorium, train station, theatre, church, cemetery and post office. It would be many years later when images coming out of the war were to show people being taken by train to concentration camps, that Ruth was to reflect upon the similarities. People with mental health conditions were brought to these asylums by train and walked the short distance to their legal incarceration where for many they would spend the rest of their lives locked away.

Entering the building through the large main doors, Charlotte would see and hear the sounds of everyday life in the building known locally as the Whittingham Asylum even though its name was changed in the early nineteen twenties to Whittingham Mental Hospital still the stigma of the asylum would remain for local people. Charlotte would see the wide corridors with wards and individual rooms leading off them and she would have heard the ever present sound of patients crying or calling out and the sound of doors being opened and closed using keys that rattled on long chains held on the belts of the nursing staff.

Charlotte would have seen patients wandering freely along the corridors patients that would have welcomed the sight of a young child in their midst but nonetheless, patients that might have been different and therefore frightening to the young Charlotte.

Charlotte was slow to recognise and go to her mother when they arrived at Ruth's room but over the course of a few weeks they re-established their relationship. The next and important test was to see how Ruth behaved in the company of Maria. That took more time as the young doctor built confidence in Ruth who slowly unlocked her concealed maternal instincts.

Life came back to Ruth; she was one of the fortunate ones who walked out of that place less damaged than when she went in. The memory of that institution would live with Ruth for the rest of her life.

CHAPTER EIGHTEEN

Ruth left hospital in the March of nineteen forty six but not before Edward had agreed, in close consultation with the hospital and with Ruth that the key to a lasting improvement in Ruth's health was for the couple to have a life of their own in their own home. Edward took some convincing before it was agreed that they would lease Bowland Moss Farm House where they would live with the two children. It was agreed that Ellen would continue to care for the children during the day but Ruth would return home each night to Bowland Moss to be with the children rather than staying with Moira in Blackpool.

Before Ruth returned home, and without anyone other than the Carmichael's being aware, Edward along with fifteen thousand others attended, by invitation an event at the Royal Albert Hall in London. It was a low key but fitting tribute that would be made to the Voluntary Interceptors, who were presented with certificates of appreciation for their work in the war. In keeping with that work, the event was not publicised and for many who attended, their visit to London was as wrapped in secrecy from their families as was their work throughout the war. The simple parchment certificate was signed by Herbert Creedy, a senior Civil Servant who had been recalled from retirement to the Security Executive, for the duration of the war. The citation message on behalf of the government was suitably vague and yet to those who served as Voluntary Interceptors it said all that was needed:

'In the years when Civilisation was menaced with destruction Edward Carmichael who served from 1940-1945 gave generously of his time, powers and technical skill in essential service to his Country'.

This opaque but meaningful tribute to people who put their own lives at risk should Britain have been occupied, captured the grateful thanks of a nation who would not know of the bravery and service of these people for decades, and for many their wartime secret was taken to their grave, the evidence of which would have only been discovered in their papers by their families. This secret was also kept from Ruth.

Bowland Moss Farm House, Ruth's new home was a delightful cottage situated alongside a farm machinery repair yard that always seemed to be busy with the comings and goings of farmers with their broken equipment. The cottage had two bedrooms and a modest size kitchen that served also as the main living space. There was an inside toilet only but the lack of a bathroom was seen as no problem, the children would do as Ruth did as a child, and bathe in the galvanised tin bath that would be brought in from the yard and placed in front of the open fire to be filled with warm water.. The cottage came fully furnished and so for the first time in her marriage, Ruth was able to play her full role as wife and mother.

The arrangement seemed to be working well for the first few weeks. Ruth was happily back in the cockpit with her friends and although the transport arrangements to and from work were tedious Ruth was prepared to cope with that for the sake of her marriage and her children. But it wasn't long before Edward had moved back to living with his parents complaining that Ruth couldn't cook, and was a poor housewife. The children were also difficult to wrench from Ellen each evening and soon Ellen was insisting 'for the sake of the children' that they remain with her on week nights.

Edward seemed to be being deliberately difficult and disagreeable and it was only occasionally that he would stay at Bowland Moss Farm with her. The long standing arrangement that Sam would take Ruth and Edward by car to Preston had evaporated and Ruth would start her day at six o'clock going to Garstang with a neighbour on the back of his motorcycle and then catching a bus to Blackpool. The return journey would see her walking about three miles home from where the nearest bus would stop and yet Ruth persisted in the hope of salvaging a marriage that was dying before her eyes.

Edward was becoming a stranger and the Carmichaels were slowly and Ruth would say deliberately easing themselves and her children out of Ruth's life. Visits to see the children were rare following a confrontation with the family when Ruth arrived at Eastbrook Farm one Saturday afternoon in late July.

On her arrival Charlotte ran to the gate to greet her mother and was abruptly stopped by Aunt Matilda who told her to go indoors. As Charlotte did so, Edward, Sam and Ellen did the same leaving Ruth at the gate with Aunt Matilda. Aunt Matilda had a sense of purpose in her demeanour and gave the impression from the outset that she was acting as the family spokesperson. In a voice of the headmistress that she was, she began by telling Ruth that she should waken up to the reality of her situation, explaining that she was and always had been tolerated rather than welcomed into the family because of her foolishness in getting pregnant. She said that Ruth's mental illness and her prolonged absence from the children had served to confirm that her two children were "blossoming" without Ruth's interference in their balanced and ordered life.

Ruth attempted to interrupt and was abruptly silenced by Aunt Matilda. Ruth persisted and spluttered that she was trying hard to be a good mother but that Edward was continually seeing Sarah. Ruth resisted Matilda's attempt to regain the conversation by explaining that their marriage had been overshadowed by Edward's continued contact with Sarah. Ruth explained that she had a first hand account from one of Edward's supervisors who had seen Sarah and Edward embracing and kissing in Avenham Park in Preston. Ruth explained that Anna, her supervisor was so shocked that she deliberately went across to Edward and asked him what the hell he was doing, a married man, cavorting in this way. Aunt Matilda was unmoved by the evidence of Edward's ongoing extramarital 'relationship' with Sarah, indeed it seemed to hasten bringing her to the point she was so eager to make.

Aunt Matilda began by pointedly stating that neither Edward nor the family or the children wanted anything more to do with her. She asked Ruth to acknowledge that her marriage to Edward was over and that whilst she remained it prevented the children from getting on with their lives and stopped Edward from pursuing the happiness he so deserved. As though to counterbalance her last point she looked into Ruth's eyes and said, "You don't fit here in this family in this part of the country and you should go back to Wales and start a new life of your own and leave us to bring up the children."

Ruth stood silently absorbing what she had heard. It was true that the children saw Ellen as their mother rather than grandmother and, yes, they were happier in Ellen's company than hers. It was equally true that she was not welcomed by the family and deep in her own heart, Ruth knew that she would never be happy unless she was out of this family and the trap she found herself in. But what she was being asked to do, to walk away from her marriage and her children was just too big a step to take to achieve her own happiness for the future ...... or was it?

Ruth suggested to Aunt Matilda that she ask Edward to come to Bowland Moss Farm that evening when they could discuss their future. Matilda agreed and as she strode back to the house her posture suggested she was satisfied that she had achieved her task and without emotion, she turned and went indoors.

As Ruth walked home, she began to evaluate what she had heard. Yes she was young, still only twenty three and her whole life lay ahead of her. Perhaps, she thought, there will be room for happiness in her life and perhaps she could put behind her the events of the past few years. Ruth started to build a picture of a future where she was back in South Wales amongst people she loved and who loved her. All of the people that knew she had married were now gone from South Wales and her thoughts constructed a scenario whereby she would simply slip back without people knowing of her marriage and her children.

Ruth began to build pictures of secretly returning to Lancashire periodically to see her children and she felt, these visits might serve to rekindle the relationship she once felt she had with Edward. As she arrived at the front door of Bowland Moss Farm, the picture was complete.

Ruth's naive belief that what Aunt Matilda had proposed was good for her only served to underscore the extent to which the Carmichael family had taken control of her life, her self esteem and her perspective of what was right and appropriate for her and her children, though she couldn't see it.

Ruth was not a simple person but she lacked the ability to put herself and her children at the centre of the discussion and held onto the belief that if she was good, if she humoured Edward and if she went along with the 'wisdom' of the family suggestions, all would come right in the end. She had no other reference points; her father and mother never took decisions preferring to put difficult problems to one side in the belief that 'things will come right in the end'. What this did for them and what was happening now for Ruth was that alternative scenarios were never explored and so Ruth was being manipulated and was slowly sleepwalking into her own future nightmare.

That evening Edward arrived at about eight o'clock expecting to be met by a hostile reception. Instead, Ruth who was dressed in a pretty summer dress had deliberately left her hair down knowing that Edward always liked her hair like this. Ruth warmly welcomed Edward into the house embracing him as he slipped by her and into the kitchen. Ruth had created a scenario in her mind that she would be able to draw Edward back into her life by making herself so irresistible that he would abandon any thoughts of leaving her. Ruth, this naive young woman thought that she could seduce Edward and in one night resolve everything that was wrong with their marriage.

Ruth had prepared a supper of cold meat and salad which was already on the table along with a bottle of stout and two glasses. The mood of the evening was flirtatious and reflective as Ruth moved the discussion towards their courtship and their first night of love together. Edward, on the other hand retained a sense of focus upon Ruth's plans to stay at Bowland Moss Farm as he put it "for a week or so" before either moving to live with Moira or moving back to south Wales. Ruth recognised that Edward was seeing this evening as a last night together but he was also suggesting that they could remain good friends and meet occasionally. Ruth leapt upon the possibility that away from the influence of the family and without the pressure of the children she and Edward might start again through nights of fun and love.

With that Ruth invited Edward to stay for the night and, at least for that night, love returned again to their relationship as they made love and reflected upon their good times together. By the following morning though, Edward's mood had changed and he was eager to leave the house saying that Ruth could stay at Bowland Moss Farm no more than a week but that she must not disturb the equilibrium that had been established for the children by visiting them without firstly asking him.

As Edward slipped out of the house, without even a backward glance, Ruth acknowledged the truth of what she was doing. She was about to leave her two young children. She was planning to continue to deny their existence to her parents and to those who were closest to her and she was about to try to ultimately find happiness for herself in a place and with someone where this part of her life would remain locked away forever. Thus a deceit that had begun with her out-of-wedlock pregnancy was to be given a new and ever more complex dimension as a whole portion of her life was to be expunged or at best embellished so as not to reveal the self made web of deceit that Ruth was now so trapped in.

CHAPTER NINETEEN

Ruth spent the next few days deciding how she was to approach her decision to leave Edward and to slowly let go of her children. She had considered an immediate move to south Wales but needed both time and a job. She left Bowland Moss Farm and moved back into Moira's home. But Moira was blunt and uncompromising in her condemnation of Ruth's decision to leave her children, no matter what the circumstances. Her only concession to Ruth was to swear that she would not divulge any of what had occurred to anyone in the family. However, Ruth read the signals and knew that Moira had washed her hands of her and she concluded that she should quickly look for other accommodation. Ruth had also decided to make a clean break from her association with Vickers and grasped the opportunity to take up a job she had been interviewed for as a post office manager at the Fulwood post office.

Fulwood, which lies between Preston to the south and Garstang to the north, sits on the busy A6 trunk road and was a large suburb of Preston though seen by many of its middle class residents more as a distinct suburban village. The attraction of the job, aside from the obvious one that it took Ruth back into post office work which she so enjoyed, was that the job came with accommodation. Ruth would be given the small flat above the post office and would run the sub-post office on a day to day basis on behalf of the elderly owners who owned the premises and had run the shop and business for more than three decades.

Ruth moved into the flat in the mid August and in so doing severed her relationship with Moira and Jack who had become such friends to her. The atmosphere on the day Ruth moved out of Moira's home was frosty and a far cry from the warmth and friendship that embraced her when she moved there in nineteen forty one. To Moira, Ruth was unrecognisable and had become someone that had lost her sense of what was right and wrong and had personally lost that charming vitality that so characterised the first years of her stay.

As Ruth left that home Moira knew that the young woman who was leaving would never again cross her threshold. She knew that Ruth was attempting to rewrite her own history and that before long there would be no place in that history for someone who knew as much about Ruth and her children as she did.

Ruth's first weeks at the post office were overseen by the owners Albert and Maud Elliot a couple in their mid sixties who were kind and considerate and keen to ensure that Ruth was settled into both the job and the flat. Ruth was quick to adjust into the work. She was friendly and chatty to Albert and Maud and very soon customers were remarking on how nice Ruth was.

But Ruth was guarded when she was asked personal questions about her family and her connections locally and this troubled Albert and Maud, not because of suspicion of dishonesty rather they speculated that she was troubled personally and they were anxious to help. Ruth's response would always be that she had served at Vickers and lived with a cousin who she had fallen out with. She would reflect the horrors of what she saw in Cardiff during the bombings but questions about her family were always met with the same response that they were 'living in Ireland' and any suggestion that a young pretty woman like her should be marred was always dismissed by the comment that she preferred her work and her own company. Indeed, as the weeks passed by Ruth was seen to be the model employee in that she never went out at night, didn't seem to entertain the company of young men and was always eager to be around the business.

This cloistered life was in contrast to the Ruth who previously enjoyed friends, dancing and company and yet it seemed to suit Ruth's current mood. Her thoughts in the loneliness of her rooms above the post office would only be for her two children. Ruth knew the enormity of what she had done and was wracked with the pain of guilt and the fear of being found out. Ruth considered how she might slip into Goosnargh village on a day when she knew that Ellen would be there with the children and secretly snatch the chance to see them.

But as these plans were formulating in her mind, Ruth was also carefully examining her diary and was noticing that she had missed her period and she was beginning to fear that she might be pregnant. Ruth counted the weeks back to the night, the last night that she slept with Edward and that was mid July. It was now early September and as each day passed by Ruth knew that there was now no doubt that she was indeed pregnant.

In the long nights alone in her flat, Ruth's mood changed. She became melancholy and tearful as she counted the days since she last saw her children, days that had become weeks and weeks that had now become months. Ruth was fearful that if Edward were to know that she was again pregnant he would demand that this child should also be taken from her. But she also so desperately wanted to see Charlotte and Maria.

Despite her fears Ruth decided that she must write to Edward and at least establish how the children were coping without her. Her letter was short, without revealing where she was living, she made clear to Edward that she had not returned to south Wales. She said of the children; '*I pine for my babies every night and as their mother I must be allowed to see them, even if you simply bring them to a park or the beach so that they can see me and so that I can hold them....please agree*'. Ruth explained in the letter the subterfuge of using a post office box number by saying that she was attempting to get on with her life and didn't want him or the Carmichaels' to turn up on her door step and ruin her chances of regaining a life of her own. Ruth remained in the grip of the Carmichaels even now.

The hold the Carmichael family had over Ruth was enormous and despite the evidence of Ruth now having written to Edward, as the months passed by it strengthened the case for them that Ruth was uncaring and had abandoned her children. The selective amnesia on the part of the Carmichael family that they were the innocent victims of Ruth's voluntary departure had become a reality for them. When asked by neighbours and friends about the whereabouts of Ruth, their mantra was to say that she had suddenly, and without warning, walked out on them and her children. Ellen was cast in the role of a saint and Edward the grieving husband. The letter was never replied to by Edward though he had received it and read it.

These long nights of reflection were taking their toll on Ruth's health and on her erstwhile friendly and pleasing demeanour. It was noticeable that Ruth was looking tired with dark rings beneath her eyes. Albert and Maud had discussed this with her and asked if she needed assistance in the shop or the post office and whenever this subject was discussed it was followed by a period when Ruth seemed happier, more attentive and eager to please.

As the weeks passed by and autumn turned to winter, Ruth was able to conceal her growing body under large frumpy winter clothes. Customers and Albert and Maud saw the small changes but most would put this down to a woman who had let herself go a little and was more interested in her work than in her personal appearance. Ruth spent her days concealing her changing shape from her employer and her customers and her nights slowly formulating her thoughts and plans for her future.

Ruth's letter writing was now limited in the first instance to a simple change of address to her mother, Auntie Lottie and Uncle Arthur and to Mary Morgan explaining that she was pleased to have left Vickers and that what she now needed was to get back to the work she so enjoyed in the post office. Ruth maintained the illusion of a contented marriage and tried hard to conceal her mood of depression. But her mother was not to be fooled.

Ruth received a short curt and damming letter from her mother in late November explaining that she had finally managed to get the truth out of Moira who she had been corresponding with for some time worried about the evident tone of Ruth's letters. Ruth was shocked by what her mother had to say in the letter. She wrote: '*You have wilfully concealed the fact that you are a mother of two children from me and your father...this will kill him. I know that you think badly of your father but in all the bad things he has ever done he would never have abandoned his children. And for me you have broken my heart, you are not the daughter I said goodbye to in England and I now disown you. You will not be welcome at my door and you will never be discussed again in my presence. God may ultimately forgive you but I cannot*'. She ended by saying, '*I will go to the priest tomorrow and I will confess my sin of disowning you before him and God but I will not ask for forgiveness...you are no longer my daughter*'.

Ruth wept the whole day and needed to be relieved of her duties by Maud who had been summoned by an anxious customer concerned for Ruth's wellbeing. At the close of that day, Maud went to Ruth's flat to talk with her. As she entered the flat that had once been her home for many years Maud was immediately struck by the sparseness. The flat had been offered fully furnished but there were no personal items such as ornaments or photographs. The flat was spotlessly clean and tidy and even the kitchen had nothing out of place.

Maud sat Ruth down and asked what had upset her so much that she could not stop crying. Ruth had difficulty speaking but explained that she had received a letter from her mother that was dreadfully upsetting. Maud asked if there had been a death in the family and at that Ruth broke down completely. All she would say was that there were problems in Ireland and no more. Maud suggested that she might take some time away from her work to visit her mother but this immediately turned down and Ruth smiled towards

Maud and said, "I'm being silly and probably making too much of what I read...I will be fine tomorrow so please don't worry." Maud was encouraged by this and left saying to Ruth that she should feel free to talk to her at any time.

Ruth had by now accepted that Charlotte and Maria were lost to her, never quite making the connection that if she really wanted her children, even now, she would need to fight for them. Despite her mother's letter, Ruth had convinced herself that she had not walked away from her children, rather they had been kept from her and it was this complex perception of what in part was true that allowed her to see herself as a victim rather than someone who had effectively but for reasons that were in part understandable, walked away from her children.

The further Ruth's pregnancy progressed, the more reclusive and isolated she became. She was an exemplary employee but Albert and Maud were becoming concerned that Ruth was too lonely and too isolated. Ruth had turned down several invitations for Sunday lunch with Albert and Maud but they were determined that they would get her out of the flat into their home where they might begin to get to know this person who was becoming an indispensible part of their lives. Hearing that Ruth planned to stay alone in the flat for Christmas, they insisted that she join them at their home on Christmas Day. Ruth tried to prevaricate for several days but on discovering that it would just be the three of them at lunch, she reluctantly agreed.

CHAPTER TWENTY

Christmas Eve was a day of great pain for Ruth. She spent much of the evening and many hours of the night recalling Christmases in her childhood. She remembered that despite hardships as she was growing up, and the family's terrible shortage of money the children would always go to bed excited at what the following day might bring. She recalled the Christmas eve of her thirteenth birthday when, after being sent to their beds the children lay awake speculating what 'Father Christmas' would bring. The older children protected the myth by playing along with the image of a Father Christmas who slipped down the chimney. Ruth remembered how even at the age of thirteen, she wanted to retain the magic of Christmas and so she was as excited and as drawn into the charade as anyone.

Ruth knew the routine well, she would wait for the noise of her father returning home from the Feathers pub happy and noisy, and this would be the signal for all the children to be extra quiet. Ruth would hear the sound of her mother imploring her father to be quiet whilst she gathered the pillow cases that were each to be hung on the banister rail, one each for the children. The pillow cases were their Christmas stockings and in each there would always be some fruit, some nuts, a small gift from their parents and in Ruth's case a gift from Auntie Lott and Uncle Arthur. There would also be a toy, often a second hand one that her father would painstakingly repair and repaint in the workshop at the pit and if the money would run to it, there would be a book and some pencils. But this Christmas was to be filled with expectation for Ruth who had begged for a bicycle and had been told on numerous occasions that if she was good there might be a chance.

And so it was that eventually, her father was sobered or quietened enough or both for her parents to make the short journey up the stairs. The exceptionally narrow stairs always creaked but Christmas Eve seemed a time for them to groan more and to creak even louder as Maeve and a rather unsteady Darragh slowly ascended the stairs. As they did so the children giggled knowing that the tight bend in the stairs with their narrowing treads would always be their father's nemesis and the point in the evening when the children's education in vulgarity would be further extended and this Christmas Eve was to be no different.

The stair was reached and it became clear that their mother had navigated the bend before their father because she could be heard whispering, "Darragh, mind the corner..." That unfortunately was his cue to blaspheme and fall all in perfect harmony. He, two of the children's pillowcases and what later became clear was a bicycle, descended in a series of bangs, scrapes and the occasional ring of a bicycle bell until the fall ended and the remaining sound was that of her father, who was clearly unhurt swearing and again attempting to renegotiate the stairs. Ruth and the children were in hysterics of laughter muffled only by burying their heads deep in their feather pillows. The pillowcases were eventually placed on the banister rail and after much delay and whispers of 'have they gone to sleep yet' the children sent Ruth to slowly bring the pillowcases into the bedroom. And yes this was to be Ruth's year to have a bicycle, one that had been rebuilt and repainted.

In the loneliness of her flat above the post office, Ruth also rehearsed the movements that she anticipated her own children would be going through that Christmas Eve. Charlotte was now at an age when she would be excited and would be difficult to put to bed. She knew that her children would each have a present from her which she had sent to the house without any return address and without any franking on the package that could reveal where she was living. Ruth had added a simple card inside the package which said, 'With much love from Mummy. I'm sorry I cannot be with you but you should know that I love you and I think of you every day' and so she did. Barely an hour would pass without her thoughts drifting to the wellbeing of her children.

That Christmas Eve and the early hours of Christmas morning were spent alone and in tears as Ruth confronted yet again the enormity of what she had done.

On Christmas morning Ruth put on her most voluminous dress and a large woollen jumper that did a marvellous job of concealing much of her large bump and off she went to Maud and Albert's home. Their home, a small bungalow, within a short walk from the post office, was set a long way back from the main road and although it was winter it was clear that the front garden was well tended and tidy.

On entering the house Ruth could smell that distinct aroma of a home cooked lunch that was so familiar to her as a child in her Senghenydd home. Maud answered the door wearing a large apron over what was clearly her best dress and ushered Ruth in from the cold air. Albert was smartly dressed in a suit and tie and was clearly anxious to make Ruth feel welcome. He took her coat and ushered her through to the sitting room with its welcoming coal fire burning in the hearth.

The fire surround was festooned with home made decorations and trimmings and the evidence of their popularity was everywhere with dozens of Christmas cards, most of them evidently hand made. Ruth passed across to Maud her Christmas card which Maud immediately opened. There was a simple card with a warm message from Ruth but in the envelope there was also a gift made over many nights in her flat. It was a simple calendar that was incorporated into a circular hanging, covered in a pastel material. The edging was a beautifully worked lace that had the finest of small stitching. Maud was taken aback, not realising that Ruth was so adept with a needle and accepted it saying that it would replace the rather ordinary nineteen forty six calendar in seven days time.

Albert sat Ruth down and went to a small drinks table with a number of glasses and a Tantalus containing two fine crystal bottles. He asked Ruth if she would like a sherry. Ruth pondered the question; she had never been one for drink unlike her father who might himself have been overwhelmed by the array of Christmas drinks bottles on and around the table. Ruth was concerned that the medical advice being given to her by her local doctor, an enlightened young man was that pregnant mothers should avoid drink. Politely she responded by saying that she didn't care to drink but accepted a glass of dandelion and burdock, a delicious hedgerow mead, flavoured with burdock root which was a favourite of Ruth's.

Despite severe ongoing rationing lunch was plentiful and a taste that Ruth had long forgotten. Maud had prepared a small chicken reared in her own garden, roast potatoes, carrots and Brussels sprouts also from her garden and this was followed by a home made Christmas pudding that had been made months ago. The friendliness and ease of the company was just what Ruth had needed but she remained guarded and cautious when the subject of the conversation turned to Christmas's past or her parents.

During the conversation, Ruth learnt that Maud and Albert had no children and it was becoming evident to her that their attention towards her was to the daughter they had never had. Ruth became increasingly nervous as the convivial conversation turned towards long term plans and in particular when she was asked outright if she would make a promise to remain at the post office. Albert alluded to the possibility of them helping Ruth to buy the sub post office by letting her purchase it over a number of years. Concern turned to alarm as Ruth realised that this wonderful couple who had taken her to their hearts were soon to be told that she would be leaving their post office to have her baby.

Albert and Maud refused help as they went into the kitchen to wash the lunch dishes. Sat alone and facing the prospect that she was about to add two more names to her list of people she had deceived, Ruth realised that she must act quickly to avoid any further heartbreak and upset of her making.

Ruth waited until about three o'clock before saying that she was tired and needed to get back to the post office before it became dark. As she left the house Ruth was warmly embraced by both Maud and Albert and a small gift was thrust into her hand. The gift was twenty five pounds in cash with a brief note to say thank you for her dedication and her hard work. This was further evidence for Ruth that she needed to resolve her immediate future as quickly as possible so that she could advise Albert and Maud, her employers and now her close friend that her personal circumstances required her to move on.

Ruth returned to her flat above the post office and set about putting plans in place that would clarify where her baby was to be delivered and perhaps more pressing where she would live and how she would fend for herself in the weeks running up to her delivery as well as the immediate period after she had given birth. Key to her planning was to give as much notice as possible to Maud and Albert that she planned to leave the post office and this meant that she would have to be honest about her pregnancy.

For Ruth this was a turning point in her life and she was determined to ensure that this cathartic moment would set her on a course where she faced up to the reality of her situation. She planned to use the experiences of the past few years to help her shape a more positive phase in her life. She knew that she would need to consign the past, and the implications of the decisions she had taken to a place in her memories that would allow her to use them to help shape future decisions and to regain control over her own life so that she could move on.

In the run up to the New Year, Ruth spent time looking for rooms where she could live until after her baby was born. Her plans, agreed with her doctor included having her child in Sharoe Green Hospital in

Fulwood. Also, Ruth accepted the advice she was being given by her doctor that Sharoe Green Hospital was appropriate for her, given her history of mental illness because the hospital had a good maternity unit and a sympathetic and sensitive mental health unit.

Ruth found that there were plenty of landlords with inexpensive flats or rooms in the Preston area but once she indicated that she was pregnant landlords refused to take her. But Ruth's perseverance eventually paid off and she ultimately was able to rent a single room, with shared bathroom and cooking facilities in a large house in Fishergate in Preston, only a fifteen minute bus journey from Fulwood. Ruth secured a six month lease but the landlord demanded that she pay the full six months' rent in advance. Although Ruth's savings enabled her to do this it left precious little for her to maintain herself once she gave up work.

Ruth knew that she would need to work for as long as possible before her baby was born if that was to be made possible by Maud and Albert.

By the end of the second week of January nineteen forty seven, Ruth decided that the time was right for her speak frankly to Maud and Albert. She felt that it would probably be better for her to speak in the first instance to Maud and so she took the opportunity at the end of a day when Maud was helping Ruth to ask her to wait behind and have a cup of tea with her. They went upstairs and Ruth made tea for the two of them and they settled down at the kitchen table.

Ruth began by saying that she felt a duty to Maud and Albert to give them as much notice as possible that she planned to resign her position at the end of February. Without pausing, Ruth went on to explain that she had rented accommodation in Preston which she would take up in the first week of February making it possible for a new employee to use the post office accommodation that went with the job without any difficulty.

Maud sat quietly listening to the information she was being given and when Ruth had finished, she placed her hand on Ruth's and said, "We have known for some time that you would be leaving and although you have omitted to mention it, we suspected that you must be pregnant...." Ruth saw no point in concealing the truth from Maud any longer and filled in the gaps by confirming that she was pregnant and that the baby was due in the first week of April. She prompted the inevitable question and told her that the father was her estranged husband who she had left for personal reasons.

Maud looked unsurprised and, continuing to hold Ruth's hand she said, "This part of Lancashire is very small my dear so we have known for some time that you were married, we also know the Carmichael family, not personally but through friends. I'm sorry to say that you are being cast as a wicked woman by them, someone who has abandoned your children, your husband and a loving extended family."

She went on, "You will probably have a different view about that portrayal but what Albert and I have seen is a hard working good woman who is clearly troubled by what has happened. But this does not colour our view of the person we have grown to know and care for." Ruth was touched and began to cry. She tried to explain her perspective of what had happened but it was hard to counter the general opinion that no matter what the circumstances, leaving your children was a wicked sin.

Maud returned to the immediate challenges and suggested that Ruth had been wrong not to take her into her confidence earlier and suggested that Ruth's plans to move out were hasty and ill considered.

That may well have been Maud's opinion, but given the shock news that Maud, and presumably many of the people in Fulwood were aware of her past, all that Ruth could contemplate was executing her plans to leave as rapidly as possible.

Whilst Ruth acknowledged and had tried to rationalise her past decisions she could see no circumstances in which she could now remain in Fulwood. Ruth brushed away her tears and in a new found assertiveness said to Maud, "I have reached a decision that I should move on in my life. Having taken that decision the most important aspect of my future is to plan for the birth of my child away from the distractions of the past and my work." She suggested that she move out of the flat as planned at the end of January and leave her job at the end of February or early March if that would help. Maud could see that Ruth was not to be persuaded and their conversation ended as it began in an amicable and understanding way.

The following day, Albert came to see Ruth and having tried to change her mind about leaving, he too accepted the inevitability of the situation. He sat her down and in a purposeful but deeply caring way he explained that he and Maud would like Ruth to come back and see them after the baby was born and discuss with them again the possibility of her taking over the post office business as previously suggested.

These kind words and expressions of continued confidence and trust in Ruth were a boost to her confidence but she was resolved to move out of the area, though she did not mention this. Albert rose to leave and explained that he and Maud had someone in mind who could step in to run the post office in the interim that would be available from the beginning of March.

As he turned to open the door, Albert thrust an envelope into Ruth's hand and gently squeezing it as he explained, "The next few months will be expensive for you so this is just a small gift to help you along the way and to again say thank you." The small gift was five ten pound notes. Ruth deposited these in her post office savings account knowing that this would provide the additional financial security she so needed.

At the same time Ruth posted a small birthday gift to Charlotte who was by now approaching three years of age. The post mark was once again anonymised this time by deliberately twisting the franking stamp to smudge the post office mark. The gift was a pretty little summer dress that Ruth had made using as a pattern one of Charlotte's dresses she had taken with her when she left Edward and the children. Unnoticed by Edward or Ellen, Ruth had taken two items as keepsakes from both the children.

To remind her of Charlotte, she had kept a lock of her hair which had been cut off by Ellen. At the time Ruth was furious that someone should take a pair of scissors to her child's hair without consulting her and she swept every hair from the floor and carefully placed them inside the folds of Beatrix Potter's book *The Tale of Peter Rabbit*. Ruth had bought the book and intended to read it to Charlotte when she was a little older. The dress she took had been one she was given by a friend when Charlotte was tiny which she had grown out of. The simple pale blue dress with fine embroidery around the collar and the short sleeves had become a firm favourite for Charlotte and Ruth knew that by making an exact but larger copy of the original, Charlotte would know that it was made with love from her mother.

In so far as Maria was concerned Ruth was compelled to take the small booties that she had worn as a tiny baby. She also took a pair of her socks, which, if Ruth closed her eyes she could still detect on them that distinctive smell of her baby. These small reminders of her children were kept in a shoe box all carefully wrapped in white tissue and always returned to the box with a reverence reminiscent of holy relics. The shoe box and its contents were to remain with Ruth for the rest of her life.

Ruth moved into her small garret room in Preston in an old Victorian property that was split into more than ten similar rooms. The room itself was at the top of the house accessed by climbing three sets of stairs. Thankfully, although the room did not have its own bathroom, there was a toilet directly opposite the entrance to her room and a bathroom on one floor below. The room was small but offered enough space for a single bed, a wardrobe two chairs and there was a sink to the side of the window that overlooked the main street of Fishergate. The room had a threadbare slightly stained carpet on the wooden floor and the only lighting was provided by a single bulb that hung from a cord on the ceiling. Heating for what it was worth, was provided by a small cylindrical paraffin heater that at least had the benefit of enabling a kettle or a pan to be heated on the top. The decoration of the room was good and looked as though the walls had only recently been papered.

Ruth was determined to make the most of the accommodation and quickly bought new bed sheets and a quilted bed cover that made the place feel more like home. Despite having to pay for electricity, through a coin meter Ruth was determined that the flat would be a welcoming place to bring her baby back to and so she purchased a second hand two bar fire for additional heat along with a kettle, a small saucepan and some simple utensils. Having inspected the communal kitchen on the ground floor, Ruth was clear that she would avoid the need to use it unless absolutely necessary particularly in her state and so being able to warm food and make hot drinks in her room was essential. Ruth also purchased a new Yale lock for her door and with skill replaced the existing one in order that she should have complete security and privacy.

Ruth noticed a pram parked in the down stairs hallway and following some discreet enquiries established that the owner and the baby who used it lived in the flat directly below hers. Ruth felt some comfort from the knowledge that any noise her baby may cause would mainly be heard by that tenant, who would perhaps be more understanding.

Ruth's flat was conveniently located near to the bus station where there were frequent services to Lancaster and Scotland all of which stopped near the post office in Fulwood.

The days went by swiftly and Ruth slipped into the routine of commuting back and forth to Fulwood. Though the room in Preston had its limitations Ruth felt that it was hers and entirely unencumbered. She found that she was both comfortable and reasonably warm in her room but it took her some time to ensure that she had sufficient shillings ready to put into the meter and on several occasions she found herself in darkness searching for her hand bag for coins.

Ruth's relationship with Maud and Albert remained strong, something she was pleased about and it helped in the final week when she spent much of her time showing the new girl the ropes. Inevitably Ruth's last Friday came and it was with some trepidation that she awaited the arrival of Maud and Albert to hand over her keys and to say goodbye. Maud was tearful as she embraced Ruth, almost as a mother would be with her daughter in similar circumstances but Ruth reassured her that once the baby was born she would come to Fulwood and let her see the baby and that she would also discuss her future. Albert was more emotional, as he insisted that Ruth telephone the house if she needed anything and as he embraced her he whispered, "You're like a daughter to us so please keep us in your life."

Ruth left the post office and boarded her bus. As she slipped out of Fulwood a sense deep inside her told her that she would never return and all the great hopes and wonderful plans of these good people would be dashed. Ruth had a feeling of excitement about her future but also a sense of foreboding recalling the words of the gypsy in Blackpool who said, "*I can see the life you have yet to live and I warn you now that you will go through your life seeing children in your shadow.*"

CHAPTER TWENTY ONE

Unknown to Ruth, throughout the period since she left her children which was by now almost eight months, Edward had intensified his contact and relationship with Sarah. They would meet every week, mostly at dance halls or ice skating. Sarah had also begun to visit Edward at Eastbrook Farm rekindling the fond relationship she previously had with Sam and Ellen.

The children never particularly warmed to Sarah who to them seemed forever concerned that her clothes or her hair and makeup might be damaged by getting too close to them. This aspect of Sarah's personality and her disregard for the children seemed to have escaped the notice of any of the Carmichaels who became incapable of rational thinking whenever Sarah came to their house. They were so obsessed by the notion that Edward and Sarah were the 'perfect couple' they were oblivious to the ever present evidence that the children were wary of her at best and disliking of her at worst. Often Charlotte, who had developed the capability of disappearing whenever Sarah came to the house, would be dispatched to her bedroom with Maria to provide peace and quiet for Sarah and Edward. The mantra of the Carmichaels, who gushed over her every word, was that Sarah 'brings life back to Edward'.

The conversation whenever Sarah was present would always touch upon two subjects, Ruth and the future for

Sarah and Edward. To her credit or perhaps to focus the minds of the Carmichaels, Sarah would always point out that there could be no long term future for Edward and herself until Edward had shaken off the shackles of Ruth.

Ruth was always portrayed as that wicked woman who had walked out on her babies. The selective nature of their memories omitted to include that collectively and individually, Edward, Ellen, Sam, Aunt Matilda and Aunt Dorothy had made life intolerable for Ruth and had driven her to the point where her options seemed limited to walking away from them all and her children. History and her maker will decide if Ruth was right or not but what was becoming clear was that the Carmichaels were intent upon a course of action that would see Sarah and Edward married.

Sarah had recently visited the Catholic priest at her church to explore their options and more particularly, to test if there was any prospect of the Catholic Church being able to marry them if Edward could secure a divorce from Ruth and if he converted to Catholicism. The news was not good. The priest explained that even if Edward was able to get a divorce which he thought might be difficult except on the grounds of desertion, the Church's views on divorce and on marrying a couple where one party was a divorcee were pretty uncompromising. The only glimmer of light seemed to be that Sarah, a devout Catholic was prepared to 'sacrifice' her life and her ambitions to become a mother to these two children. It had not escaped the notice of the parish priest that if Sarah could marry Edward, the Church would receive three new converts, one adult and two children.

Edward had also decided to visit the family lawyer to take advice on what his options might be. The solicitor was rather more optimistic than Sarah's parish priest. He advised that for a divorce on the grounds of desertion to be granted the law required that Edward would need to register his application and then wait for three years. During those three years the court would need assurance that in those years there was no contact between Edward and Ruth.

The solicitor indicated that 'desertion' was an uncommon ground on which to divorce because desertion requires a party to 'walk out' on the marriage with the intention to never return. He suggested that intention is extremely difficult to prove but evidence that Edward had tried to find Ruth would help. However, it was explained that for a successful application, there must be no evidence of contact and a complete absence of evidence of where Ruth was living for the whole of the three years. This buoyed Edward who immediately instructed his solicitor to proceed to draw up the necessary papers. Edward omitted to tell his lawyer that Ruth had written to him asking for a meeting, an omission he would compound repeatedly as a result of more contact in the years to come.

Sarah continued to make it clear to Edward that she remained uncompromising on two issues. If a divorce for Edward was possible she was prepared to marry him and take on the children but only if she could marry in a Catholic church which would require Edward and the children to convert to Catholicism. Furthermore, she was quite clear that heavy petting was as far as their physical relationship would go before marriage. Edward's previous unwillingness to become a Catholic for Sarah had evaporated in the light of her offer to take him and the children and the latter matter was considered by Edward to be not an insurmountable problem!

Ruth's move into her cold draughty room in Fishergate coincided with one of the worst winters on record. Two relatively short spells of cold weather, one in December nineteen forty six, the other in early January led to what became known as the 'main event' which persisted from late January to March. Intensely cold weather conditions affected much of England and Wales with temperatures breaking all records. These severe weather conditions resulted in Ruth's small room being constantly cold with ice regularly forming on the inside of her window.

Ruth's final few weeks before she was due to give birth went well though she found the intense cold, penetrating, leaving her feeling chilled at all times. She also found the climb to the top of the house to her room an increasing challenge. On one occasion when she was taking a rest between landings laden down with shopping, her downstairs neighbour stopped and introduced herself as Marilyn and, pointing into the pram she introduced Gareth her four month old baby.

The strong Welsh accent prompted Ruth to ask where Marilyn was from and discovered that whilst she was originally from Cardiff her home was on Anglesey a small island off the north Wales coast where her husband worked. She explained that her husband was on a training course with the RAF in Preston and that she had rented the room in order that she could see him on weekends and that he could see the baby. Marilyn asked Ruth to mind Gareth for a moment whilst she carried

Ruth's shopping up to her flat and then invited Ruth into her flat for a cup of tea.

Over tea Ruth simply explained that she had left her husband before knowing that she was pregnant, omitting to mention that she had two other children. This prompted Marilyn to offer advice to Ruth from the perspective of the novice mother which was so reminiscent of how her own mother had advised others. Ruth enjoyed Marilyn's company and they agreed to meet up once Ruth had returned home with her child, and that day was to come very soon.

On fifth of April nineteen forty seven at about five thirty in the evening, Ruth recognised the early signs that she was due to deliver her baby quite soon and she also knew from her experience that she would need to get herself to Sharoe Green Hospital in Fulwood fairly quickly. Ruth was organised and well prepared with her small case packed and waiting by the door.

Ruth was calm and composed as she quietly locked the door to her room behind her and carefully negotiated the stairs to the pavement outside the building. She had taken the precaution of establishing that there was a taxi hire company just one hundred yards from the flat and so she made her way slowly but purposefully the few steps to their offices. As she did, she suddenly came to a halt. It wasn't the baby or the imminence of its likely birth that brought her to a halt but the sight of Edward and Sarah walking, arm in arm on the other side of the road.

Sarah dressed in a smart long coat and wearing a little red felt hat with a velvet top was distracted by the shops and clearly didn't see Ruth, but that was not the case for Edward. Their eyes met and their gaze was held as

Edward tried to reassure himself that this plump young woman hunched over as she carried her suit case was indeed Ruth.

Edward's face was like thunder as he tried to veer Sarah into a position that if she tried to look across the road, she would not be able to see Ruth. As they reached the point where they were level with each other, separated only by the width of the road, Edward broke into a smile and in a jaunty self assured way, he raised his hand to his hat as though to doff it.

Ruth was transfixed as the couple moved out of her sight into a side road. Eventually, Ruth continued her journey to the taxi hire office and was immediately ushered into the back of a smart black car.

As the taxi passed the point where Ruth had seen Edward and Sarah, she looked in vain to see if she could identify where they had gone. In the matter of two minutes, she had seen Edward for the first time in nine months. Ruth wondered if she had concealed the evidence of her pregnancy from him but concluded that you would need to have exceptionally poor eyesight not to have recognised that she was nearing her day of delivery. Moreover, Edward had seen her pregnant on two previous occasions so was well aware of how large she could get.

On arrival at Sharoe Green Hospital, Ruth took a couple of moments to compose herself before presenting at the front desk of the maternity unit. The hospital was a grey Victorian building that at one time had been a work house and in that regard it was an imposing slightly fearsome structure that suggested it had many memories. Alongside this image was that of a popular cottage hospital maternity unit which served this demanding middle class area of Preston. For Ruth however, her baby would be delivered under the public assistance plans which meant that although she paid a nominal sum of five shillings per night that she was there, the rest was paid from the assistance funds.

Ruth reported to the reception desk and was immediately chastised firstly for not attending a clinic appointment two weeks previously and secondly for presuming that she could simply turn up, unannounced and expect to be delivered of her baby. Ruth was shown to a room where the midwife she had previously met, a jolly large lady ushered her towards the couch and examined her.

The midwife confirmed Ruth's assertion that she would not be long before she had her baby and with that she was shown to a small ward of six beds of which only two were occupied. Both ladies in the ward were also awaiting their delivery and both were first time mothers.

By midnight, Ruth's contractions were a matter of a few minutes apart and she was moved into a delivery room for the final stages. Ruth who had never experienced a delivery in a clinical setting before found the array of instruments, bright lights and sterile trays frightening and alien. Her two previous deliveries had been straight forward and within the bounds of child bearing, relatively pain free. It was soon clear that Ruth was about to be delivered of her child rather quicker than the planning in the delivery room had allowed for and in the time it took for the junior nurse to get the midwife back to the room the baby's head was presenting.

Within a further few minutes and at precisely twelve fifty three on the Sunday morning of April sixth nineteen forty seven, Ruth was delivered of a baby boy. Having dealt with the cord, and having weighed him and checked him over the restless Ruth was finally given her baby. He was adorable and the image of Edward but without Edward's birth mark on his forehead. Ruth fell in love once again.

That night Ruth's baby was taken from her, the normal practice of the day and placed in a small room alongside the other babies. Ruth was irritated by this administrative arrangement but like others fell in line and did as she was told. Ruth had no trouble breast feeding and so when her baby was put down to sleep he was full and comfortable and seemed to sleep well. The following day Ruth was able to have her baby for most of the day and skilfully dealt with all his needs.

The staff were aware that Ruth was an 'assistance' delivery so sensitively steered away from questions about the father. They did however ask if she had decided upon a name and in the manner in which her own mother named her babies Ruth announced that the name would be Michael to commemorate her beloved brother who was so tragically killed in Singapore during the war. It had always been Ruth's intention to call her first born son Michael and as she looked into the eyes of her baby and for the first time called him Michael she looked for those small characteristics that might remind her of Michael but there were none apart from the little dimple in his chin.

Ruth and Michael were examined every day to make sure that they were both well before discharging. The staff were showing some concern that Ruth was suddenly finding it difficult to breast feed her baby and called in the doctor to see her. He examined her and remarked that she was very under nourished and that her weight was considerably below what he might have expected from a woman of her age. He decided that for the sake of her own health, Michael should be put on a formula feed.

Ruth was disappointed but there was more concerning news about Michael who was showing early signs of having Eczema. These signs were present on his feet and hands but as each day passed they seemed to spread despite the application of creams. Ruth became overly alarmed and the doctors were concerned that this uncertainty was impacting upon Michael's emotional bonding and reassurance. However their greater concern was that Ruth was constantly tired, eating little and fretting for her baby.

Despite their concerns it was agreed that Ruth should be allowed to leave the hospital, having been there for three weeks on the strict understanding that she would attend the outpatient clinic on a weekly basis so that the doctors could monitor the development of Michael and satisfy themselves that Ruth was coping well. Ruth reluctantly agreed and enthusiastically arranged for a taxi car to take her home.

Ruth arrived at her room in the early afternoon of Monday twenty eighth of April with Michael, her suitcase and her medication and gratefully accepted the offer from her driver to help her to her room. Her first chore was to buy food for Michael and herself and then return to the room and settle Michael into his new surroundings. Despite the irritation that the Eczema must have caused Michael, he was a quiet contented soul during his first few days which allowed Ruth time for sleep and to recover from the birth.

The living arrangements were less than perfect with lines of towelling nappies and clothes hung near the paraffin heater and the two of them sharing the same bed. The paraffin heater produced plenty of heat for cooking and general heating but gave off terrible fumes that sapped the air of oxygen. The two bar electric heater was hardly enough to warm the room and Ruth was finding the cost excessive. Because of Michael's health Ruth rarely stepped out of the flat other than to buy food and on this day to return to Fulwood for her check up.

The outpatient clinic staff expressed concern about Michael's breathing and diagnosed bronchitis. The Eczema was not getting better and different creams were provided in the hope of improving what was by now a rash over much of Michael's body. However, the doctors were most concerned for Ruth who was also diagnosed with Bronchitis but whose weight had continued to fall and she was looking drawn and deeply unwell.

Ruth left the hospital agreeing to return in ten days. On her way home from the hospital, Ruth called into the registry office for Births, Deaths and Marriages to register Michael's birth. She had with her the certificate from the hospital and quickly completed the necessary documents. Because she was married Ruth had no difficulties registering the birth and showing Edward as the father but she needed to show Bowland Moss Farm as the family home as this was, correctly the place that she had seen as home with Edward.

Armed with Michael's birth certificate Ruth found a slight spring in her step as she walked home with her baby wrapped in a shawl across her chest. Her positive spirits lasted for only a short time as by that evening she became much weaker and found it difficult to manage simple tasks like making up a bottle. For his part, Michael was chesty but seemed to fret mainly as a reaction to the worsening health of his mother, Ruth.

Ruth and Michael managed to get through the next days but Ruth's health was by now very poor. As May drew to a close Ruth rarely stepped out of the house and this was becoming noticeable to Marilyn who had still not seen Ruth and her baby. Marilyn decided to call on Ruth and invite her to have tea with her. She knocked on Ruth's door at about ten o'clock in the morning and was surprised to get no response though she could hear the gurgling sounds of Ruth's baby. Marilyn became concerned and knocked harder and for longer.

Eventually, Ruth came to the door and opened it very slightly. Marilyn was shocked by what she saw and resisted Ruth's attempts to keep her outside the room pushing at the door and entering. The room was tidy though the evidence of drying nappies gave the room a slight odour and a feel of dampness. Marilyn's great concern was for Ruth who looked weak. Ruth had dark lines beneath her eyes and her deep chesty cough was evidence that she was very unwell. Ruth apologised that she had not yet been to see Marilyn and explained that both she and Michael had bronchitis and that Michael was suffering from Eczema.

Ruth was anxious for Marilyn to leave, partly because she was embarrassed that Marilyn should see her like this and partly because she was concerned not to pass on any germs to Marilyn and her son. As Marilyn moved to the door she drew Ruth to her and put her arms around her and it was at this point that she realised that Ruth was abnormally thin and weak. Ruth agreed that Marilyn should do some shopping for her something she repeated over the next seven days.

Marilyn begged Ruth to return to the hospital but she refused. Ruth was concerned that if the hospital was to see her like this the doctors would take her baby from her. For Marilyn, there were no concerns about the welfare of Michael, yes he had bronchitis which simply wasn't shifting and the Eczema seemed to be contained, but her concerns were for Ruth's health which was deteriorating before her eyes.

Marylyn decided to contact Sharoe Green Hospital and spoke to the Matron. The Matron was grateful for the call and assured her that they would send a doctor to see Ruth that day. When the doctor arrived a couple of hours later, he initially had difficulty getting Ruth to open the door and it was only the intervention of Marylyn that ultimately persuaded Ruth to open the door. The doctor spent about twenty minutes with Ruth and Michael expressing serious concern for Ruth who he diagnosed as having pneumonia. He felt that Michael was well cared for but that he too needed to be treated for the Eczema. Ruth refused to go to the hospital and abruptly showed the doctor to the door.

On the doctor's return to the hospital he reported his concerns for Ruth's health to his consultant which began a chain of events that would change the course of Ruth's life.

The only address the hospital had on their records for Ruth's husband, Edward was Bowland Moss Farm and so they dispatched a nurse in a car to the farm to try to get Edward to persuade Ruth to come into hospital. On arrival at the farm, the nurse found that the Carmichael's lived just a short distance away at Eastbrook Farm. The nurse rapidly found the new address where she found Ellen, Sam and Sarah sitting at the kitchen table.

The nurse explained that Ruth had given birth to a baby in April and that she was now desperately ill, living in a flat in Fishergate, Preston and that the hospital was keen to admit her but there was an issue about who would care for the child. She explained that the boy, named Michael was recovering from bronchitis and that he had a severe but treatable Eczema.

The family looked to one another each exploring why they should become involved when frankly they had no real connection with Ruth anymore. However, it was Ellen who, for whatever reason said that the family would take in the baby.

Still reeling from the shock that Ruth was again back in their lives, Sarah suggested to the nurse that it might be better if they arranged to take Ruth's baby that night and they would then phone the hospital and arrange for them to send an ambulance for Ruth. Content that there was a plan that would take care of the baby and that Ruth could be in hospital soon the nurse left.

As she was leaving, Edward arrived from work and was told what had happened. His reaction was to immediately suggest that this was none of their business and they should leave well alone matters that didn't concern them. With that, Sam turned to Edward and said, "Look me in the eye and tell me that this could not be your child, it was born on sixth of April, what were you and Ruth doing nine months ago?"

Sarah was distinctly interested in Edward's response which was painfully slow in coming. "Yes" he said, "I suppose it could be mine but that was the last time I had anything to do with her." Turning to Sarah, he said,

'Honestly, if it is mine it would have been the last time we were together and the very last time I have seen her." Angry but keen to see something happen Sam suggested that Ellen and Edward go to Fishergate and get the child.

In the confusion, no one had thought to ask the nurse where in Fishergate Ruth was living. Sarah, who seemed to have a plan for every occasion suggested that Edward should go to her sister's boy friend George, who lived in Fishergate and see if he knew people who would know where Ruth was living.

Edward and Ellen left immediately in his father's car and drove directly to George's home leaving Sam and Sarah to care for the children. On arrival at George's mother's house, George agreed to help Edward. They left Ellen at George's home but before they started their search George turned to Edward and said, "Where is she Edward? Knowing you as I do, I bet you have a good idea."

Edward sheepishly asked George not to divulge that he knew Ruth was previously working and living in Fulwood because a friend had seen her. He went on to explain that he had seen Ruth in early April only a few yards from George's home but he had not mentioned this to Sarah. George, not known for beating around the bush said, "You're a bloody fool thinking that you can ditch a wife by pretending not to know where she is." George was referring to the fact that Edward had recently and proudly announced to the family that on the eleventh of April he had filed for divorce on the grounds of desertion claiming not to know of Ruth's whereabouts.

George and Edward walked across the road to where Edward had seen her and within a few minutes and a couple of conversations with people who knew George well they were knocking on the door of Ruth's flat. George told Edward, "Shut up and leave the talking to me." As Ruth opened the door, she staggered backwards as she saw George, who she had last seen some years ago. But as she absorbed that shock, she saw Edward who was clearly intent upon entering her room.

They entered the flat and despite George's warning, Edward turned to Ruth and with some apparent concern said, "The doctors at the hospital are very worried about your health and want us to send for an ambulance to take you into hospital." He then looked at the baby in Ruth's arms as indeed did George and any doubt that this was not Edward's child was immediately dispelled. Michael was the image of his father even down to the distinct long ear lobes and that 'Carmichael nose'.

Edward went on, "We're here to take the baby home with us until you are feeling better and then we can discuss you and your baby's future." George was taken aback by what appeared to be a generous offer of help. But George was wily, and knew Edward well. He could see that Edward had no intention of giving up this child who was clearly his son. There was no point in Ruth struggling as Edward gently took Michael from her arms, she was too weak and was defeated. Without taking a toy or a comforter or clothes Edward left with Michael, his medication, a bottle and some powdered milk. As the door closed Ruth collapsed to the floor.

George and Edward dashed across the road to a waiting Ellen who was surprised by the speed of their return. She took the sleeping child in her arms and having studied his features she turned to Edward and said, "Oh Edward what have you done? This child is

clearly your son ....and what of Ruth, how is she?"
George explained that she was extremely unwell and
with that he went to the telephone and rang the Hospital
to advise them of the situation.

Some time later, as Edward and Ellen drove onto
Fishergate they saw Ruth being carried on a stretcher
into the back of an ambulance. Again Ellen turned to
Edward and said, "Oh Edward, what has this family
done to that poor child?"

Emotionless and without a second glance, Edward
passed the ambulance and sped on his way to Eastbrook
Farm and Sarah who would be there waiting for him.

CHAPTER TWENTY TWO

Ruth was admitted directly to Preston Royal Infirmary suffering from acute and life threatening pneumonia. There she stayed for three weeks during which time the sickness almost took her life. She was weak, delirious and for most of the time she was sedated. Her health deteriorated so much in the first week that doctors were constantly asking for her family to attend her in hospital. Sadly, all the hospital knew of Ruth was the address where she had been brought to hospital from and they knew nothing of her family other than the Carmichael's who were conspicuous by their absence.

As Ruth's strength slowly returned and she was again able to talk she would simple say that she had no family. The hospital doctors became increasingly concerned by her mumblings and questions about her baby and it was only when she became lucid and arrangements were being made to transfer her for convalescent care, coincidentally to Sharoe Green in Fulwood, that they discovered Ruth had delivered a child there in April.

On admission to Sharoe Green Hospital the staff were concerned to establish the whereabouts and the welfare of Ruth's baby and were not satisfied until they had made contact with the Carmichael family and could confirm that Michael was safe in their care. Despite Edward knowing the state of Ruth's health when he last saw her and knowing that she had been critically ill he didn't once visit Ruth in the hospital.

Following the revelation that Edward had fathered a third child and that the child, Michael had been brought to Eastbrook Farm, the future plans that Edward and Sarah had been making to marry seemed to everyone to be at serious risk of unravelling. But the Carmichael family had under estimated the bond of love that existed between their son and Sarah and their capacity to drive forward with those plans despite the reappearance of Ruth.

A family meeting was arranged following a couple of weeks during which Edward and Sarah had carefully analysed their options and their future plans. Sarah had returned to see her parish priest, this time with Edward who explained that he had filed for divorce on the grounds of desertion and that they would need to wait for three years to marry. The conversation with the priest included the fact that when Ruth had left Edward she was pregnant with his child. They shared with the priest that the child had now joined his sisters at Eastbrook Farm and their plans once they were married would be to take all three children into their home as a family. Sarah and Edward were careful to skirt around the matter that within weeks of filing for the divorce Edward knew the whereabouts of Ruth and indeed had met with her.

The parish priest was no more encouraging than on the previous occasion about their prospects of marrying in the Catholic Church though he did agree to write to the Bishop for advice particularly as there were now three children involved. The priest was encouraged to hear that Edward had agreed to start the necessary 'Instructions' to become a Catholic and to convert to Catholicism at the earliest possible date. The priest explained that the course of Instructions was the process by which an adult becomes a member of the Catholic Church and includes Catholic teaching in beliefs and practices, prayer and scripture reading. Finally, they made plans that Michael would be the first of the three children to be baptised into the Catholic Church.

The family, without any discussion or reference to Ruth had taken control of Michael with the firm intention that despite the additional burden on Ellen, Michael would not be returned to Ruth. As a concession to Sarah who was determined to undermine the last vestige of Ruth's connection to the child, Edward agreed to her demand that at the baptism the child's name should be changed from Michael to Robert. Had Ruth been aware of this calculated and cruel act it would have destroyed her.

A date for the Baptism was set for November and it was agreed that immediately afterwards Edward would formalise the name change by instructing the office for Births Deaths and Marriages. This decision was to become the precursor for a raft of changes that would marginalise Ruth to being simply the mother of three children she ultimately abandoned.

Ruth was discharged from hospital in early July and with the help of Marilyn her neighbour who had visited her every Sunday during her stay in hospital, she was able to return to her flat in Preston. Ruth had managed to regain some of her weight and outwardly at least she had recovered well. Mentally however, she was scarred by the loss of her third child and despite several letters to Edward during the course of her hospital stay, begging for an opportunity to see him and the two other children there were no replies.

On Ruth's return to her flat she spent days scrubbing, polishing and cleaning to restore the room to that of a single person. All remaining reminders of Michael were removed from the room and the window was opened to bring much needed fresh air into the room. Ruth met with the landlord who was aware that Michael was no longer with her. He agreed to extend the lease on the room on a monthly basis and this gave Ruth some stability whilst she decided what she was going to do next with her life.

Ruth's first priority was to make a trip to Senghenydd following a letter from Auntie Lottie to say that Uncle Arthur had been unwell. Ruth replied and excitedly informed Auntie Lott that she would come and stay with them over the last weekend in July knowing that by then she should look and feel much better.

Ruth boarded a train in Preston and made in reverse the journey that she had embarked upon all those years ago to come to the north of England to do her bit for the war effort. As the train made its journey south she recalled the flirting of the young men who shared her journey to the north and wondered what course their lives had taken, were they still alive, had they found a sweetheart and married, did *they* have children too?

On this journey, the train was much quieter and there were not the eyes looking at a young, beautiful desirable woman, what glances there were almost seemed to marginalise rather than engage her. Though Ruth was on the road to physical recovery, she knew that she had lost the sparkle of youth. The curvaceous seventeen year old was now a twenty four year old mother of three, burdened by the baggage of guilt, scarred by terrible memories and introverted to the point of appearing cold and distant.

Ruth arrived in Senghenydd at about five thirty, weary from a long train and bus journey and drained from her hours of soul searching. She knocked on Auntie Lott's door something she had never done before remembering that when she lived in the village she would simply walk in and shout, 'It's Ruth', indeed, doors would only be closed and locked at night.

Lott answered the door looking ill but finding the strength to warmly take Ruth into her arms. She held Ruth in an embrace for what seemed like minutes before bringing her into the kitchen. Ruth looked towards Arthur's chair which was empty. She turned to Lott and knew in an instant that Arthur had gone. Lott wept as she explained that Arthur had died the previous week and that the funeral had taken place the previous day.

With tears still rolling down her face Lott spoke with pride as she made a cup and tea and told Ruth about the funeral that was attended by the whole village. Typically for these Welsh valleys, the funeral service started at the house with Arthur's simple coffin being taken from the front room where it had been for the past forty eight hours.

Lott explained, much to the inner amusement of Ruth, that she had put the crocheted table runner on the top of the coffin along with her crystal vase but not before she had given the coffin a good polish which she did each day, "I like my home to be clean and tidy" she said as she carried on with her story.

Sitting in her chair alongside the fire place, with Ruth kneeling at her feet, Lott explained, "As the hearse slowly pulled away from the house my neighbours and friends, young and old, fell in behind me and slowly walked to the junction where more friends were gathered, and they too joined the funeral cortege. This was repeated again and again as we slowly walked past each street or road junction all the way up the hill to the church. As the funeral party reached the church so the men of the village broke into Arthur's favourite hymn, Cwm Rhondda."

Ruth clasped Auntie Lott's hands in hers as Lott described how she turned to look behind her at the villagers. "There were as many as three hundred good souls who had gathered to say goodbye to a much loved friend and neighbour" she said, and how true that was.

With pride in her voice, Lott explained that as the coffin was carefully taken from the hearse, the men, still singing had slowly and quietly come together and formed up as a choir. "The air was filled with the sound and the harmonised voices of more than one hundred great Welsh singing voices and if I had been in Treorchy I could have heard this choir singing for Arthur." Ruth knew the importance of this wonderful hymn which for every Welsh man or woman is the very embodiment of the 'hwyl' or good bye.

Lott explained that only the men sang and as though to respect them and their great voices as much as the passing of Arthur, no one moved until the final words were sung:

> *Guide me oh Thou great Jehovah*
> *Pilgrim through this barren land*
> *I am weak but Thou art mighty;*
> *Hold me with Thy powerful hand,*
> *Bread of heaven, bread of heaven*
> *Feed me till I want no more;*
> *Feed me till I want no more.*

Lott brought her story to a close by saying: "Before they closed the coffin, I placed in Arthur's right hand a photograph, taken many years ago of Arthur, me and Dai and another of you Ruth, forever the daughter we never had." Ruth was overwhelmed that on this saddest of days Lott had taken the trouble to ensure that her love for Arthur was remembered.

As they sat drinking tea, and eating Auntie Lott's Welsh cakes in the fading light of the evening the door opened and in came Dai who had personally walked to every house in the street to thank them on behalf of his mother for "giving Arthur a good send off." He had also been returning plates and cups and saucers to neighbours who had provided them for the tea and sandwiches after the funeral.

Ruth was overjoyed to see Dai once again and as she embraced and kissed him it brought joy to Lott to see this childhood friendship which spanned an age difference of twenty years held in a loving embrace. The remains of that evening were spent reminiscing over hot tea, soup and sandwiches and, of course, Lott's famous Welsh cakes. Lott and Ruth retired to bed at about ten o'clock and with the house only having two bedrooms they left Dai down stairs to sleep on the sofa in the front room.

Ruth slept well, perhaps the most refreshing sleep she had enjoyed in months but she knew that this return to the womb of her childhood could last only for two more days before she must return to her other life, the life that she had so carefully managed to keep from the people of Senghenydd.

The following day, a Saturday, Dai and Ruth walked to the local shop to get groceries but took time to stop at the recreation field, known to the locals as the 'rec' where they sat on a bench to talk. Dai, in a touchingly open way, shared with Ruth the dramas of his marriage which he described as "explosive and unpredictable." He explained that his wife, who was 'English', was a feisty individual whose mood swings saw her move from loving and caring to moody and intolerant. He explained that in the ten years of their marriage, they had two children, a boy and a girl but that in the last year, he and his wife had spent as much time apart as they had together.

He then turned to Ruth and said, "I haven't told Mam yet but I suspect that she has guessed, that I have moved out from my wife and so far, she has no idea where I am." He went on, "If she found me she would insist that we get back together but it just wouldn't work. She gets money for the kids and money for the rent so she is well off but I've had enough of her temper and her demands." Ruth was taken aback by the candour of his revelations knowing that she simply could not reveal any of her life for fear that this open friendship would dissolve in the light of what she had done.

Dai explained that his war had been spent with the Welsh Guards initially with the British Expeditionary Forces in France in nineteen forty, before going on to Tunisia in nineteen forty three, ending up in Italy between nineteen forty four and nineteen forty five. He gave no explanation of what he saw or what he went through simply saying that he had met and lost some fine friends and good soldiers along the way.

Dai was demobbed in nineteen forty six and explained that he immediately went into the motor trade buying and selling army surplus vehicles of any size or shape and trading in cars and motorcycles. Before turning to Ruth to fill in her gaps since they last met, he explained that he was now living outside London "Where the wife cannot find me."

He repeated several times that he wanted to see his kids but not her and that the only way this could be achieved was by him occasionally waiting to see them at the school or seeing them when they stayed with his wife's mother and father. He explained that his wife's parents had sympathy with Dai describing their daughter as mad not to realise what a good chap Dai was. Dai concluded by explaining that his children were living in Chiswick and he was living above his garage near the Elephant and Castle, south of the river in London.

It was now Ruth's turn to fill in her gaps and she explained at length her time in Cardiff and her work in the aircraft factory in Blackpool. She glossed over her three children by simply saying that she had previously met someone and that the relationship had broken down so she was on her own. She pointed out that she had only recently been discharged from hospital having had a particularly bad bout of pneumonia and that she was trying to convalesce before starting to find a new job.

They wiled away more than two hours slipping from memories of her childhood and Dai playing ball with her in the street or reading stories to her to the tragedy of broken relationships and how both of them would like to turn back the clock.

There was for Ruth and Dai a deep set of roots that bound them together in a way that only childhood friendships can. They both remarked that when you have known each other for more than twenty years and you have family and friends that bind you together there are no secrets and no hiding places. And yet there were gaps in both their lives, these were people with futures and distinctly opaque pasts.

Having made their purchases from the local shop and stopping many times to speak to people who were keen to see both Dai and Ruth they eventually arrived back at the house. Lott was not surprised perhaps she was even pleased that their short errand had taken so long. It was clear from the previous evening's conversation that she was keen to see Dai and Ruth together despite the tremendous age difference.

Lott could see that Ruth was comfortable in this older man's company and for Lott, as she neared the twilight of her own life she needed to see her son and her dear Ruth happy. And it was the matter of Ruth and happiness that led Lott to send Dai off to the Feathers for a drink to allow her the time alone to speak to Ruth. Ruth knew this conversation was going to be inevitable and she was braced for Lott's questions.

Over a cup of tea, Lott asked about Ruth's family in Ireland saying that she had not heard a single word from them since they went there. This was the first clue that if Lott had not heard from them she was unlikely to be aware of any of her life since leaving to work in Blackpool. Ruth explained that she had seen them off on the boat from Heysham and had seen nothing of them since then. Ruth spoke about her letters and broke the sad news of Michael's death in Singapore.

Her story flowed for some time and when she was finished Lott looked at Ruth in the way a mother does, with her eyes penetrating Ruth's and reaching deep inside her soul. "Ruth there is something you are not telling me, something that has turned the happy girl I once knew into a nervous, guarded and unrecognisable shadow of the person you once were." Lott went on, "When you were young, you would tell me everything, your deepest secrets knowing that I would not judge you....so tell me now, what is troubling you so much that even now your eyes are darting everywhere to avoid meeting my gaze."

Ruth was expecting this level of questioning from Lott and was prepared to give nothing away except to say, "I am in love with someone who I was hoping was going to be my husband for the rest of my life and now slowly the woman that was his first love is taking him from me and it breaks my heart. His family don't like me because I'm Welsh and working class and they are determined that there will be no future for us." Ruth said no more, there was no emotion, no tears and certainly she was going to say no more on the subject.

Lott knew there was more to say but resisted the temptation to probe further. She did however make one final remark before taking the empty cups to the sink, "It is clear to me Ruth O'Connor that there is more to this story than you are telling and if you decide to go through your life keeping whatever dark secret is inside your soul from those who love you now and who will love you in the future, you will deny yourself the chance to know real happiness and you will forever be looking over your shoulder at the shadow that never lies."

Ruth needed to hear the wise words of a dear friend and there would be times in her future when she would reflect upon the guidance Lott was attempting to give her, but not today. Today she was pleased that the interrogation was over and that her subterfuge on the surface at least, had held together.

The short break was over all too soon. On the Sunday morning Dai and Ruth left the house together with plans that he would drop Ruth at Cardiff railway station before he set off on his own long journey to London.

Lott sent them on their way with sandwiches and Welsh cakes and a long warm embrace. To Dai her parting words were, "Get on with your life, provide for your children and find someone with whom you can spend the rest of your life."

To Ruth she said, "You are already a broken woman and you need to do the same. Settle down with someone who knows the good person that is still deep inside that sad sorrowful soul and make sure that person brings life back to that beautiful face."

At Cardiff station there was an awkward moment as Dai embraced Ruth and kissed her on the cheek. He hesitated and then said to Ruth, "What I really want to do is this" and he slowly drew Ruth to himself and gently kissed her on the lips. Ruth was not ready for this though she had become aware that Dai cared for her rather more than she had realised. She also found the protective nature of his warmth towards her strangely attractive and reassuring and so she was careful to leave Dai with the feeling that she welcomed his attention, his embrace and his kiss, but that the time was not yet right for there to be the future that his mother was hoping there might be for the two of them.

Ruth's journey back to Preston was filled with emotion. She felt that life had returned to her body by being back in the familiar places of her childhood. She had not realised the extent to which she pined for the hills, the warmth of the people and the anonymity from her recent past. She knew at that moment that no matter what the next months and years would throw at her, her future and the chance of any future happiness would ultimately rest in the Welsh valleys of her birth.

Chapter Twenty Three

Back in Preston, Ruth needed to get a job to top up her funds and to give her the means by which she could decide her future. She pondered the possibility of seeing if there was a chance of returning to the post office in Fulwood but on reflection, there were too many memories, lost opportunities and just too much explaining to do. Factory work was available but Ruth felt she had seen that phase of her life and didn't really wish to return to it. There were several jobs in shops but Ruth was fearful of bumping into people she knew and so that was ruled out. And then came a job she knew she could do.

The taxi car company Ruth had used previously, just one hundred yards from her room in Fishergate was advertising for an accounts clerk a job she knew she could do well. Ruth didn't apply in writing as requested on the advert in the local shop window; she simply ran around the corner and breathlessly asked to see John Russo the taxi company owner who she had previously met.

Ruth was lucky, at that very moment John stepped into the outer office and picking up on the threads of the conversation said, "So you're after the job, come on, come in and let's have a chat" he said. Ruth could not believe her good fortune and dashed behind the counter, quickly following the man she hoped would become her new boss.

They went into his office and John's first question to her was, "So how's your baby?" John's own young daughter, Sofia was running around the office happily playing and entirely content in her 'Papa's' company. Ruth explained that she had been unwell and that her son was now with her husband. She went on to say that she and her husband were having difficult times but that time might resolve their problems. She gave John her work history and explained how she had run the post office in Fulwood.

Having listened intently he raised his head and said, "You must resolve what is happening that keeps you from your baby but that is not my business. However, I would like you to start work tomorrow and I would also like to give you a pound a week extra if you will agree to be the key holder considering that you live so near." Ruth leapt to her feet and shouted "Yes, yes." She left the office with a spring in her step knowing that with a job she could begin to think more about her future.

Ruth started her new job in one of the hottest Augusts' in recent years but it was also a busy period for the taxi car business. The apparently small business was in fact quite large providing taxis for short journeys, wedding cars and a funeral hearse. She also discovered that through family connections the business was also able to provide charabanc day trips to local resorts and for extended holidays. Ruth learnt that before the war and the ongoing rationing, the business had run trips to Scotland and Wales and the occasional trip to London.

However, Ruth's first responsibility was to organise the accounts and all the paperwork in such a way that it would be easy for the accountant to do the audit and the business accounts at the year end. Ruth was in her element. She quickly had the office running smoothly and order was slowly brought to the chaotic business accounts. Debtors who took too long to pay were visited by Ruth and a combination of her Welsh tenacity and her female guile rapidly saw the cash flow in the business improve.

∾

It was by now late September and with the night's drawing in and a chill in the air, Ruth was sitting at home alongside her paraffin heater listening to the wireless when she was disturbed by a knock on the door. She opened the door, expecting to see Marilyn, but there, framed by the open door, wearing a smart grey mackintosh, a trilby hat and fine quality leather gloves stood Edward.

Ruth's eyes traced his face looking for any signs as to why he might have come to see her. Uninvited, Edward walked into the tidy but sparse room and removed his hat and gloves. "I thought I might come round to see you and to find out how you are doing and to enquire about your health", he said. Ruth showed Edward to a chair put a kettle on top of the heater and began to prepare to make tea for the two of them.

Ruth turned to Edward and said "Why Edward, after ignoring all my letters asking about the children, why have you come here today and at this hour?" Edward acknowledged that he had received the letters and reassured Ruth that the children were well and in particular he noted that Michael's health was much improved. In answer to the question why he had decided to come and see her out of the blue like this, his mood changed.

Edward explained that despite all their differences he still loved her and that he thought constantly about her. Ruth retorted, "Well if you love me that much and you're constantly thinking about me have you ever wondered what it must be like for me to go day after day without seeing my babies?" She went on, "You and your parents and the wicked Aunts have driven me out and you have gone along with it because what you want is Sarah on your arm and me out of your life."

Edward, looking distinctly uncomfortable tried to explain that he was torn between Sarah and Ruth and that until he had resolved this dilemma he needed to ensure that the children's welfare was guarded by not bringing Ruth back into the family. He explained that he had considered arranging to meet with Ruth, with the children but explained that Ellen had forbidden it saying that it would be too distressing for them. Ruth was not to know that this was a horrible lie.

They talked for more than an hour largely about their early days together and by the time Edward rose to leave they were at least talking civilly to each other. Ruth agreed that Edward could come back to see her the next week but Ruth insisted that he should bring an article of clothing from each of the children so that she could at least try to feel close to them again. As Edward reached the door he turned to Ruth and kissed her on the cheek.

Ruth was completely taken in by Edward's charm and believed him when he said that he was torn between her and Sarah.

Nothing could have been further from the truth. Unbeknown to Ruth, Edward and Sarah had moved on their plans for the christening and entry into the Catholic

Church for Michael and they were planning to take Charlotte and Maria through the same process quickly.

The relationship between Sarah and Edward was solid as was her integration back into the bosom of the Carmichael family where she was treated as the daughter-in-law elect. Edward however, was making no such progress with Sarah in his attempts to convince her that as they were "as good as married" they should consummate their relationship. She was holding firm to her stated belief that there would be 'none of that business' before they were married.

Ruth was therefore unsighted to the reality of the situation between Sarah and Edward and was simply being very cynically wooed by Edward who returned to Ruth's flat the following week with a small bunch of marigolds and chrysanthemums'. Ruth was touched by this because Edward had never bought her flowers in all the time they were together. Indeed, Ruth reflected that she could not remember Edward ever buying her a gift always saying that presents were a con dreamt up by shopkeepers to make money. This was therefore a big gesture on his part and she was curious but flattered.

Edward explained that he was not able to bring an item of the children's clothing for Ruth but promised to do so next week. Ruth thought this was a bit presumptuous but equally she felt that it might support Edward's previous suggestion that they should try to get to know each other again. Ruth was intrigued that Edward was hovering by the window and as they spoke he seemed preoccupied by the comings and goings in the darkened street outside. Eventually, Ruth said, "What on earth are you looking for out there, I thought you had come here to see me." Embarrassed, Edward returned to his chair by the heater and regaled Ruth with stories of how the children were happy and content in Ellen's care and how they were developing well.

However, any attempt by Ruth to move the conversation towards a discussion about seeing them or about a future for the two of them was met with the same response that they would need to rediscover the spark that had brought them together all those years ago.

Edward seemed on edge and eventually said that he would need to go. Ruth suggested that next week they should go to the cinema as she was keen to see a film, any film because it was so long since she had visited a cinema. Edward was very cool about this or any suggestion she made about spending some time outside the flat brushing them off by suggesting that this was supposed to be time for them to talk and get to know each other again.

Edward rose to leave and as he did, he again looked to the window. It was at that point that Ruth asked again what on earth he was looking for and asked, "Are you expecting to see someone or are you meeting someone?" Edward again shrugged off the question and went to the door. Once again as Edward was leaving he drew Ruth into his arms. However, this time he lingered, and as he kissed her there was a closeness that she remembered from the past, a warmth and an intimacy that she had forgotten in herself and in Edward.

As Edward left Ruth turned out the light and went to the window. Being careful not to be seen she waited for Edward to appear on the street below and she watched him as he carefully navigated the traffic in Fishergate and walked purposefully to the other side of the road. He walked the few yards to the side junction whereupon he turned left and disappeared into the side street.

It was at this point that Ruth recalled the incident back in April, when she had seen Edward and Sarah do exactly the same thing. Ruth wracked her brain to try to understand why Edward or indeed Edward and Sarah should walk into a side street away from the bus stops and the shops. The following morning before going to work Ruth strolled across the road and into the side street and to her surprise all she could see were three houses and a large piece of open space. Ruth could only surmise that Edward was visiting someone in those houses, she was intrigued.

As October gave way to November, Ruth and Edward had been seeing each other on and off for some weeks. Their evenings together always followed the same routine: Edward would spend an hour or two with Ruth mostly talking about the early time together with Edward being extremely attentive. It was clear to Ruth that Edward was becoming increasingly close to her. He spoke little of Sarah and when pressed he was inclined to say that they were not seeing much of each other, inferring that their relationship was cooling if not ended. Ruth was drawn to the only conclusion that made sense, that being the possibility that she and Edward could get back together if their current courtship progressed in the same positive vein it had done in the past few weeks.

And so when Edward called to see Ruth in mid November, her mood was lighter than previously and she was happy to see Edward. They talked as usual and picking up on Ruth's cheerful mood, Edward opened up the conversation to the prospect of Ruth seeing Michael, perhaps from afar initially on a visit to Avenham Park in Preston.

Ruth was overjoyed and like a child being promised a treat by its father she pressed, "When...when can we do it when can I see Michael?" Edward was calm explaining that he would need to make the arrangements and then let Ruth know.

And so it was that in this mood of euphoria Ruth succumbed to Edward's charms and ended up in bed with him. Every cell of her subconscious mind was telling her that this was the most stupid thing she could ever contemplate and yet the prospect of seeing Michael again clouded her better judgement so much that she simply gave herself to Edward.

As Edward left, Ruth knew instinctively that she had made a terrible error of judgement. Perhaps it was the smile that could have been read as a smirk on Edward's face or perhaps it was the evasiveness about meeting the next week or perhaps Ruth knew as Edward skipped down the stairs that she had been seduced in the most cynical of ways.

And so she had! It had only been the previous day on Sunday the seventeenth of November that Edward and Sarah had attended the Catholic Baptism of Michael in Sarah's Church. Before the Carmichael family witnesses and in the grace of God, they had callously stripped this small child of a name that had been given to him so lovingly and with such poignancy by his mother Ruth and replaced it with the name Robert. In so doing Sarah and Edward had begun a process through which Ruth's children would begin to learn that their mother did not exist. That message would evolve into one in which the children were to grow up being told that their mother was dead.

CHAPTER TWENTY FOUR

Ruth waited for four weeks before Edward came knocking on her door again once and it was obvious from the outset that his intentions were to bed Ruth once again. Ruth was firm and determined that this would not happen. Before Edward could remove his coat, Ruth demanded to see the little tokens from the children that Edward had been promising for weeks. Ruth was not surprised when Edward again offered a lame excuse and again suggested that he would bring them on his next visit in a week. Ruth considered the situation and decided to put all her cards on the table.

She started by casting Edward's mind back to their last meeting four weeks previous and as she did she could see Edward's mind going in an entirely different direction to hers and she was quick to correct any thoughts he might have that she was there simply to meet his carnal needs. She pointed out that in all the weeks of promise that there was hope for their relationship all they had done was to remain in her one room flat bringing no external expression to their thoughts of getting back together again. Theirs was a "secret relationship" she said and with that she turned to face Edward and confronted him with a stark question, "Edward, do you have any intention of getting back together with me?"

Edward spluttered intending to respond but Ruth carried on, "Let me put it this way, are you prepared to go from here now and take me back to the farm and declare to your parents that we are back together again. Are you also prepared to reintroduce me back into the lives of my children and are you prepared to once and for all stop seeing Sarah?"

Edward was ill prepared for any one of these questions. Still fumbling with the words to answer Ruth's questions, Ruth provided one more fact to stimulate his mind, "And whilst you are pondering all of that you might also wish to know that I am pregnant."

The jauntiness left Edward as did the ability to speak but they were replaced by a flushing of his cheeks and an anger that Ruth had never seen before. Edward rose and walked over to the chair where Ruth was seated. He placed his hands on each of the arm rests of the chair and drawing his face to within a couple of inches of Ruth's he spoke in an intimidating and deeply threatening tone.

"You stupid, stupid woman" he said. "What makes you think that by threatening me with the suggestion that you are pregnant is going to change my plans for my future; neither you nor anyone else is going to do that." He rose and in so doing pulled Ruth to him and said, "And if you are pregnant, and if you ever so much as utter the fact that I am the father I will search the country for you and I will take that child from you just as I have done with the other three." He went on, "I will not have to do much to take this child I will simply have to point out to the authorities that you are not fit to be a mother and that you have abandoned three of your children already."

Ruth was sobbing partly out of fear and partly because she was clear that this meeting marked the absolute low point in her life. At that moment, at that precise moment Ruth knew she would never again see her children.

Edward's parting comment was threatening and frightening for Ruth, "You can expect to see me calling at the flat every week until you have disappeared from the face of the earth." He was crystal clear in his repeated warning, "My deal with you is this, if you go and you take that child with you, you will hear nothing more from me. But if you attempt to ruin my life by letting people know that I'm the father I will, and I repeat, I will find you and I will take that child from you too....mark my words."

Ruth trembled with fear. This was a determined and frightening Edward and someone she knew she needed to take seriously, for her own safety and her own sanity.

Edward left the room descended the stairs and went out onto the street. Once again, he crossed the road and at the junction he turned to his left and disappeared. Despite Ruth's traumatised state, she was curious about where Edward was going and before she realised what she had done, she threw on her coat and her shoes and dashed into the street. Ruth reached the street corner where Edward had turned and as she did so, she saw Edward getting into a car. Hiding in the shadows she waited a few moments and then saw a young man leave a house and step into the car with Edward. It was hard to see who it was but as the car approached the junction with Fishergate, Ruth could see the man clearly and knew immediately who it was.

It was George Morrison Sarah's sister's boyfriend. Ruth knew George from his visit to the flat with Edward in the April and from several years previous when she had met him in Blackpool when she was ice skating. Indeed she remembered that Sarah had been out on a number of dates with him but these fell by the wayside when Edward came on the scene.

Whilst Edward was now regularly meeting George, he had made no mention that Ruth was still living in the flat across the road. He like most of the family had assumed that Ruth had left the north of England and Edward was not going to disabuse them of this notion.

Ruth returned to her single room that night, a room which felt darker, less homely and far colder than previously. She sat huddling around her heater and began the process of deciding what she should now do with her life. She was indeed pregnant, that was not a bluff and Ruth was determined that she would have this child and she would keep it. To do this Ruth knew she would need to move out of the flat and in the short term she would have to be extra vigilant when she was walking to work to ensure that she was not seen by anyone who might know her or Edward.

The following day, Ruth's employer's wife Jane was alone with Ruth in the back office and Ruth took the opportunity to have a quiet chat with her. She took the bull by the horns and decided to be absolutely honest with Jane about the events of the past few weeks.

Jane knew that Ruth was married but estranged from her husband and she also knew that her child, Michael was now with Edward. The rest was hazy largely because Ruth ensured it stayed like that. Ruth told Jane that over the past many weeks she and Edward had been seeing each other and for Ruth at least she had hoped that this would lead to reconciliation.

Ruth confided that she had mistakenly slept with Edward and was now pregnant. She told Jane that this news had outraged Edward and that his threats towards her were frightening and felt very real. Ruth completed her story by explaining why she needed to move out of the flat quickly and pointed out that she would understand if she and John felt that she should leave the company.

Jane listened quietly and offered no judgement but when Ruth had finished she slipped her arm around her shoulder and said, "You're a friend and part of the business and John and I will help you to do what you think is right for you." She went on, "Stay in your flat tonight and in the morning the three of us can talk about how we can help you." They spoke no more on the subject and by mid morning Jane and Sofia who had been out in the garage with her 'Papa' were ready to leave. Jane again slipped her arm around Ruth and said, "We won't pry but we will help as much as we can."

Later that day one of the drivers was wasting time between jobs in the outer office and knowing that he lived nearby, Ruth asked him if he knew where George Morrison lived as she knew him through a friend of a friend. The driver hardly moved as he pointed across the road and said "number ten Guild Street, he lives there with his mother." Ruth felt a shiver run down her spine as she considered the number of times that she had been in Fishergate when she might have bumped into George.

As Ruth returned to her office she began to feel frightened realising that the future for her unborn child depended entirely upon her ability to put distance between herself and Preston and in particular, herself and Edward. That night her journey of only one hundred yards or so home, was taken in the shadows of the buildings where she tried hard to blend into the background.

The following day, Christmas Eve, Ruth went into work half an hour early as usual but on arrival she was surprised to see John waiting for her. He quietly asked Ruth to sit with him and explained that Jane had filled him in on the background to her circumstances. He asked Ruth if she was looking to move home and her job locally or to move completely out of the area. Ruth explained that she was afraid that if she remained in the area for too long, it would not be long before Edward would get to know and she would end up losing this child too.

John listened sympathetically then explained to Ruth that she could move tonight into the flat above the business which was currently empty. He went on to explain that he had a friend, in the motor trade business in Wythenshawe near Manchester who desperately needed someone to help him with his business accounts. He explained that he had spoken to him by telephone and that if Ruth wanted the job she could move there after the Christmas holiday. He also explained that whilst the wages would not be quite so good, the job would come with a flat that she could use.

Ruth was overjoyed by with the news though saddened that once again she would have to leave people who had become good friends and who had taken her to their heart. She asked John if she could telephone his friend and confirm the arrangements which he agreed.

His friend turned out to be a cousin called Victor and he was delighted to hear that Ruth would be arriving after Christmas explaining that she would need to prepare herself for a great deal of work if he was going to be able to present his business accounts on time to his accountant. The thought of moving was saddening but the challenge of being able immediately to be useful and busy was a wonderful counterbalance to Ruth.

Having declined an offer to have Christmas lunch with John and Jane, Ruth moved her few belongings into the flat above the taxi company and settled down to a quiet Christmas alone with letters to write and planning to do. But before any of this she took advantage for the first time in years to run a hot bath and soak there in the knowledge that she would not be disturbed. She thought about her children but her mood was less melancholy than the last Christmas. Tonight her thoughts were only about protecting the unborn child inside her and doing whatever she needed to do to ensure that her whereabouts both now and in the future were not discovered by Edward and his family.

༺༻

Ruth had continued to write to her mother though she received no replies. This was heartbreaking but Ruth knew that she had visited this upon herself by not sharing with her mother what was happening in her life when she first became pregnant. Nonetheless, Ruth wrote again to her mother telling her that she was moving to Wythenshawe near Manchester and that she would provide an address in due course. The address would be a post office box number as previously so that her whereabouts could not be passed on, no matter how innocently this might happen.

Ruth had been in regular contact with Mrs Morgan until earlier in the year but this lady of character and style had now moved to Colorado in the USA with Colonel Arthur Brockenbeck or 'Hawkeye' to his friends. Reading between the lines of her letter, before she departed for Colorado Mrs Morgan may have conveniently forgotten that she was married but this was probably for her a minor oversight. She was clearly happy and, for Ruth that was a great blessing. However, Ruth pondered whether the USA was really ready for the likes of Mrs Morgan. Ruth feared that the letter from Mrs Morgan would probably be the last and the end of a wonderful relationship with a larger than life character and someone for whom rules were generally for other people. Notwithstanding the fact that she may not hear again from Mrs Morgan, Ruth wrote if for no other reason than to convey a more positive side of her personality but also to attempt to keep open a dialogue with someone she really cared for.

In so far as Mary Morgan was concerned, her letters had become less frequent but none the less enjoyable. They were prosaic always gushing with excitement, love and passion for her ability to move amongst a circle of friends that saw the world the way she did.

The letters had previously spoken of several friendships but now the letters carried one name and that was Clarissa. Mary was in love with Clarissa and her letters were full of the ups and downs of that relationship but what penetrated the narrative was a clear sense that Mary had found her soul mate in life and that their love was as intense and as honest as that of any couple Ruth knew. Naively Ruth once asked in a letter if Mary and Clarissa held hands and did they kiss. "Kiss my darling" she replied, "we snog and we laugh and we cry and well, darling we do everything." Ruth could detect the influence of Clarissa in both the writing and the content of her letters.

Ruth was determined that it was now her turn to carve out a piece of happiness for herself and if that meant putting her past in a special place to be visited but not dwelt upon then so be it. Ruth's letter to Mary rejoiced at her good news and her happiness and spoke of a day in the future when they might meet up and when she could also meet Clarissa.

Ruth decided to use this letter to explain that she and Edward were no longer together without providing too much more detail. She did however explain that she was expecting a baby but omitted to mention that she had three others that she had previously walked away from. To Ruth this was as honest as she was prepared to be even with someone who she regarded as her closest friend.

On completing the letter she reflected upon how good she felt and how these first steps towards her new future were uplifting. Feeling in a state of moderate contrition, Ruth decided to also write to Auntie Lott.

Her letter to Lott was carefully constructed to provide some of the background facts of a less than happy marriage with Edward. She admitted to having known Edward for some years and that they had married in nineteen forty three. She also explained the other person in Edward's life, Sarah, and she carefully wrote about how Sarah had won the tug of love and had taken Edward from her. Finally, she told Lott of her pregnancy and that she was going to keep the baby and bring it up on her own however difficult that might be.

Ruth walked to the post office and as she dropped the letters into the post box she felt that for the first time in many years she was on the journey towards regaining control over her life.

CHAPTER TWENTY FIVE

On New Year's Eve Ruth packed her few belongings and took them downstairs into the garage. John had insisted that he drive Ruth to Wythenshawe which would provide an opportunity for his family to see his cousin again. And so by mid morning Ruth, John, Jane and Sofia climbed into one of the company cars and set off.

Their journey of a little more than forty miles was symbolic for Ruth as she was putting distance between her and Edward and she was leaving a place where everyone knew each other and many knew her. For Ruth, the journey had the additional effect of being able to close the lid on bad experiences and it gave her the energy and focus to think positively about her future. As always her children were never far from her mind but she knew that there was nothing she could do now to get those children back. Her thoughts were only for her unborn baby.

On arrival in Wythenshawe, Ruth was taken immediately to Victor's house which was only a few yards from the business. Victor was a carbon copy of his cousin John, affable, kind and evidently very hard working. Victor was single and seemed to live to work being successful in several small businesses. However, this new venture, a vehicle repair business which he had only recently bought had many problems, not the least being the state of the accounts.

Having enjoyed a cup of coffee, a completely new experience to Ruth, they walked down the road to the garage and Ruth was taken to her flat. Ruth was shocked; the flat had a sitting room, kitchen, bathroom and two bedrooms all furnished. The feel of the place was masculine which was no surprise once Ruth realised that the previous owner of the garage had also been a single man. However, Ruth was sure that she was going to be happy here and quickly carried her few personal belongings into the flat.

Before John and Jane left to drive back to Preston, Jane took Ruth to one side and explained that Victor was fully aware that she pregnant and knew that at some time in the future she would need to take time away to have her baby and to decide where she was ultimately going with her life. Jane explained that Victor was entirely comfortable with this, concerning himself only with his business and the state of the accounts.

Ruth spent the following eight weeks completely submerged in the accounts of Victor's new business. She discovered that the accounts were virtually non-existent but that there were no material concerns about the integrity of the business. At the end of February, having been undisturbed by Victor and left to get on with the accounts, Ruth asked Victor if he could spend a couple of hours with her to fill in some gaps prior to her taking a further couple of hours in which she would give him a forensic assessment of the business accounts.

Ruth had discovered a real flair for this kind of work as Victor was to find out at the first intensive meeting about the business. Victor was shocked by what Ruth had achieved. She had chased the many debtors and had brought in more than one thousand pounds of money owed to the business that Victor was unaware of. She had also cleared all the creditors most of whom were known. Ruth asked many questions about the stock and stock control systems and when she was finished she announced that she would be able to present the final accounts on time for the meeting with the accountants in April but that she wanted to let Victor have sight of the state of the business the following day.

The following morning, looking tired but excited, Ruth disclosed to Victor that when he bought the business, the full extent of the stock had not been recorded and that having recovered most of the aged debtor monies, the business was in a healthy state and, surprisingly trading at a small profit. Victor was staggered. He could not believe that Ruth had achieved so much in such a short time and that she had grasped the workings of the business so quickly. This was something that was confirmed by the accountant when he met separately with Victor.

Victor reported all of this back to Ruth and in so doing he gave her an envelope saying that this was her bonus. It was only later when Ruth opened the envelope that she discovered there was fifty pounds in crisp notes. This money was immediately banked in her 'baby fund' as she called it in the post office savings account.

Ruth's pregnancy was uneventful and by July she had seen her doctor several times and she had already been booked into the local hospital for the delivery. She, like the rest of the country was getting excited about the plans to launch the National Health Service which would mean that she would no longer have to pay at the point of use for her care.

Throughout the nineteen forties it had become apparent that a health service run by the government would be introduced but only in the teeth of opposition from large sections of the medical profession. However, the war had increased the sense of social solidarity, and many saw the advantages of a centrally funded health service. Many doctors had military experience and knew that service personnel had, from a health perspective, been looked after better whilst they were in military service than in peacetime.

On the *appointed day*, the fifth July nineteen forty eight, having overcome political opposition from both the Conservative Party and from within his own party, and after a dramatic showdown with the British Medical Association which had threatened to derail the National Health Service before it had even begun, Anuran Bevan's *National Health Service Act* came into force. The reassurance that healthcare free at the point of use provided to Ruth and to post war Britain was overwhelming. Ruth saw this also as an omen for her new baby, knowing that she would never have to face the question of whether her child's health needs could be afforded.

The fifth of July nineteen forty eight was also a memorable day in the life of the Carmichael family but for entirely different reasons.

CHAPTER TWENTY SIX

In the period since Edward had last seen Ruth, he and Sarah had been moving forward with their plans for marriage. These included Edward's and the children's conversion to the Catholic Church. Having baptised Michael, and changed his name to Robert, Sarah and her parish priest moved swiftly to baptise Charlotte and Maria, something that was achieved in the January of nineteen forty eight. Edward completed his Instructions in the Catholic faith and in the April of the same year he too was baptised and converted to Catholicism in a service attended by the whole Carmichael family including the children.

The irony of the situation had not escaped Edward that had he succumbed to Sarah's demands to become a Catholic all those years ago, he would not have found himself in the predicament he was in today. But for Sarah the symbolism of attending her church with Edward and the three children and demonstrating both her faith and her commitment to ultimately marry this man was powerful and placed her centre stage for the nine o'clock service.

There were however mutterings from some members of the parish who felt that it was unbecoming to be making a public commitment to a man who was still married and they could be seen turning their heads away from Sarah and Edward as they walked down the central isle together having taken communion. Some members of the parish, who only attended the nine o'clock service, boycotted the mass for the same reason. None of this impacted upon Sarah and for the most part Edward was simply taken along on this emotional wave.

Edward had visited Ruth's flat in Fulwood on a couple of occasions only to find when he visited in April that she had left. He tried hard to establish where Ruth had moved but no one knew. This irritated Edward because his intention was to ensure he kept Ruth in his sights so that he could at the same time ensure that she didn't attempt to make any contact with the family in order to disclose that he had been cheating on Sarah.

The children were settled into the family life on the farm but it was a life where their mother was never mentioned. The only one of the three who had a memory of their mother had been actively discouraged from speaking of her. Should Charlotte make the mistake of mentioning her mother, the punishment, particularly if the other children were nearby was to be sent to her room.

On one occasion when Sarah had visited the house Charlotte was determined not to do as Sarah asked of her and blurted out "You are not my mother and I won't do it." The reaction from Sarah was instant, as she asked Edward, "Are you going to let the child speak to me like that"? Rather than playing down the comment, Charlotte was told to apologise and was then sent to bed without her evening meal and told to never speak of her mother again.

This was but one of many occurrences where Sarah's influence over Edward and her lack of any empathy with the children came through. Sarah was not predisposed towards children and showed regularly that she simply tolerated them rather than attempting to get close to them.

Slowly but cynically, the concept that Ruth was dead was introduced into the conversation with the children so that the idea of her ever returning was slowly removed.

During early June, Ellen developed bronchitis and this rapidly became a matter of some concern to the family doctor. He was so worried about her deteriorating health that he visited Ellen three times a week and towards the end of the month his visits were daily. Ellen was weak and becoming weaker by the day and though she was comfortable there seemed to be no way that she could shake off the bronchitis. Suggestions that she should go into hospital were shrugged off, primarily because she still saw herself as the only person capable of caring for the children.

Without Ellen managing the house, Charlotte at the age of four was doing chores and taking on work for Ellen as her own mother Ruth had done before her. Neither Sam nor Edward seemed capable of doing anything with the children or for themselves.

The wife of a neighbour was drafted in to help each day as Ellen's health appeared to be taking a turn for the worse but she could not offer to the sensitive and bewildered children what they needed. There was no one to draw the children into a loving embrace and to tell them that everything would be alright. Only Ellen herself as she lay sick in her bed was able to stop Robert's cry though Charlotte did her best. Maria sat in the corner of Ellen's room for hours refusing to leave even when Ellen's coughing became so bad that she could barely breathe.

Sam and Edward were beside themselves with concern knowing that they could not expect the neighbour to help out indefinitely. Father and son had very similar views about women. Both saw them as 'bearers and carers', bearers of the children they would single handedly bring up, and the long term carers for them both now and in their dotage. The thought that Sam or Edward might do anything about the house during this crisis had never even crossed their minds. They had no relationship with the children and therefore knew nothing of their routines, needs, likes or dislikes. Ellen did everything for the children, and for her husband and her son.

On the occasions when Sarah visited during Ellen's illness, she offered no support with the children preferring to be taken out for a walk or even to be taken into Preston or Blackpool by Edward. Their trips out were never with the children, always alone, always as a courting couple and always without a care in the world. Sarah seemed oblivious to the deepening crisis in the Carmichael household and simply distanced herself from the problems and especially from the children.

Ellen was by now weak. The mood of the house was tense with a growing sense of foreboding. And so it was that in the early hours of July the fourth nineteen forty eight, Sam woke the house, grief stricken wailing that Ellen had died in the night.

A doctor was called immediately and when he arrived at about six in the morning he confirmed her death and said that in his opinion she had died as a result of a heart attack. Ellen was fifty years of age.

∽

The neighbour was again called to the house and she took Maria and Charlotte to her home away from the grief and away from the chaos. As the news of what had happened spread around the near and distant neighbours, another neighbour took Robert as they rallied around this family in shock.

Ellen was removed from the house and taken to Preston hospital where a post mortem examination would be carried out. As the undertakers pulled out of the farm yard, Sam and Edward stood looking at each other neither knowing what to do. Sometime later Sarah, then Aunt Matilda and Aunt Dorothy arrived and it was at that point that the enormity of what Ellen's death would mean to the children dawned upon them all.

Sarah made clear her position on the subject when she said, "There is nothing I can do to help, not until we are married and so you will need to cope yourselves or speak to social services about what they can do." Aunt Matilda and Aunt Dorothy similarly felt that they would not be able to assist and as though paralysis had set in, they simply sat there in silence. Sam was incapable of doing or saying anything in his grief and it was Edward who eventually rose from his chair and asked Sarah and Aunt Matilda if they would accompany him to Preston to visit the Council offices.

At this stage as Edward drove out of the driveway, no one from the family had spoken to the children, and yet it was evident to them as they were being bundled out of the house in the early morning that something dire had happened to their grandmother. Charlotte had absorbed everything and though she could not fully explain to herself what was going on, she knew that her grandma was dead.

At four thirty on the same day, Edward returned to the house followed by a social worker. The social worker sat with Edward and Sam and explained that she had a foster family in Inglewhite, a small village quite near to the farm that would be able to take Charlotte and Maria as soon as they were packed and ready to go.

In so far as Michael was concerned, of course he was now being called Robert, the social worker explained that he would be taken to Preston and placed with a Catholic foster family. Sarah had been influential in this placement through her own contacts with the parish priest and the social services department were grateful for the help. Although the war was over there were still many children who had been orphaned by the war who were in the care of the overstretched social services system in the country.

The social worker asked that the children should be brought back to the house to prepare them for what lay ahead. However, she was startled to learn that the whole day had passed and no one had seen fit to visit the children nor had anyone spoken to them about what had happened to their grandma.

She immediately took control and asked Sarah to arrange for the two girls to be brought to the house. When they arrived, Charlotte was holding the hand of Maria and neither would let go of each other. The social worker asked that everyone other than Edward should leave the room so that Edward and she could talk to the Children.

Edward, who had very little relationship with the children, not surprisingly was lost for words. With a sympathetic voice, the social worker sat the two girls down next to their father and began the painful task of explaining to them that their grandma had died. The girls once again turned to each for comfort with Charlotte holding Maria almost as though to protect her from the shock.

It was then the social worker's responsibility to explain that they were being taken to stay with a family in Inglewhite and that they would stay with that family for some time until their father and the Council were able to decide what to do next.

Asked if they had any questions, Charlotte said, "So grandma has gone to heaven to be with mummy." The social worker turned to Edward but held back her question until the children had been sent to their bedroom to get a toy and their pyjamas. It was only when the children were out of earshot that she sharply asked Edward, "Why would your children think their mother is dead when you have told me only a couple of hours ago that she has deserted you?" Edward mumbled that it seemed easier for the family to build a picture in the minds of the children that she had died rather than to say she had abandoned them.

The social worker was clearly irritated by Edward's response and turned again to him and asked, "You told me this afternoon that you have no idea of the whereabouts of Ruth your wife and that the last time you saw her was in nineteen forty six when she walked out of Bowland Moss Farm, I am asking you once again Mr Carmichael, do you have any information that could help us to trace your wife so that we can see if we can work with her in possibly reuniting the family, or at least the children with their mother."

Edward looked towards the half open door and seeing Sarah and Aunt Matilda in the shadow, he said, "I have told you, she left in nineteen forty six and I have seen nothing of her since." Edward had conveniently omitted to note that he had been to her flat in Fishergate to take Robert in nineteen forty seven and he not surprisingly omitted to tell her that he had been having a relationship with her again resulting in her being pregnant with their fourth child!

The children returned to the room with a parcel of clothes and their dolls. The social worker turned to Edward and reminded him that the family in Preston was expecting him that night with Robert and urged him to leave immediately she and the girls had left the house. With that Charlotte turned to her father and said, "Daddy, will you come to see us?" He nodded and with a gentle tap on their heads, two of his children were taken away. There were no tears, there was no affection shown to them by anyone, they simply walked down the driveway into the uncertainty of their own future.

Later Edward and Sarah took Robert to Preston and handed him over to the waiting family at the door of their home. Once more, there was no emotion. Now all his children were in care and it was all handled as though it was a transaction.

And so, as the day drew to a close, a day that had started with the death of Ellen, and ended with Edward and Ruth's three children being taken into the care of the local authority, Sarah and Edward drove alone back to the house.

Five days after Ellen's death the family was provided with the Coroner's findings from the post mortem examination. Those findings confirmed the family doctor's view that Ellen had died of a heart attack exacerbated by the bronchitis.

A funeral was immediately arranged and the following week Ellen was buried before a small family gathering and six local neighbours at the local church in Goosnargh. The family, but not the friends returned to the house where plans were formulated that would see Edward and Sam leave the smallholding as soon as they could find a buyer for the lease.

Plans for the children were on hold until the next meeting with social services but the emerging view was that it would be unlikely that Edward could resume his direct role as the children's father until such time as he and Sarah had married and that was still two years away.

CHAPTER TWENTY SEVEN

Unaware of the death of Ellen in early July and the turmoil this had created in her children's lives, Ruth's mood of optimism and improved self esteem was strengthened by continued praise for the work she was doing for Victor at the garage. She had used time between her ongoing work for the garage to assist Victor with the accounts of one of his other businesses which again demonstrated her grasp of the motor trade business and her excellent book keeping and accountancy skills.

Ruth was touched by the fact that Victor made no references to her pregnancy or the fact that by now she was getting quite large. The other staff in the office seemed to avoid sensitive questions but regularly asked after her health and took pleasure in reporting back to Ruth that since her arrival Victor seemed far less stressed about the business.

Ruth had attended regularly at the antenatal clinic in the hospital and was often taken there either by Victor or, on his instructions, another member of staff was asked to do this for him. Ruth felt a real sense of belonging within the small team where she knew she had made a very real difference.

The letters that Ruth had sent to Mary and to Lott had by now been responded to and again Ruth took great comfort from what she interpreted to be genuine support.

Mary was effusive in her letter offering the 'ladies of London' as a collective for support should she need it. She also and very genuinely offered Ruth a home for as long as she wanted it in London with her and Clarissa.

As always, Mary's letter moved rapidly from the substantive matters in previous correspondence to the intimacy of the ups and downs of her own relationship. Ruth loved the window into Mary's world, not so much for the unorthodox nature of her relationship with Clarissa, but because of the evidence that two people can love each other so much that it withstands the daily challenges of life.

The letter from Lott was lengthy and intimate. She opened her letter by saying that several of her friends had become pregnant attempting to fix a broken marriage but in her experience it only put off the inevitable break up if that was the direction it was going in.

Lott explained that the good thing about a close community such as Senghenydd was that people *were* close and cared and that they would soon be there to help and to assist.

Lott closed her letter by saying, '*Come home little Ruth, come home to your valley to the people who love you and to the people who care*'. She went on; '*People will talk for a while and perhaps they will gossip but they will always have time for you and they will always regard you as one of their own; come home and let me look after you until you are ready to do what you feel you must do*'.

Ruth was overwhelmed by the generosity of Lott's offer and it certainly opened up opportunities for her that she had not yet considered. But it was the unexpected letter from Dai, which took Ruth completely by surprise. Clearly, Lott had given Dai Ruth's address and she must have outlined much of what Ruth had confided in her earlier letter.

Dai's letter was lengthy and covered a wide range of issues. He spoke firstly about the state of his marriage explaining that whilst he was paying into his wife's bank account money for his two children, his wife was chasing him down asking for more money. Dai explained that because of this and her anger at him leaving her, she was refusing to agree to a divorce.

Dai talked a little about his business and explained that the car sites were doing well with a big demand for old motorcycles and an increasing demand for small cars as the impact of petrol rationing was lessening. However, he spoke also about wanting to return to Wales planning to do so as soon as he could find a buyer for the businesses. He expressed a concern to be nearer to his mother in Senghenydd something he hoped to achieve within the next couple of years.

Dai's final comments were touching and sincere as he acknowledged how difficult Ruth's decision to leave her husband must have been and how brave it was of her to take such a decision. Ruth stopped reading the letter as she reflected upon how little Dai really knew and if he would be quite as considerate if he knew that she had three other children.

Dai's final comment was to offer help, support and any assistance he could even to come to her and take her to south Wales if she wanted to take Lott's offer of a home back in Senghenydd. He spoke of his feelings for Ruth and how much he had enjoyed meeting her again making a particular point of expressing how easy they both seemed to be with each other.

Ruth read Dai's letter several times as she tried to tease out of it what he was saying between the lines so that she could respond appropriately. Ruth was certain that the warmth they both felt for each other when they parted in Cardiff was clearly coming through from Dai in this letter. She looked back over their short time together when she visited Lott and recalled several occasions when Dai was looking intensely at her and on reflection she realised that though she didn't pick up the signals she could see them now. Indeed, on further reflection Ruth could see that they were exceptionally close over those couple of days and picked up easily on their lifelong friendship.

Ruth asked herself over and over again, was Dai trying to suggest that if she returned to south Wales there could be the prospect of the two of them getting together? Ruth carefully crafted a reply, being circumspect not to draw too many conclusions but using the opportunity to make it clear to Dai that she welcomed his interest in her wellbeing and being clear that she would 'really like to get together again as soon as possible'.

Ruth made it as clear as she could without crossing the line he had set in his letter that she liked him a lot and felt really at ease in his company. She closed her letter by saying that she had responded to Lott thanking her for the offer of spending time with her but making it clear that she would take no decisions until after her baby had been born. .

It was by now August and whilst there was still plenty of work for Ruth to do, Victor was assiduous in ensuring that Ruth spent at least a couple of hours resting in her flat each day. Ruth welcomed the kindness but also acknowledged that she needed the time to put her feet up and rest. The weather was oppressively hot making Ruth feel uncomfortable unless she was in her flat and stripped down to her underwear.

What Ruth also enjoyed in her afternoon rest period was listening to the wireless and joining in the nation's excitement at the Summer Olympic Games being held in London. These were the first to be held after the War and whilst they were referred to as the 'Ration Book Olympics' the nation embraced them and the world wide competitors warmly. Fifty nine nations attended with the notable exclusion of Germany and Japan and whilst British athletes did not fair too well, for Ruth the Olympics was another sign of Britain getting back on its feet.

Ruth sought out a meeting with Victor to address arrangements for the period when she would be away from her work having the baby. Victor had avoided the conversation not wanting to face up to the inevitable question of what Ruth would do once she had given birth. The meeting did little to help, with Ruth asking if they could cross that bridge once she had returned home from the hospital. Victor was relieved but detected in Ruth a hint that she would wish to move on fairly soon after the birth of her child.

On the late evening of the first of September, Ruth went to the hospital quietly and without any fuss, simply leaving a note for Victor to say that she expected to be away from work for about a week having the baby and that the accounts were fully up to date.

Ruth checked into the newly rebranded National Health Service hospital in Wythenshawe an old building that was much in need of refurbishment. However, for

Ruth the most important feature of the maternity unit was its reputation which was excellent.

Ruth was taken to the maternity unit by a young nurse resplendent in her new blue uniform with a starched white apron, cuffs and collar and a large white hat. She explained as they slowly walked to the ward that the new nurses' uniforms were one of the first things the hospital provided when they were taken over by the National Health Service. However, she pointed proudly to her silver belt buckle at her waist explaining that this was given to her by her mother when she qualified as a nurse.

Ruth settled down knowing fully the experience of child birth and that it could be several hours before this baby was born. Ruth was relaxed, happy and very positive spending the next few hours contemplating her future something that was only interrupted by the quickening labour pains.

At three twelve on the morning of the second of September nineteen forty eight Ruth gave birth to a little boy. The delivery was straight forward, and both she and her baby endured the delivery without harm and in good health.

✍

Ruth was thrilled to once again have a baby in her arms and relished every moment she was allowed with her child. When asked if she had decided upon a name she quickly announced that the name would be Huw, "A fine strong Welsh name and one to be proud of" she said. The name Huw Carmichael was placed at the head of the cot tied on with a simple blue ribbon.

Ruth happily breast fed Huw and her contentment and her ease with the baby were noted by the staff when after four days she pestered them to be allowed to go home. Ruth returned to the subject of when she could leave the hospital when Victor called at the hospital with flowers from him and the staff. He confirmed to the nursing staff that she would be taken home on discharge and would not be expected to work until she felt ready to do so. It was therefore agreed that Ruth could be discharged at one o'clock the following day after the eleven o'clock ward round and that Helen, Victor's sister would be there to take her home.

Ruth was anxious when the doctor and the ward sister arrived the following morning with their folders and charts but she was soon relieved when she overheard the sister say to a nurse that Ruth could be discharged immediately after she had seen the matron.

In the few days that Ruth had been in the hospital she had not seen the matron and rather hoped that as she was now so close to being discharged this final step would not delay her, especially as Victor had arranged for Helen to pick her up sharply at one o'clock.

At about eleven thirty, Ruth was taken to a side room with her baby and a few minutes later the door opened. As Ruth turned towards the door with Huw in her arms she gasped as she realised who was standing there looking at her. It was Aunt Dorothy in her matron's uniform, and flowing red cape with her arms crossed and her face like thunder, glowering at her. "I have just returned to the hospital and was intrigued to see who the 'Mrs Carmichael' was in my hospital and now I see that it's you" she said.

Before Ruth could say any more, Aunt Dorothy continued, "And what unsuspecting individual is the father of this child" she said in a superior, cutting and dismissive way. Ruth was angered by the attack on her and looked Aunt Dorothy square in the eye and said, "I suggest you take a look and you will soon see that this is another of Edward's children."

Aunt Dorothy came close and looked carefully at the infant in Ruth's arms. The look of shock on Aunt Dorothy's face was palpable as she slowly drew away from Ruth and returned to the doorway. "Does Edward know about this", barked Aunt Dorothy to which Ruth answered, "Of course he knows about Huw, why do you think I have tried to get as far away from him as I can?"

Gone was Aunt Dorothy's air of superiority and authority replaced by bewilderment and shock. But it was obvious that as Dorothy tried to absorb the information, she was rapidly doing some calculations in her head that might place Edward with Ruth together nine months ago.

But it was now Ruth's turn to experience uncertainty and worry as it suddenly dawned upon her that it would now only be a matter of hours or at best a couple of days before Edward would become aware through Aunt Dorothy that Ruth was living in Wythenshawe with his baby.

Dorothy turned to leave the room but before she did she had one parting comment for Ruth. She looked at Ruth and Huw very carefully before finally saying, "Oh what have you done Ruth, Edward already has to cope with so much and now this....."

Ruth was not to know the hidden awful background and meaning of what Aunt Dorothy was alluding to, but she was now afraid of the consequences of Aunt Dorothy knowing her whereabouts and sensed that she would very rapidly be speaking to Edward. Without another word said, Aunt Dorothy opened the door and left.

Ruth was in a state of complete shock when Helen sought her out to take her home. Gone was the confident, self assured Ruth of a couple of hours ago. Ruth's protective instincts had taken over and she found herself scouring the area to see if Dorothy was watching as they drove out of the hospital grounds. Her instinct was flight, her very being said grab everything you can carry and run, putting distance between Edward and Wythenshawe.

When they arrived at the flat, Helen was so concerned about Ruth that she immediately asked Victor to come and talk to her. When Victor arrived Ruth had calmed down a little as her immediate thoughts and energy were transferred to ensuring that Huw was settled and comfortable. Victor didn't detect the same anxiety that Helen had and so he spent much of the time with Ruth looking at her baby and reassuring her that she should take whatever time she needed to settle Huw into the flat. Helen immediately offered to provide whatever help she could and by the time they decided to leave, Ruth was feeling somewhat calmer. Before Victor left, Ruth asked if she could make a telephone call from the office which Victor agreed to immediately.

Once Ruth was alone she sat down and began to mull over in her mind what Edward's reaction would be once Aunt Dorothy spoke to him about the child that it was evident she, and presumably the rest of the Carmichael's were unaware of. She quickly concluded that he would be furious and want to find her and again that reinforced in her mind that her only option was to run and run as quickly as she could.

Once Ruth was satisfied that Huw was settled she slipped downstairs to the office which by now was empty and dialled the telephone number for Dai. The phone was immediately answered by Dai who was delighted to hear Ruth on the other end of the call. He immediately deluged Ruth with questions about her health, had she had the baby and when would they be able to meet up. Ruth's tone was warm but worrying to Dai as he listened to her explain the events of the past week, the joy of her child and the fear that Edward might very soon try to find her.

Calmly Dai absorbed the information and when Ruth had finished he said, "You need to get away from there as soon as possible and what you should do is to take up my mother's offer to go and stay with her in Senghenydd for a while." Ruth saw the sense in what Dai was saying and with that agreed the immediate plan was for him to telephone the post office in Senghenydd the following morning to arrange to speak to his mother. Once this was accomplished, he would telephone Ruth with plans to drive to Wythenshawe and take her to Senghenydd.

Ruth met with Victor at eight thirty the following morning and explained that she needed to leave very soon to take her baby to south Wales. She gave no more detail but made it clear that whilst she would be eternally grateful for the job, the flat and the friendship she had received from Victor and the staff, her immediate priority was to return, as she put it, "To the valley of my birth and to the family that will love me unconditionally."

Victor was resigned to the implications of Ruth's decision and reluctantly agreed that she could move on as soon as she had finalised her arrangements. Ruth went on to spend the rest of the day in her room resting and waiting for Dai's telephone call which came at precisely one minute past six in the evening.

Dai was so excited that it was some time before Ruth was able to piece together all the facts that poured out and which mingled into a jumble of excited and emotional feelings coupled with crisply articulated immediate plans. These plans were built upon an enthusiastic agreement from Lott that Ruth, and Huw should move into her home 'immediately if not sooner!' The second part of the plan was that Dai would arrive the following day at about midday to collect Ruth and Huw and drive them to Senghenydd a journey that Dai estimated would take about eight hours.

The following morning Ruth spoke again to Victor who pre-empted their meeting by arranging to make up her wages and by preparing a letter of reference for her. Ruth thanked him for both and explained that her friend would pick her up at about midday to drive her to south Wales.

Dai arrived at about eleven o'clock, enthusiastically anticipating the opportunity to spend time with Ruth. As he went into the flat, Ruth picked up Huw and showed him to Dai. His reaction was to immediately take Huw from her and to expertly cradle him in his arms.

Dai spent some time looking at Huw before turning to Ruth and saying, "He is beautiful and looks so much like you." Ruth walked over to Dai and put her arms around him and Huw. She placed a small kiss on the forehead of Huw before kissing Dai warmly on the cheek. "Let's take things slowly" she said.

Ruth sat Dai down and explained that she did have strong feelings for him and that she, like him could see the day in the future when they could get together. But she also pointed out that both of their lives were sufficiently complicated right now that they should not make them worse by entering into a relationship right away. Ruth was clear that Dai should face up to his commitments to his wife and children first, before embarking upon a relationship with her. Ruth surprised herself as she explained that they must both show restraint and patience until such time as the complications in their separate lives was resolved or at least more stable.

Dai acknowledged the voice of reason and explained that his own children would be out of school and off his hands very soon and perhaps that would be the point in the future that they could explore getting together.

They rapidly packed Ruth's few belongings and whilst Dai sat in his car with Huw, Ruth slipped back into the office to say goodbye to her work colleagues and Victor. Victor held her in his arms and said quietly, "Should you ever need to come back there will always be a job and a home for you." Ruth cried as she turned to leave Victor and a place where she had been so very happy.

During that same morning, Aunt Dorothy had made her way from Wythenshawe on an unannounced visit to Eastbrook Farm. She had resisted the temptation to telephone Edward, deciding instead to speak with him about her meeting with Ruth and his fourth child.

She arrived just as Edward was about to leave and he was clearly taken aback by her unannounced presence. As he walked towards Aunt Dorothy to greet her he was struck by her obvious anger. Firstly, she snapped at her taxi driver to wait and then she proceeded to take Edward by the arm, as a mother would do with a naughty child and march him back into the house.

As they went into the kitchen, Sam was sitting at the table oblivious to Aunt Dorothy's arrival and was startled when he heard her voice. Aunt Dorothy walked over to Sam who was still coming to terms with the loss of Ellen and gave him a swift peck on the cheek. She then turned to Edward who was looking somewhat sheepishly at the angry Aunt Dorothy trying to understand her mood.

Edward was soon to discover why she was so obviously angry: "Whilst this family has been bending rules and trying to mitigate your stupid attraction to that woman Ruth so that you can marry Sarah, what have you been up to?", she snapped at Edward. He looked at Sam who was by now engaged with the conversation and then turned to Aunt Dorothy and said, "I don't know what you're talking about." Aunt Dorothy was enraged as she sat Edward down next to his father and explained who she had seen in her hospital in Wythenshawe.

She finished by saying, "I looked into the face of that child and I know it's yours so don't insult my intelligence by trying to deny it." Edward was speechless and it was his father who was able to absorb the information first. He slowly turned to Edward and said, "I will take your silence to mean that what Dorothy has said is true. I share Aunt Dorothy's anger and disgust that you have misled this family, the church, and your lawyers not to mention Sarah, into believing that you were done with that woman." He continued to berate Edward, "I take it that whilst your mother was caring for your children, you were cavorting around with Ruth?"

Edward eventually found his voice and said, "Please, please don't tell Sarah, I know I have been foolish but Ruth is behind me now and all I want to do is to marry Sarah and get the children out of care." Dorothy was unimpressed as was Sam. Edward left the room with his head down appearing to be contrite.

Sam and Dorothy talked for some time before Sam went outside to fetch Edward back into the room. Once again, Edward stood there like a naughty child, his head down and his whole demeanour confirming the parlous position he now found himself in.

It was Sam who spoke first as he explained to Edward that they were both shocked and disappointed in him that he could cheat on Sarah and that he could lie to the family by suggesting that he had not seen Ruth. He asked Edward what he felt Ruth's plans would be now and whether he felt that Ruth would make any claims upon Edward, or whether she might turn up with the child.

Edward explained that he had made it clear to Ruth when she told him that she was pregnant, that if she kept out of his way he would be happy for her to keep his child. Dorothy and Sam looked to each other both raising their eyebrows at the coldness of his action then.

Sam shook his head and after a moment of silence he went on to explain that Dorothy and he were prepared to keep secret what they knew but Edward would need to promise that he would never see Ruth again. Edward lifted his head and simply said, "Thank you both and I promise that I will never see her again."

Dorothy left the house without speaking to Edward and as she was driven away, Sam turned to Edward and said, "I plan to give up the farm as soon as I can get rid of the lease, when I have done this you should find yourself a place of your own and get your life back in order." He went on, "I will not tell a living soul about this but it will be a matter of conscious to you whether you plan to ultimately tell Sarah".

CHAPTER TWENTY EIGHT

Ruth, Dai and Huw left Wythenshawe at a little after midday on this late September day in brilliant sunshine and with a sense of adventure in their minds. They talked nonstop as they travelled south through the beautiful towns of Shrewsbury, Ludlow, Leominster and Hereford before passing into Wales. The journey was long and tiring but they stopped along the way to eat sandwiches that Ruth had prepared and to make hot tea using a small primus stove that Dai kept in his car. Huw slept for much of the journey and rested comfortably in Ruth's arms as the miles clicked away.

Their journey took them onto the Heads of the Valley road signalling that they were now not far from home. When they reached Quakers Yard a matter of a few miles from Senghenydd, Dai stopped the car and turned to Ruth. He slipped his arm around her and said, "Ruth you know that I love you and you know that I am now there for you for the rest of my life if that's what you want." He kissed her gently on the cheek and said, "We will go at your pace Cariad." Whilst Ruth knew little Welsh she knew the tender meaning of the word Cariad which is a Welsh term of endearment for darling. Ruth drew Dai close to her and with a tear in her eye said, "Always call me Cariad, Dai and I will always be happy."

They drove the final few miles to Lott's home arriving at eight o'clock weary but palpably happy as they were greeted by Lott on the doorstep of her house. They were whisked into the kitchen which was wonderfully warm with a kettle merrily whistling on top of the black range. Lott put the kettle to one side and turned to Ruth and said, "Give little Huw to me for a cwtch whilst you two settle in."

Dai brought Ruth's few belongings into the house and took them upstairs. Ruth was already in Dai's bedroom in which Lott had put a small cot, some soft toys and her rocking chair which Dai pointed out had been the one his mother had used to nurse him when he was a child. Ruth turned and looked at the bed that had clearly been Dai's for many years. Dai caught Ruth's eye and immediately reassured her that he would be sleeping down stairs.

Dai stayed at the house for only the one night, anxious to get back to London to his businesses. On the morning he was leaving, he witnessed a stream of neighbours entering the house anxious to get a glimpse of Ruth and her baby and to see if they could piece any more of the jigsaw of gossip together that was sweeping through the village since their arrival.

But they were no match for Lott who was by now very much the matriarch of the village, highly respected and certainly not to be crossed. To each she said the same thing, "Ruth will be staying in my house with her baby for as long as she likes and that makes me a very happy old woman and I will hear nothing of the tittle-tattle that this village is so famous for."

For Ruth, there was nothing but happiness in being back in south Wales. She had been a popular child and young woman in the village and the stories of her heroics in the Cardiff bombings continued to circulate in the village making her something of a local hero. In so far as little Huw was concerned, whilst there would be gossip and some more robust questioning by the more direct neighbours he would be seen as a son of the valley and was therefore one of their own.

As the last of the visitors were leaving, Dai called upstairs, "Cariad I'm leaving now" and in a public act of affection he firstly kissed his mother, who then took Huw from Ruth as Dai warmly embraced Ruth and kissed her goodbye. This would have done little to stop the gossip but at least it served to demonstrate that Ruth and Dai would be a talking point for some time to come.

Ruth and Lott quickly settled back to the friendship they had enjoyed during the years when she lived in Senghenydd. Lott was old and tired easily but took great comfort in nursing Huw to sleep and doing the same herself. Ruth was able to cook for Lott and do some of the house work that Lott found increasingly difficult and this pleased her. Ruth was grateful that Lott didn't pry into the past but the past suddenly and without warning came back in the person of Edward.

It was only a week after Ruth had moved back to Senghenydd that she was disturbed by a knocking at the door at about three o'clock in the afternoon when Lott and Huw were sleeping upstairs. Ruth answered the door to be confronted by Edward who looked angry and intimidating. He pushed past Ruth into the house and when he reached the empty kitchen he said, "Are we alone?" Ruth had the presence of mind to say that Lott and Huw were upstairs and she asked him to lower his voice as she took him into the front room so as not to disturb Lott whose room was at the rear of the house.

Edward had difficulty in keeping his voice down as he explained that Aunt Dorothy had confronted him with the news that she had seen Ruth and her baby. Edward spent no more than about ten minutes in the house but in that time he managed to make it abundantly clear that if Ruth was ever to try to make contact with him, or if she were to make it known to anyone that the child was his, he would return as he had threatened before and he would take the child from her.

Ruth was terrified as she observed the raging anger in his demeanour and his voice. He neither asked to see Huw nor did he ask after his health. Importantly, Edward also failed to tell Ruth that her three children were now in the care of the local authority because of the death of his mother. We will never know what Ruth's reaction to that news would have been or if that might have marked a watershed in her life when she might have begun to try to get her children back. As far as Ruth was concerned, her children were in the loving care of their grandmother and were happy and adjusted.

As he left the house, Edward could see that several of the neighbours were on their door steps anxious to see who was visiting Lott's house with a car. Edward leant towards Ruth and in a lowered voice said, "I bet these people don't know about your past or the three children you abandoned and I bet you would like to keep it that way, so mark my words, keep away from me, my family and the north of England or they will know everything." With that he climbed back into his car and sped off leaving the neighbours to speculate what all of that was about.

As she entered the house, Lott who was a little deaf and still sleepy from her nap asked who was at the door.

Ruth simply said that it was someone from the National Health Service here in Wales to remind her that she must register the baby with the clinic as soon as possible.

The experience of meeting Edward again and the intimidation that came with his threats deeply upset Ruth which she was unable to hide from the ever attentive Auntie Lott who sat her down and asked her to explain why she was so upset. "Now tell me Ruth, who was that who came to my door and upset you so much?" Ruth relented and explained that it was Edward her husband and the father of her child. She went on to say that Edward, far from wanting to play a part in the upbringing of her baby was making it clear to her that he didn't want to see her or the baby again. Lott accepted the explanation and spent time consoling Ruth who asked her not to disclose to Dai that Edward had been to the house.

The weeks passed by and it seemed to become a routine that Dai would return home to see his mother every two or three weeks and those visits proved enjoyable for Ruth too. At one level it meant that she had someone a little younger to talk to and at another level, Ruth was able to take time to herself without the feeling that she needed to be looking after Lott.

Ruth found it difficult during Dai's visits to meet the matchmaking expectations coming from both Dai and Lott whilst he was still embroiled in marital difficulties with his wife and she continued to stress this upon Dai. For her own part, whilst she acknowledged she too was still married to Edward, Ruth regarded her marriage as over with, and so would be able, when the time was right, to consider Dai's proposition that they get together.

This latest visit proved to be exceptionally difficult as she listened to Lott asking for information about her grandchildren and she listened to Dai's outpourings about the latest attempts by his wife to find out where he lived or to seek more money. Ruth felt in the middle of a difficult and unresolved problem that she was determined not to become entrapped in. This came to a head when she happened to overhear Lott ask Dai if her grandchildren would be visiting for Christmas which was only a matter of a couple of weeks away. Dai dodged the question when he saw Ruth enter the room but she was not prepared to do the same.

Ruth sat down beside Lott and put her hand on hers before she turned and spoke. She began by saying, "Lott I have been very happy here and I'm grateful for the care you have lavished upon me and Huw but it's time for me to move out so that you, Dai and his family can get on with your lives."

Dai looked shocked but Ruth continued as she turned to face Dai, "I cannot become an obstacle between Auntie Lott and her grandchildren and I cannot have you sleeping on the couch in your mother's home, that's why I will be moving out soon to take up a job and to let you resolve your marital problems without me being part of them."

Ruth then turned to Lott and said, "When the time is right Auntie Lott, and one day it will be, Dai and I will get together but that will not be for a while until Dai and his wife and children have resolved whatever needs resolving. In the mean time I will not be far away and I will be able to see you every day."

Dai was about to respond when Lott interrupted saying that Ruth was right not to become embroiled in the dying embers of Dai's marriage and that it was indeed important that her grandchildren should feel able to visit. She then turned to Ruth and said, "So you're going back to the post office are you?" Ruth looked shocked as Lott squeezed her hand and said, "Who do you think suggested to Mrs Thomas that you should move in and run the post office?"

Lott explained to the bewildered Dai that Mr Thomas the postmaster had recently died and that Mrs Thomas felt unable to run the post office which was next door to her house on her own. She explained that Mrs Thomas had been thinking of selling up when Lott reminded her that Ruth was back to stay and might soon be looking for some independence and a job.

Ruth filled in the remaining gaps for Dai by telling him that Mrs Jones had invited her into her house for a cup of tea about ten days ago. Whilst there, she had offered Ruth the postmistress job and the unused living quarters above the premises. She had also assured Ruth that between her and Lott they would be able to look after Huw.

Clasping a letter in her hand Ruth said, "It was only this morning that I received confirmation from the head post office in Cardiff that I can take on the post office."

Dai looked despondent and remarked that he felt as though he was completely outside of this arrangement. Ruth slipped her arm around his shoulder and reassured him that this would be an excellent solution. She explained that she would no longer feel compromised by living in his bedroom; his mother would be able to see her grandchildren whenever they wanted to come over and that she and Dai could still see each other every time he visited.

Later that evening Dai and Ruth went out to the Feathers for a drink and were able to find a quiet corner where they could chat. Dai recognised the merit of the new arrangements and was genuinely happy that this meant Ruth was here to stay in the village. Dai also admitted that putting his children first now would in the long term give him the satisfaction when they did get together that he and Ruth could feel they had done the right thing.

Dai also seemed to put into perspective their ambition to one day get together realising that this could be a year or two away. Somehow, that perspective and timescale took pressure off them both without lessening their affection and feelings for each other. Ruth summed up their conversation by saying it would be a lengthened courtship but with a known destination.

For those observing Ruth and Dai in the pub that night their body language and the intensity of their conversation served only to reinforce that whatever the nature of their unconventional relationship they were a couple that appeared to be in love.

Dai returned to London with plans to spend Christmas Day in London and then to go to Senghenydd for two days over the New Year to be with his children. For her part, Ruth moved into the rooms above the post office three days before Christmas with plans to spend Christmas day with Lott and Huw.

Ruth had very fond memories of both the post office and the rooms above and as she moved in, she felt she knew every corner of the place. Mr and Mrs Thomas had lived on the post office premises at the time that Ruth was working there but she remembered well their excitement when the house next door came up for sale and the soul searching that went on when they considered if they could afford the purchase. It was then that they decided to rent out the rooms above and to create a completely separate entrance avoiding the need to enter via the post office.

The rooms were small but more than adequate for Ruth and Huw. There were two bedrooms which pleased Ruth as she was keen to get Huw used to sleeping in a room of his own. Next to Huw's room was a small bathroom with a bath! Ruth's room had a feminine feel to it with pastel colours and bright floral design curtains at the window that overlooked the garden. The garden itself was looked after by a neighbour who used it exclusively for vegetables and soft fruits sharing the produce with Mrs Thomas. Down the stairs, behind the secure door that led to the post office were a sitting room with an open fireplace and a small kitchen with a door that led out into the garden.

There was room enough outside for Ruth to put Huw in his pram and once he was walking, the rudimentary fence that separated the garden from the pathway would provide sufficient room for him to play.

Ruth was deliriously happy on that first night when she settled Huw down to sleep and retired to her own room to contemplate her good fortune. Here she was having come full circle in her life returning to the place where she first worked and the place that gave her the taste for post office work that had formed such an important part of her life. She felt safe, at home and for the first time in a little while she felt at peace with herself.

Christmas for Ruth brought the same period of intense reflection this year as she considered again what her three children would be doing. Her image of their Christmas was the one she took from the last Christmas in Eastbrook Farm, a frozen in time image with a roaring log fire in the inglenook and the once yearly table that groaned with food from the farm. Ruth's selective memory had conveniently forgotten that this special day for children in the Carmichael household bore all the hallmarks of the Victorian values the adults were brought up with where the children should be seen but not heard. As Ruth contemplated Christmas's past she never diluted in her own mind her culpability or her role in what Edward would always refer to as her 'desertion' of the children.

Ruth enjoyed a happy and intimate Christmas day with Lott and Huw, a day that was interrupted regularly as children knocked on Auntie Lott's door, as Ruth herself had done all those years ago to bring a small gift. These gifts would be small and a gesture of the love each child and each parent felt for Lott. This reinforced for Ruth the certainty that she had taken the right decision in returning to Senghenydd. Ruth's own gift for Lott was a hand knitted bed jacket, which was a delight and a surprise as Ruth explained that Chris, a dear friend in her past, had taken the time to teach her to knit.

New Year's Day nineteen forty nine was spent in her new home where Ruth deliberately stayed to enable Dai to spend as much time as he could with his children and Lott. The children were by no means young, Harry was thirteen and Elisabeth was eleven and would be twelve in February. Ruth had never met the children and had been quite explicit with Dai that she felt it was completely inappropriate for her to do so. Dai and Lott agreed to this which ensured that there would be no chance of Dai's wife making any connection between Ruth and Dai.

Late on New Year's Day, Dai called by to see Ruth and spent about an hour with her before returning to be with the children. Before he left he gave her a new address where he could be contacted explaining that he had to move because his wife had been calling at the house in his absence and the landlord had asked him to leave. This had been a repeat of a similar incident a year or so ago and Ruth reflected how grateful she was that she had taken the decision to step back from Dai until their marital disagreements were behind them. None of this lessened the feelings that Ruth and Dai had for each other but they both knew that these would need to be on hold for the time being.

Dai returned to London and Ruth embarked upon her new career as the post mistress of Senghenydd and her shared responsibility with Lott and Mrs Thomas for the upbringing of her four month old child.

CHAPTER TWENTY NINE

Ruth soon settled into the role of full time postmistress and part time mother. She could not have been more fulfilled as she demonstrated to both the post office and Mrs Thomas that their decision to appoint her was sound. Ruth was already popular with the older folk in the village and many who had drifted away from the shop and post office when it became evident that Mrs Thomas was having difficulty coping were coming back to be greeted by the young, enthusiastic Ruth.

Huw was blossoming in the company of his two 'Aunties' and Ruth's bond with him was strong. She spent every morning dressing and feeding him before taking him either next door to Mrs Thomas or the few minutes' walk to Auntie Lott. Huw was rapidly becoming well known by most of the village who all knew him by name and would regularly stop for a chat with him. This was the childhood that Ruth remembered and in that respect she could have wanted nothing different for her child.

Ruth rarely ventured out of the village and had a morbid aversion with the thought of visiting Cardiff. She recognised the issue but had difficulty in pinning down quite why she simply could not go there. This became a problem when she was asked to attend the occasional post office training day. Ruth explained why going to Cardiff would evoke the terrible memories of the bombing and it was agreed that instead she would go to Bridgend or even Swansea. Other than this, Ruth was well and completely fulfilled.

Ruth paid a nominal rent to Mrs Thomas for the rooms and their arrangement was that she received the postmistress wage but that she and Mrs Thomas would share in the profits from the sales in the store. With business improving, and Ruth's natural frugal lifestyle, she was able to return to her previous habit of saving as much as she could. She could never shake off the sense that all of this could end tomorrow and that she needed to have money to care for Huw and herself.

As the year passed by, Dai continued his visits to Senghenydd but they were less frequent mainly because he was exceptionally busy in his business and because he didn't want the children to suggest that he had a regular pattern of visits to see his mother in case his wife turned up on Lott's doorstep. However, Dai's visits were always a reminder to them both that their friendship was increasingly enduring and their fondness, perhaps even their love for each other was growing.

Dai continued to call Ruth Cariad, a name that reached deep into Ruth's heart, because of the depth of feeling it conveyed. Ruth had learnt some Welsh at school and so she understood some of the common words used in the village but she was foxed when as Dai was leaving her one day he said "Cariad, Rydw i'n dy garu di" and dashed out. It was weeks before Ruth was able to translate that what he had said was Welsh for 'I love you'.

Dai was a deeply sensitive and highly emotional person whose soft spoken voice and innate kind and caring personality drew people to him. He seemed to

Ruth to only have friends, people who spoke kindly of him and people who wanted to always be in his company. Their age difference seemed immaterial to Ruth as she looked upon Dai increasingly as a soul mate and potentially a partner for life. But she could not yet reconcile how if they were to 'get together' it could be done without breaking one of society's most valued principals that two people, intent upon a lasting and loving relationship could come together unless they were married.

For her part Ruth could not contemplate asking Edward for a divorce and Dai seemed to be bound into a marriage where for whatever reasons, his wife would be unlikely to release him from their marriage too.

These matters were never allowed to get in the way as Ruth and Dai continued their pact with each other of looking forwards and not back. This became a powerful force in their relationship and as their time together passed by they were creating their very own past.

This second phase of Ruth's life and in particular her return to the valley of her birth turned into one of the happiest times in her life. She arrived back to Senghenydd in nineteen forty eight with her baby barely weeks old and now in the September of nineteen fifty three and at the age of five she was preparing Huw for his first day at the local school.

Ruth and Dai had previously discussed the need to pre-register Huw at the school and at Dai's suggestion she agreed that it would be less difficult for Huw to explain, if his name on the register was to be Huw Evans, and not Hew Carmichael.

Both Ruth and Dai saw this as an important commitment to each other and a symbol to remind them that one day very soon they would live together as a family. This whole transition went unnoticed by Huw, who had been calling Dai, Pop since he could speak. The presumption in the village had always been that Huw was Dai's son and so registration was no more than a formality.

Ruth remembered well her own first day at school and she was determined to ensure that Huw was as prepared for the excitement and the apprehension as she was. Lott who by now was showing her seventy five years, and Mrs Thomas who were as much a part of Huw's life as Ruth, had arrived at the post office at eight o'clock to wave Huw off to school. Huw was excited and could not see what all the fuss was about. But he would learn in years to come that this rite of passage, where symbolically a child enters the journey to adolescence and then on to adulthood marks a time in a parent's life when they have to let go.

This was never going to be an easy day for Ruth who had never seen any of her secret three children on this same journey. As she prepared Huw for his big day she sobbed alone in her room as she thought of those children all of whom would be returning to their schools today. Ruth asked herself who would be brushing their hair, or polishing their shoes, who would tie a ribbon in the girls hair and who would be kissing them goodbye at the school gates. There was never a day that went by without Ruth thinking about her children, but some days, birthdays, Christmas and days like today which marked lines in the sand for them were especially difficult.

Auntie Lott and Mrs Thomas warmly kissed Huw goodbye and waved as Ruth walked him the short distance to the school, meeting up with other mothers and their children doing the same journey with the same apprehension. The scene at the school gates was the familiar mixture of anxious and clingy goodbye's and those, like Huw who could not get through the gates soon enough to be with friends.

CHAPTER THIRTY

As Ruth walked back to the post office alone she felt a deep sense of loneliness as she began to realise that her 'baby' was now on his inevitable journey to independence. Ruth recalled her own sense of liberation as she walked for the first time through the school gates all those years ago. But then she was a child and now she was an anxious mother coming to terms with having to let go.

Ruth meandered her way back to the post office deep in thought. But as she turned the corner into her road, her heart sank as she saw a small group gathered around someone lying on the pavement. In an instance she knew it was Lott.

Ruth felt her heart beating rapidly as she ran to Lott's side and dropped to her knees beside the still figure of Auntie Lott. As she drew Lott to her and placed her arms around her so the small crowd respectfully moved three or four paces back leaving Ruth at the centre of a circle of onlookers, alone with her dearest friend. Ruth wailed at the crowd "get the doctor, get the doctor" but it was already too late.

Ruth cradled Lott in her arms rocking back and forth calling to her to waken up. But the more people gently told her that Lott was gone the more she rocked, and the more she wept. It was only when the village doctor arrived and knelt beside Ruth that she released Lott from her embrace. Within minutes of his arrival, the doctor confirmed that Lott was dead.

Ruth was inconsolable and refused to leave Lott demanding that she should be taken from the cold street to her own home and her own bed. With great reverence two burley men slowly lifted Lott and carried her the few feet to her home and placed her, at the insistence of Ruth on top of her own bed with her head resting on the soft feather pillow.

Mrs Thomas tried to prise Ruth from Lott's side but she refused to leave. It was only when someone returned to say that Dai had been called and was already on his way that Ruth agreed to leave Lott's room and speak to the doctor and senior members of the community.

The doctor gave Ruth a death certificate on which it recorded that Lott had died from the effects of a heart attack. It was only then that Ruth realised that Lott had been treated for a heart condition for some years. The doctor suggested that the Co-op undertaker should be called to remove Lott to the funeral home insisting that she should not be left on her bed until Dai arrive which could be several hours away.

Ruth returned to Lott's side and in a vigil that lasted more than an hour Ruth held Lott's hand as she slowly felt the warmth of her body drain away. Ruth wiped Lott's face and hands, removing the evidence of her fall and lovingly brushed her white hair out from its familiar bun. Ruth looked into the face of a woman she had known all her life and her own sense of loss was total.

Eventually, the undertaker arrived and it was at this point that Ruth had no option but to relinquish her physical and emotional hold on Lott. Lott was removed from the house and placed in the waiting hearse outside.

As the hearse moved out of sight the lonely figure of Ruth in the deserted street reflected the immense sense of emptiness that Ruth felt inside. As she turned to walk down the road to the post office Ruth was touched by the respect given to Lott as each house observed the tradition of closing their curtains and shutting their doors.

The usually busy streets were deserted with the exception of Ruth who dragged her shocked and emotionally drained body back to her rooms above the post office which itself was closed.

Ruth was intercepted by Mrs. Thomas who coaxed her into her home and gave her a cup of hot sweet tea. Slowly Ruth regained her composure as Mrs. Thomas impressed upon her the importance of being strong for Huw so that she could help him to make sense of what had happened that day. Ruth saw the sense in this but asked if Mrs. Thomas could take Huw once she had picked him up from school and explained what had happened to Auntie Lott.

Ruth went to the school at about twelve o'clock and met with the head teacher who was aware of what had happened and anticipated Ruth wanting to take Huw out of school. Huw was brought to the office confused at seeing his mother there and concerned when she said she was taking him home, especially as this was his first day in the school.

On their way home Ruth stopped at the Recreation Ground where she slowly and sensitively explained that Auntie Lott had died. Huw calmly listened and when Ruth had finished he slipped his arm around his mother and said, "Are you alright Mam, are you very sad?" He went on, "My friends at school told me that Auntie Lott was dead so I knew."

Such is life in a small village that news of this kind can bypass the best laid plans of teachers and parents and where a child is told by his five year old friends that his Auntie has died. Perhaps in the great scheme of things this was right for Huw to hear the news in this way; he was saddened but accepting of this inevitability in life.

Later that day Dai returned home to be greeted by Ruth who took him into his mother's house. Dai had spent the past six hours coming to terms with the news but he was none the less grief stricken as he walked into his mother's empty home. Ruth spent several hours with Dai consoling him and also helping him to remember the vast number of happy times and events he had shared with Lott. Dai's outpourings of love for his mother were deeply touching to Ruth and showed a side of him that she had never come across before.

The comings and goings of neighbours anxious to pay their respects to Dai meant that it was difficult for him to talk to Ruth and it was clear that he was keen to discuss something. Ruth left Dai as he made plans to go to the undertaker to see his mother alone and to make the necessary arrangements for her funeral. Ruth invited Dai to come to her for a late tea so that he could see Huw before he went to bed and to give them time to talk.

At about five thirty Dai arrived at Ruth's home to be greeted at the door by Huw who threw himself into Dai's arms. He had always been close to Dai but it seemed as though tonight more than any other night he needed the company of a man.

They ate tea and chatted and when it came to the time when Huw needed to go to bed he was insistent that Dai should take him. Ruth prepared Huw for bed and then observed the scene as he trotted off to bed hand in hand with Dai. It was more than half an hour later that Dai returned and explained that Huw talked none stop about Auntie Lott asking questions about why she had to die, where she had gone and would mummy be happy again soon.

Ruth and Dai settled down to talk as Dai explained that over the past few months he had managed to sell his business in London and that he had agreed in principal to purchase a garage and petrol forecourt in Bridgend, not many miles from Senghenydd. He explained that his plans were to move back to south Wales in November to work in the garage and also to complete the purchase of a house in Bridgend where they could live.

Dai drew a letter out of his pocket and explained that he had written to his mother only a week ago about his plans to return to Wales and that in her reply she had said, '*I am pleased for you Dai and if I should have one final wish granted in my life it would be to see you, Ruth and Huw settled as a family, I will then truly be a happy woman*'. Ruth cried as she leant over and embraced Dai.

Dai explained that thankfully his wife was no longer chasing him and that he had not heard from her for some time. His children were now out of school and working and he felt free and able to ask Ruth to come and live with him in Bridgend.

Ruth knew that with the loss of Lott now was indeed the right time for the three of them to set up home together as a family. Ruth was overjoyed in the midst of the great pain of the day and over the next hour or so she and Dai formulated plans that they had previously never dared to make. They agreed that no one would need to know that they were not married and so Ruth would simply adopt Dai's name immediately they moved to Bridgend.

Their planning brought light into an immensely dark day and as Dai left Ruth to go to his mother's home, he kissed her goodnight and as he turned to walk away he said, "Cariad, I love you" and in reply Ruth said, "Rydw i'n dy garu di."

Their love and their plans would now form the third phase of Ruth's journey through life.

CHAPTER THIRTY ONE

Lott's funeral took place on the Friday morning a day that was cool but filled with bright sunshine. The planning for the funeral had been difficult for Dai as so many people wanted to attend each looking to be there to 'give her a good send off'. The village church where Arthur had been buried was aware of the numbers that might come and arranged with the village hall to have dozens of chairs delivered to be placed outside the church for those who could not get inside. Dai's children were not going to be present and so it fell to Ruth to stand by Dai and to support him on this saddest of all days.

The hearse carrying Lott arrived at the house at nine forty five. Two wreaths lay on the simple coffin one from the family with its personal message of love and another, from the families of Senghenydd that ran the length of the coffin which simply said 'Auntie Lott'.

The arrival of the hearse was the signal for Dai and Ruth to step outside and lead the mourners through the streets of the village and up the hill to the church. The scene was overwhelming for Dai as he witnessed the outpourings of love and affection for his dear mother with hundreds of people walking the difficult journey to the church. As they came into sight of the church the full throated sound of a male voice choir could be heard singing Lott's favourite Welsh song the beautiful

'Myfanwy'. There is not a Welsh man or woman who is not moved to tears when they hear this most evocative of Welsh anthems.

The funeral service was harrowing for Dai and Ruth the two people who owed so much to one of God's kindest creatures. As the service drew to a close, the Vicar turned to the congregation and signalled to Ruth to come forward. Dai was not prepared for what was to follow. Ruth spoke quietly and without falter in her voice of Auntie Lott the mother, friend, confidant and the village Auntie. She ended by explaining that she was going to recite from a poem that Lott found comforting following the death of her beloved Arthur, Dylan Thomas's powerful, 'Do Not Go Gentle into That Good Night'.

The congregation was spellbound as Ruth delivered this challenge to the perceived wisdom of a quiet passage to the gates of heaven. As she read the final words her heart broke into a thousand pieces. Dai rose from his pew and helped the distraught Ruth back to her seat as the ripple of voices from outside the church collected with those of the congregation inside to sing the only hymn to close a funeral in Wales 'Cwm Rhondda'. Ruth knew the importance of this wonderful hymn which is the very embodiment of the 'hwyl' or good bye.

Following the burial, the mourners Ruth and Dai went back to the village hall where there were sandwiches and tea and an opportunity for friends to reflect upon the life of this extraordinary woman. It drained Dai to hear the many stories from the young and the not so young whose lives had been touched in very personal ways by the kindness of his mother, Auntie Lott was destined to remain a legend in this small village for many years to come.

That evening Dai and Ruth cried and laughed, sat in silence with their own thoughts and shared many of the personal stories told to them by the people who came to say goodbye to Lott. They laughed at the number of people who didn't know quite what to say to Dai and Ruth and who simply said with a great honesty and reverence, "She's got a good day for it anyway." Ruth and Dai parted company agreeing that they should spend the following day together and with Huw thinking about their future and planning for their move.

The following day, Dai took Ruth to Bridgend firstly to see the business he had decided to buy and secondly to look at the house he was proposing to buy for them to live in.

Their journey to Bridgend would normally take a little under an hour and would bring them through villages and towns that Ruth had never visited but whose names were so familiar to her. As they passed through the village of Upper Boat, Dai pointed out the house where his Auntie Mary lived and as they swept into Tonteg he pulled up at a house on Main Road telling Ruth and Huw that they were going to say a quick hello to his Auntie Violet and Uncle George.

Dai sprung out of the car took Huw by the hand and dashed to the house pulling Ruth behind him. He was like a young boy as he rushed into the house desperate to show off his new family. Dai's uncle and auntie were overjoyed to meet Ruth and to see Huw. Auntie Violet turned to Ruth and asked if she remembered her from when she was a child visiting Lott. In an instance Ruth did remember the lovely lady who would spend Sunday afternoon playing cards with Lott and Arthur and was so patient with Ruth who was always eager to play herself.

Ruth hugged Violet as the memories of her childhood again came flooding back to her.

They left Tonteg with a promise to return again in the very near future and headed back on the road to Bridgend. As they passed through Llantwit Fadre, Dai hooted the horn and waved to a man on a bicycle who Dai explained was his Uncle Edmond, "Never worked another day in his life after he was laid off by the colliery and now all he does is odd jobs for people....but he has a heart of gold" explained Dai and they descended the hill towards Cross Keys. Once again, Dai reminded Ruth of his family's deep roots in the valleys as he named another three members of the family who lived between here and Llanharan.

On arrival in Bridgend Dai's first port of call was to show off his new garage. Ruth was disappointed not to have gone to the house first but recognised in Dai that he needed to demonstrate to her that he would have a substantial job and therefore the garage was his first priority.

Dai introduced Ruth as Mrs Evans to the current owner something she was not expecting but a name she felt had a certain ring to it. Huw was fascinated as the outgoing owner showed them around the forecourt with several used cars for sale and the small showroom with its three gleaming new cars. There were two fuel pumps that seemed to be busy serving a constant stream of people in cars and on motorcycles. Finally, they were shown the offices that were above a busy workshop.

Ruth remarked to Dai just how familiar the surroundings felt to her as she whispered in his ear that she would rapidly knock the office into some shape if he wanted her to do. Dai smiled and said, "I hoped you

might say that because it is certainly not my forte."
There were three people working in the office, one on the
forecourt and one in the car sales section which
prompted Ruth to do some quick calculations about
Dai's costs and the likely sales he would need to make to
cover those costs and the other overheads.

As they drove away from the garage Ruth mentioned
these costs to Dai who smiled and remarked that this is
just the kind of open and honest partnership he was
looking for in the business in the future. Ruth questioned
the word partnership and Dai commented, "You and I
are a partnership and it's important to me that you
become a partner in this business and in the others I will
buy in years to come."

He went on, "You have a lot of experience and in no
time, I'm sure you will learn the business so that in the
future, if anything should happen to me, you and Huw
....and any children we might have, will have a secure
future." Ruth laughed of the reference to his age but
squeezed his arm and said thank you.

They arrived at the house Dai was proposing to buy.
It was an end of terrace property that overlooked a
large green play area that was lined by elm and oak
trees. The front of the house instantly reminded Ruth
of Mrs Morgan's house in Cardiff with its small front
garden and wooden gate. Dai left Ruth and Huw on
the doorstep as he was greeted by the next door
neighbour Mr Owens, with the keys for the house. He
was the son of the previous owner and was acting on
behalf of the family in the sale of the property. Once
again, Dai introduced Ruth as Mrs Evans and also
brought Huw to say good morning and to shake Mr
Owens hand.

Huw opened the front door and they entered moving slowly from room to room most of which had little furniture as this had been sold following the death of the previous owner. But Ruth could see that the house was substantial and very much a family home.

Downstairs there was a beautifully decorated front room and a large, extended kitchen with plenty of room for eating. Upstairs there were four bedrooms and a bathroom. Ruth was overwhelmed by the size of the house and as she was thinking about what they would do with such a large property so Dai whispered to Ruth, "Wouldn't you love to have more babies and bring them up in this lovely house." Ruth paused before responding and what she said brought tears to Dai's eyes, "Yes of course I want more children and I want to have them with you." He hugged her and lifted Huw into their embrace.

They spent about thirty minutes in the house before Dai confirmed with Ruth that the house was what she wanted. Having agreed, they returned to Mr Owens's house and with a shake of a hand the deal was done. As they walked to the car, Dai told Ruth that the house would be purchased for cash and placed in her name. He explained that there were two reasons for this, firstly to ensure that at no time in the future could anyone make a claim over her home and secondly to make life easier for her because of the age difference as they became older.

CHAPTER THIRTY TWO

The following eight weeks were like a whirl wind for Ruth. She firstly needed to tell Mrs Thomas that she would be leaving the post office at the end of November to move to Bridgend. The news came as no surprise to the ever observant Mrs Thomas who predicted that it would not be long before Dai and she moved out of the village. Mrs Thomas made this task easy by explaining that she had received several offers for the business and it would not be difficult to sell.

The next step was to secure a place in the local school in Bridgend for Huw something that was achieved three weeks later when she and Dai went to Bridgend to sign the papers for the house. The school was within walking distance of their new home and though much larger than the Senghenydd school it had a village school feel to it. The plans were that Huw would join the school at the beginning of December when he could settle into the pre Christmas activities where he would soon feel a part of the school.

Ruth was overwhelmed by the generosity of Dai's gesture to place the ownership of the house in her name. As they sat outside the Solicitors office, she gave Dai her post office pass book and said, "This is all my savings that I have been putting aside for many years, this should now be placed into a joint account with you." Dai held the book in his hand unopened for a couple of seconds before he passed it back to Ruth saying, "No, you must keep this for a rainy day, I will provide for you and our children and I will ensure that we are able to add a few pounds more to your nest egg as the years pass by." Dai ensured in his tone that Ruth would understand that for him, this was the end of the subject about money.

They entered the Solicitor's office where an array of papers was awaiting their signatures. The first transferred the house into Ruth's name but not before Dai counted out one thousand two hundred pounds in cash to secure the ownership unencumbered by any mortgage. Ruth had never seen such sums since she left the central post office in Cardiff. With one signature from Ruth and another from a clerk in the solicitor's office acting as witness, the house was Ruth's.

The second papers placed the freehold of the garage in Ruth's name and the business in Dai's once again in an attempt to provide security for Ruth. Again Dai paid for the freehold, the business and the good will by cash. Finally, the Solicitor held a document in his hand and said to Ruth, "I have a last Will and Testament here for Dai and I have his permission to tell you that in the event of his demise, he has made proper and generous provision for his children from his first marriage and the rest of his estate will pass to you." For Ruth this was a day of shocks and surprises.

Dai and Ruth went next to the auction and sale rooms where they made arrangements to purchase the furniture they would need to turn the house into a home. Despite the large sums of money that had changed hands that day the frugal nature of both Ruth and Dai meant that they saw no difficulty in purchasing perfectly good second hand furniture for their home.

As they came to settle the bill, Ruth stopped Dai and said, "From what you have said this may be the last opportunity for me to use some of my money on our home and therefore I beg you to let me pay." Dai knew this was important to Ruth and after a dash to the post office down the street Ruth returned and settled the account.

On their return journey to Senghenydd Dai informed Ruth that he had decided to sell his mother's house and that the proceeds would be placed into a bank account for his children.

❧

By the end of the last week of November, Ruth and Dai had managed to move furniture from Lott's house to Bridgend and they had spent time making sure the Bridgend house was ready for them to move in to in December. Strangely, Dai refused to move into the house until he could do this simultaneously with Ruth and Huw preferring instead to sleep in the office above his new garage. Huw was excited about the move to his new school having visited there twice and seemed eager to start his new life.

At eight thirty on Saturday fifth December nineteen fifty three the Evans family collected their final belongings and set off for Bridgend. Their goodbyes were all done the previous night and whilst these were sad goodbyes it was clear that Senghenydd would never be far from their thoughts.

The journey to Bridgend was filled with excitement and anticipation. For Ruth this would be her first family home, for Dai it would be a new life with his first love and for Huw it would be the first time that his 'father' would be living with them.

The move to Bridgend, the home and the business fully lived up to the expectations of Ruth and her family. Huw quickly settled into school and Ruth and Dai rapidly became a good team in the garage. Ruth managed the accounts whilst Dai oversaw the garage and repair shop.

They adapted to new routines and for Ruth she also adapted to having Dai in her bed at night. Dai was the second lover in her life and she could not be happier. His gentle nature and his commitment to love and care for Ruth seemed to find no limit. He was good with Huw and settled quickly into the role of father to 'their' child. Huw loved to spend time in the garage with Dai and was never happier than when he was in the pit in the garage looking up at the underside of a car or when he was helping the mechanic take an engine apart.

Christmas was a happy time but this was also the first time that Dai saw Ruth in one of her melancholy moods as she privately reflected upon what her other children might be doing. At first Dai thought he was at fault but was soon reassured by Ruth.

No matter how hard he tried to understand Ruth's sadness she would not let him into her thoughts and secrets. On one occasion he entered the bedroom and saw Ruth putting her small suitcase back on top of the wardrobe. As he approached her he saw the keys in her hand and looked worried. Ruth sat him down on the bed and said, "We both have pasts and some of mine are locked in that small suitcase. Please understand that I love you and that the past is in the past but sometimes I have to open the case to remember." She paused and then said, "Please don't ask me what's in the case and please don't ever open it."

Dai put his arm around her and said, "If your past is in that tiny case then I'm happy and I give you my word that I will never look into it." However, he gave Ruth a warning that in his experience it was children who look into places they should not and he suggested that the best thing for her to do was to put the contents of the case in the Bank. As always, Dai was sensitive and practical and the following week she took the small case of her memories and placed it with the Bank for safe keeping.

Some weeks later, Ruth went to see the solicitor and at his suggestion she too made out a last will and testament. She took all the advice given by her solicitor but insisted upon one additional insertion into the will. That request, recorded her wish that on her demise, her private bank box contents should be handed over in their entirety, unopened to Mary Morgan.

The solicitor was instructed that the contents of the small case, papers of no monitory value and some simple private items of baby clothes were only to be given to Mary. The solicitor was given a set of keys to the case and was also instructed that if Mary should predecease Ruth, the contents were to be taken by him and destroyed. The solicitor agreed.

CHAPTER THIRTY THREE

By the beginning of June nineteen fifty four, Ruth realised that she was pregnant. She was overjoyed as was Dai when she broke the news to him. Huw was rather more concerned that it should be a boy so that he would have a friend to play with. But for Ruth and Dai this news would symbolise fully their commitment one to the other, the depth of their love and a real joy at being able to have a child of their own. But it also brought into sharp focus their age difference. Dai was a young looking fifty six whilst Ruth was still young at thirty two.

In the February of nineteen fifty five, Ruth gave birth to a healthy boy fulfilling the dearest wishes of Dai and Huw. Returning to her family tradition Ruth told Dai that she wanted to call the boy David Michael. He was delighted never knowing that the second name, Michael would celebrate not only her beloved brother Michael but the son Ruth could never talk about.

Ruth barely had time to settle David into a routine before she was to announce that she was again pregnant. Ruth delivered a second child in the second week of the following January, this time a girl. She named the child Joan Charlotte. Once again, Ruth would capture the name of one of her long lost children in the names of her new family.

It was to be a further two and a half years before Ruth would give birth to another child, again a girl and again the name was to capture that of one of her children from the past. She named her third child with Dai, Deborah Maria.

Throughout this period Ruth and Dai brought up their children in a home filled with love. They gave generously of their time to the children each in their own way trying to compensate for the deficiencies in their past. Ruth was over protective and Dai the complete opposite seeing childhood as the time when children should explore and take risks.

They brought the garage business from strength to strength with Ruth managing the accounts either with a child on her knee or at her feet in the office or late at night at home given that Ruth was not a great sleeper. Together Ruth and Dai were a partnership of giving rather than taking and each worked extraordinarily long hours to make their family happy and their business a success.

As the years passed Ruth suffered nightmares regularly, something that deeply troubled Dai as he watched the tormented Ruth cry and shout until she woke herself up. The outpourings of her nightmares was always shouts of 'give them back to me' and 'I'm sorry please help me I'm sorry'. Dai knew not to pry knowing this was territory both had agreed not to enter.

Visions of the gypsy haunted Ruth as did her prophetic words, '*In your life you will have the blessing of many children but you will endure lifelong sadness. I can see the life you have yet to live and I warn you now that you will go through your life seeing children in your shadow.*"

Ruth was also a prolific smoker, as indeed was Dai and often her nights were spent in a smoke filled kitchen as she prepared food for the children's breakfast or ironed clothes. Ruth was obsessed by many small things but her greatest obsession was that her children should never, ever play further away from the house than she could see them. She was tormented by the thought that someone might try to snatch them something that was the subject of her many nightmares. The 'someone' was always Edward who stalked her mind regularly with the threat of taking away Huw and she saw these threats extending to her other children.

Ruth was most protective of Huw something that was noticed but never spoken about by Dai who was placid and always tolerant of Ruth's sometimes strange ways. Their love was deep and resilient and there was never a cross word spoken. Ruth was moody but Dai began to see the signs and kept out of her way when a moody phase was approaching.

As a family they spent summers on the nearby beaches of Llantwit Major or the Gower coast and in the winter they gathered together around the fire for stories and games. Ruth resisted the call from Huw for a television believing that it would interfere with the interaction of her growing family. Ruth was strict and her old fashioned values were occasionally regarded by Dai as being out of character with someone who wanted her children to grow up with an independent streak drawn from her.

By the late summer of nineteen sixty Ruth was again pregnant with a child that she delivered in July nineteen sixty one. This child was to be called Mary in memory of her dearest friend Mary Morgan.

Ruth was by now thirty eight and her recent life of child bearing, not to mention the three she had many years ago was having an impact upon her. She constantly looked tired, was becoming rather grumpier and was now having to look after Dai who at sixty one was not in the best of heath. But no matter what the world threw at Ruth she was stoic and generally cheery. Her life was her children, then Dai and then the business in which she was taking an increased interest as Dai stepped back to only working a few days per week.

∽

By late nineteen sixty two, Dai was diagnosed as having lung cancer. He remained positive but it was becoming obvious that the cancer was weakening him. However, for Dai the news in the October that he was again to become a father seemed to rally his spirits but this would be a false dawn.

In the middle of December nineteen sixty two after bravely fighting the cancer, Dai died in the arms of his darling Ruth.

For Ruth the world caved in. Her lover, her friend, her soul mate and the father to her children was gone and Ruth was now alone with her children, her secrets and the business.

There was no time for sentimentality after the funeral. Ruth knew that all that stood between her and another disaster for the children she had brought into the world was her. She insisted that Christmas should not be put on hold and drew the children to her to understand that they must now work for each other and for her so that she could become the breadwinner and mother. The fourteen year old Huw rose to the challenge and stepped in as the man of the house organising the children and ensuring they turned as much to him as they would to their mother for support and help. The tight knit family of five children was soon to expand to six with the birth in May nineteen sixty three of another girl.

Ruth pondered the name for some time before, with the help of the children she alighted upon a name that would remain a lasting tribute to Dai. The name that was very carefully spelt out at the registry office to ensure no mistake was Daianne.

Ruth managed to keep the garage business running drawing upon the excellent relationship she had established with the staff. The sales manager brought in when Dai died was made general manager and with the careful help of Ruth the business grew with two new dealerships being added over the next few years to cement the modest income Ruth was able to draw from the business. Ruth's nest egg continued to grow but her frugal nature resisted all calls from the children for holidays though she did eventually agree that there could be a television in the house.

Ruth's nightmares continued as did her long nights alone in her smoke filled kitchen escaping the call to sleep where once again she would be awoken by terrifying nightmares confronting her past, despite the joy and happiness her children with Dai brought to her.

Ruth's new fear was that the eighteen year old Charlotte from her past may try to find her and in so doing, would shatter the image her children had of their mother. On the other hand, Ruth was obsessed by trying to find a way in which she might possibly see her three children in the north of England without compromising her new life.

Ruth regularly visited the Bank to sit in the bank deposits section reviewing her box of memories. She never took the box or its contents out of the bank in part because the memories were all too vivid and in part because she continued to heed Dai's words that children get into every corner of a house and will find anything that has been hidden.

Though Ruth had lost touch with Mary, during her trips to the bank she left her diaries in the hope that one day Mary would read them. These diaries would fill in the gaps but would also remind Mary that she was never far from Ruth's thoughts.

CHAPTER THIRTY FOUR

It was now October nineteen seventy and Ruth's children were rapidly growing up. Huw was twenty two and very much Ruth's man about the house and a willing and capable surrogate father to the young ones. Joan was a sensible fifteen year old and the others were generally very well behaved. This drove Ruth to discuss with two dear friends and neighbours if they would spend a few days at the house helping Huw to care for the children whist she took a trip down memory lane to return to Blackpool.

The children were excited that Simon and Karen, who were in their late thirties, would spend time with them. They had two children who were the same ages as Mary and Daianne and they went to school together. The children helped form the plans that Karen, her daughter Isabel and Ruth's girls would sleep at Ruth's house and Simon, his son Benjamin and the boys would sleep at Simon's house.

Happy with the plans and content that the children would have a wonderful time with Simon and Karen, Ruth embarked upon her epic journey of rediscovery. The first real challenge was to again enter Cardiff a city that still brought flashback memories of the death and destruction she witnessed as a young woman during the bombings.

Ruth's train journey from Cardiff to Preston also brought back memories of the young alluring woman that turned heads on her journey to Blackpool all those years ago. Though smartly dressed Ruth could see that she no longer turned heads, she was now forty seven, a mother of nine children and she had dark secrets that would certainly turn heads but for a completely different reason

On arrival in Blackpool, Ruth returned to the guest house Mrs Morgan and Mary stayed in when they came to see her during the war. Little had changed in Blackpool except that the khaki uniforms and the austere greys and browns of the nineteen forties had been replaced by the mini skirt, hippies wearing shaggy Afghan coats, Indian cheesecloth shirts, and patchwork gypsy skirts. The suits and trilbies of the war years had for men been replaced by tight fitting shirts with large collars, and flared flannel trousers were now out replaced by American jeans and platform shoes.

Ruth spent the majority of her days in the library reading through old newspapers looking for any pointers that might lead her to understand where her children may be. She assumed that Edward would have remained local to Blackpool and so she combed the electoral rolls but found nothing. On her second day of visiting, a kindly lady sat next to her and said, "I'm the librarian and I could not help but notice that you are obviously searching for something or someone in our records, can I assist you." Ruth was immediately concerned not to reveal too much simply saying that she lived and worked here during the war and wanted to see if she could find any names of people or stories about people she knew from that time. Her response was unconvincing to the librarian who had seen many women pass through the library in search of information, mainly of long lost sweethearts.

Ruth's evenings were spent sitting on the benches on the promenade people watching, looking for the figure of a teenager who might be one of hers or an adult she may recognise. The person she didn't seek out was cousin Moira who through her research she discovered still lived in the same house. Somehow, whilst Ruth was here to discover she was not prepared to confront the ghosts of the past.

There were many names she recognised in the register and to pay a call upon them might have dug up too many painful memories or might have placed Ruth too close to people who might still be in touch with Edward.

On her last evening Ruth made her all too familiar journey back to the guest house. She was a lonely figure on the busy pavement as she saw again the sign for the gypsy she had visited with Mary Morgan during the war years. She recalled the now prophetic words of the palmist: *"In your life you will have the blessing of many children but you will endure lifelong sadness."* She remembered the hushed tones in which the gypsy said, *"Your name is Ruth ... and I can see the life you have yet to live and I warn you now that you will go through your life seeing children in your shadow."* And she shivered as she recalled the final warning: *"Ruth, you will walk many paths in your life but before the sun sets every day, you will see those children in your shadow."*

As Ruth drew level with the entrance to the gypsy, resisting the inner temptation to go in she heard someone call, "Ruth come on let's go in." She turned and looked around but there was no one there, just the distant memory of a youthful Mary.

∽

As the years rolled by, Ruth made the same journey on many, many occasions, searching and not finding, hoping and having those hopes dashed. These journeys were certainly not cathartic but they fulfilled what to Ruth became a pilgrimage of hope and a chance, perhaps a last chance to become as close as she could to, Charlotte, Maria and her beloved Michael. As each visit ended and she returned to her home in south Wales, a home in which few of her children now lived, her hopes of one day seeing her three children from her past was fading.

Throughout the eighty's and nineties, her family met their own soul mates and married. They moved out of the house, some to live locally, and others to live in places throughout England and Wales. Each left a piece of themselves behind in that house and each would rush home at the very mention that their mother needed something or that she was unwell.

And sadly, Ruth's health was deteriorating, the result of years of smoking, raising her many children and running the business. She concealed the news for many weeks but the cancer was aggressive and it became clear to those of her children who lived nearby that their mother was very poorly.

CHAPTER THIRTY FIVE

It was in December nineteen ninety three when the devastating news that Ruth was suffering from lung cancer descended upon the family. The ripple started when one of her children was told the news by Ruth in confidence and in confidence she told another a sister and brother and by the Christmas of that year the whole family, children and grandchildren knew that Ruth was dying. All of Ruth's children along with their spouses and their children descended upon Bridgend to celebrate Christmas all knowing but not saying that this might be Ruth's last.

In the comings and goings over the Christmas and January and February each of her children who were taking their turn to stay at the house to care for Ruth, pursued the same line of questions, begging their mother to open the book of her life and tell them more of the snippets she had revealed when they were small. But Ruth jealously guarded those facts that might enable the fragments of her life to be pieced together to create a fuller and more revealing picture.

She spoke of being a post mistress but failed to mention her heroics in Cardiff during the war. She mentioned her 'bit for the war effort' but omitted to reveal that she held down a responsible job as an aircraft inspector on the Wellington Bomber production line. She spoke of dear friends she had lost touch with and she spoke of her love in her youth of dancing. But her greatest secret her marriage and her three other children, sisters and a brother to these children was kept locked in her own memory.

Throughout February and March Ruth's health deteriorated with her doctor simply providing palliative care and medication. The family was alerted that Ruth had little time left and one by one they gathered at her bedside, a vigil that was to last three weeks. During that time she drifted in and out of lucidness mumbling often incomprehensible words and names. But the names she repeated the most were Charlotte, Maria and Michael. Time and again she would cry out their names to the confusion and surprise of the gathered children.

Ruth's torment continued day after day as her body weakened. As the morphine eased the physical symptoms so the mental pain became worse enabling Ruth to relive her life over and over again. She pictured Charlotte, Maria and Michael as children and her question that was never answered was, "What became of my children have they forgiven me?"

Ruth would never hear the answer to her own question but to complete Ruth's story in the hours before her death, it is necessary to return to October nineteen forty eight when Ruth last saw Edward.

Having travelled to south Wales and warned Ruth never to return to the north of England or to ever try to contact him or the family, Edward returned to Eastbrook Farm. His children were with foster families placed there in the May of that year following the death of Ellen their grandmother.

Edward and his father were both preparing to leave the farm house and find homes away from the memories. The conspiracy of silence entered into by the Carmichael family had withstood its greatest test following Aunt Dorothy's discovery that Ruth had given birth to Edward's fourth child. But relationships between Edward and his family were never going to be the same again.

Edward rented a small flat in Preston and by December nineteen forty eight he had moved there. His new home in the Deepdale area of Preston meant that he was now living a matter of minutes from where Sarah lived. Their relationship had gone from strength to strength and their long range plans to marry were getting much nearer.

Edward had filed for divorce in April nineteen forty seven on the grounds of the desertion of his wife Ruth and needed to wait the statutory three years before a divorce could be granted. The illusion that he had not seen his wife in that time was one that Sarah and the authorities had bought into, but Edward and his family knew different and were steadfastly holding the line of secrecy with Edward.

Edward's children were still in the care of foster families, Charlotte and Maria were with a loving and caring couple in Inglewhite and Michael, whose name had been changed to Robert by Sarah and Edward, was with a Catholic foster family in Preston. Edward had not seen his children since they were taken into care but maintained an understanding of their wellbeing through the social services department's regular contact with him.

Edward had left Vickers in Blackpool and had taken a position with a local entrepreneur as Chief Designer in the development and early local production of a small family car. The enterprise was run on a shoe string but produced employment for a handful of committed and dedicated engineers and fabricators. As the car went into pre-production, Sarah spent many hours with Edward helping with the design and sewing of the upholstery of the car seats. To the world around Edward and Sarah they were the perfect couple, deeply in love, young and without a care in the world.

Those who knew them rather better and were aware that Edward's children were in the care of social services were seen less frequently and ultimately were abandoned. For those who were closer friends there was a great championing of their planned wedding and Sarah was continually portrayed as the saint who would enable Edward to bring his family back together once they were married. Indeed, Sarah herself began to see her pre-destiny to save the children as one shaped by God himself. But her inner secret was that she disliked children and simply saw Charlotte, Maria and Robert as part of the baggage she would need to take on if she was to marry Edward.

In the April of nineteen forty nine, at the age of two Robert was removed from foster care and placed into the care of a Catholic run children's home in Preston. In the May of the same year the foster parents who were caring for Charlotte and Maria informed the social services office that they were finding it difficult to cope with the two girls who were by now five and approaching four years of age. The couple offered to adopt Charlotte something that Edward could not agree. He was however prepared to agree to them adopting Maria but it was always Charlotte that they wanted. This precipitated the removal of both the girls and their placement into separate Catholic run children's homes in the June of nineteen forty nine.

Charlotte was sent to an orphanage in Preston and Maria to one in Lancaster. It was Edward that influenced the separation of the children and the recommendation that they too should be placed in the care of Catholic priests and nuns, very much influenced by their recent baptism into the Catholic faith.

Edward was obsessed by keeping secret his past life with Ruth and was convinced that if Charlotte and Maria were placed together they would openly talk about their mother who they had been told was dead. The social services department and the children's homes were very much aware that Ruth was certainly not dead but had never been given the information they needed to trace her.

Once placed into the children's homes Edward and Sarah would visit each child separately about once every two months. There were the rare occasions when Charlotte and Robert were taken out together but these were extremely infrequent. The children were becoming strangers to each other and for Charlotte the sibling relationship she had begun to establish with Maria was slowly fading as they both adapted to their new circumstances and their new surroundings.

By the April of nineteen fifty, Edward was on course to receive the Decree Nisi, the preliminary to the dissolution of his marriage to Ruth. Well prepared plans for his marriage to Sarah in the June were being dusted off and invitations to the wedding were prepared.

On Monday seventeenth of April Edward received the Decree Nisi meaning that barring a complete catastrophe he would be granted the Decree Absolute on Wednesday thirty first of May.

Wedding invitations were sent to family and friends and as planned, the Decree Absolute, issued in the High Court of Justice was received on thirty first of May. The grounds for the divorce were that since the celebration of their marriage in nineteen forty three Ruth had '*deserted*' Edward, '*without cause for a period of at least three years preceding the presentation of the petition*'. This would have required Edward to have had no contact with Ruth in that period, which, with the conception of Huw in December nineteen forty seven, and his trip to south Wales in nineteen forty eight was a betrayal of Ruth, Sarah and himself.

∽

Edward married Sarah in her Catholic parish church before God, his family and friends on Saturday third of June nineteen fifty. The ceremony and the wedding breakfast that followed fulfilled the glittering expectations of Sarah. She had eventually secured the marriage she so dreamed of.

This young couple would now embark upon a future together that in their eyes could be lifted from the pages of a love story. But theirs was not a relationship built upon trust, openness and no secrets, theirs was one in which Edward's natural instinct for secrecy and Sarah's need to be the centre of his life would come into sharp conflict and shape theirs and his children's lives forever.

From June nineteen fifty, to the summer of nineteen fifty two, Edward and Sarah lived the carefree lives of any newly married couple. They lived in Edward's flat in Preston, they went to the cinema and they continued their love of ice skating and dancing. They also continued to take the children out of the children's homes for short trips to the countryside but these were trips that increasingly for Maria and Robert, were with apparently well meaning strangers. For Charlotte, there were memories, distant images of happy times with her mother and her grandmother, but she was already astute enough to know that she must never allow these memories to surface.

Edward took a number of jobs over this period, always in engineering and always on the cutting edge of development and ideas. He moved slowly into more senior roles which offered him the prospect of being able buy a home where he could bring his children back together with him. Sarah always went along with Edward's plans but for her, the longer that others could have the responsibility for the children's upbringing the better. She was neither maternal nor practical around children and when she encountered them she tended to patronise them with her silly childish behaviour. But she was prepared to see their idyllic life change and share the responsibility for the upbringing of the children in order to support Edward, something few women of her age would contemplate.

In October of nineteen fifty two, having secured a good job in Morecambe, Edward and Sarah moved to a house in the suburbs of Lancaster. The arrangement they had with the owner who was actually trying to sell the property was that they would rent it for a period of three months with the option to buy it.

The property was a three bedroom semi detached, with a large living room and dining area and a small but adequate kitchen. The house was on the corner of the road which meant that, it also had a driveway and garage. The rear garden was particularly large and overlooked a green public space. This was very much a step up to upper middle class living for Edward and Sarah. By the January of nineteen fifty three they had purchased the house and began to slowly furnish it.

Whilst Edward was happy in his job in Morecambe, Sarah knew that she would need to work in order to help pay towards the mortgage costs and the increasingly expensive middle class lifestyle they had adopted. Edward had purchased a newer more reliable car to go to work and there was the need to budget for the expense of having the children come to live with them.

Sarah quickly found a job in Lancaster working as an assistant in a fashion shop and this was the turning point Edward would claim for considering bringing the children to live at the house. But in truth, the social services were exasperated by the years of prevarication and were now openly discussing a deadline for return of Edward's children or their adoption.

At the age of six and having experienced a year in foster care and almost five years of institutionalised life Robert was the first to be brought out of the care of social services and the children's home. In the July Sarah travelled by bus to Preston and collected Robert from the nuns at the door of the orphanage. Like a character from Dickens he stood there in short faded trousers and a shirt that was far too large. He wore calf length grey socks and a pair of sandals that were old and scuffed. Under his arm he carried a small box of personal items. Robert knew only that he was going to Daddy's house with Sarah, who he now must call Mummy.

Prior to leaving the home his friends in the dormitory who looked on in envy as he packed his box teased him that he would be back within weeks. Such was the life for many of these boys that they were often returned by families who either couldn't cope or who didn't like the child they hoped to adopt.

Robert was settled into the small bedroom at the front of the house in Lancaster before it was the turn of Maria to be collected from the orphanage in Lancaster and taken to her new home. Two weeks later Charlotte was brought home and moved into the rear bedroom which she would share with Maria.

These early days living in a house were difficult for these three institutionalised children. Their lives had been ordered and directed with few freedoms to express personality or character. It was hard to change to a new regime and particularly to one where the children constantly felt they needed to gain the individual and collective approval of their new mother. Sarah fumbled her way through the following weeks until the children were placed into their schools for the new term and she could return to work.

∽

The following years were difficult for the children who needed to adjust to living in a home where it became increasingly obvious that they were far from the priority of Edward and Sarah. The house became a place where they ate and slept but it was never a home.

Sarah could not abide having toys and play things in the house and these were all placed in the garage. She was also obsessed by order and tidiness and refused to allow the children into the house unless she or Edward was there. This resulted in the children retuning from school in the late afternoon and spending until six thirty in the garage no matter what the season or the weather.

Sarah simply could not cope with the emotional needs of the children and her coping strategy was to select one child at random sometimes for a day, sometimes for several days during which she would entertain that child's needs to the complete exclusion of the other children. But the children were wise and wily and quickly realised that it was futile to attempt to change Sarah and her ways. They adopted a code of conduct between them and would often start the day by asking each other, "Who's in favour today".

Sarah was also engaged in an emotional battle with Edward to gain increasing access to his time and his attention. She would take a small insignificant issue and create a drama of it during which she would threaten to walk out on Edward who she would accuse of putting the children before her. She demanded time away from the children craving for the carefree life before the children.

Sarah insisted upon a strict Catholic upbringing with the family attending church every Sunday and on all Holy Days of Obligation. But when a new church was built about a mile away from where the family lived, Sarah insisted that Charlotte should walk the other children to that church whilst she and Edward went to the Cathedral as a couple. Sunday afternoons were generally spent travelling to Preston where Sarah's sister and brother-in-law lived though occasionally they would visit Lancaster.

The home in Lancaster was rarely visited by any friends or work colleagues of Edward and Sarah. Their life and their past was a closely guarded secret from all but the very closest of family. The children rarely brought friends to the house because they recognised from what they saw in their friends homes that the Carmichael house was different and especially uninviting.

But for the children the summers were their time when they could be free to explore their surroundings together. Every day during the six week school holiday, the children would plan their next adventure. They each had a bicycle and their journeys of discovery would regularly start at eight or nine o'clock in the morning and not end sometimes until early evening. This little band of children would have gladdened the heart of Ruth had she been able to see the resourcefulness and the bond that existed between them.

Charlotte, Maria and Robert lived two distinct lives, the one when they were under the control and manipulation of Sarah and Edward and the other where they allowed their imagination and their youthful sprit to shape their lives. They were close and their acute interpretation of their parent's complex relationship allowed them to compensate for the indifference and lack of love that came from Sarah and the disinterest that came from Edward.

These children were free spirits, bright, witty and resourceful and as they grew into adulthood these attributes defined them and shaped their characters. But they were also inquisitive and absorbed the unguarded comments of an adult or the deliberate slip of the tongue from Sarah when she was demanding more attention from Edward. Their parents always referred to their mother Ruth as being dead though the children secretly believed that there were many flaws to the story. But this was to be territory the children would only venture into when they were no longer living under the same roof as Sarah and Edward.

The children's lives went in different directions once they left home. Each left the family home at the earliest possible moment. The three children were academically bright but each was directed away from going on to university by Edward though they were more than capable of this. Edward's only interest when the three children left school was to see them get jobs and leave home. Each did just this in swift order.

But Ruth would be proud that despite the terrible direction their early lives had taken the children had gone on to fulfilling and happy lives.

∽

Ruth's family continued their vigil at the bedside of their dying mother who was now lucid for very short periods of time. She was weak and the family knew that the end was near.

And it was in this period of heightened emotion that there was a gentle knock on the front door on the morning of April fifth nineteen ninety four. Ruth's youngest child, Daianne, slipped from her mother's bedside, descended the stairs and answered the door to a smartly dressed, grey haired elderly woman who looked frail and unsteady as she rested uncomfortably on her walking stick. Daianne, noticed another, older lady slip quietly away from the doorstep and return to a large car that was parked directly outside the house. The elderly woman asked Daianne, "I wonder if I might speak with Ruth?"

Daianne explained that her mother was very ill and that the whole family was with her fearing the worst might happen very quickly. The woman was visibly shaken by what she heard and appeared to Daianne as though she might collapse. Daianne saw a tear slip down her pale face and that was followed by another and then another. Gently placing a hand on the lady's shoulder Daianne asked, "I'm sorry; do you know my mother well?" The woman paused before replying, "Darling, I know your mother so well that I grieve as you do for a woman I love dearly."

The old lady turned to leave and Daianne could see that she was about to speak but the evident shock and distress she felt rendered even a few words an impossibility. Daianne, who was now also weeping took the woman's arm and gently brought her into the hallway of her mother's house. She took the stranger into the front room, sat her down in a chair and knelt at her feet. As she did, she took the strangers hands into her own and gently held them as she looked into her intensely blue eyes that gave only a hint of the youthful beauty of this sick and grief stricken woman.

After a moment had passed and when the woman seemed slightly more composed, Daianne asked, "I can see the news about my mother is deeply distressing to you, how long have you known her?" "My dear" she said, revealing a faint Cardiff accent, "My dear I have known Ruth since we were both young girls when we worked together in Cardiff. We have remained dear friends through the long journey we both have taken in our very different lives. My name is Mary, Mary Morgan and I too am facing the final chapter in my life. I have only weeks, perhaps a month or so to live and because of this, I wanted to say a final farewell to my dear, dear Ruth."

Mary explained that she and Ruth had lost touch over the years but as the aggressive nature of her cancer suggested that she would need to go into a hospice very soon she had set about trying to find Ruth. "It has taken Clarissa and me weeks to find your mother but I shall see out my own days in peace if I have a moment to say goodbye to my dear Ruth."

Daianne, by now completely overcome with emotion slipped out of the room asking Mary if she would wait whilst she went back upstairs to see her family.

Daianne explained to the family gathered around her mother's bed that an old friend of their mother, someone called Mary Morgan, was waiting in the front room asking if she could see their mother.

The family hardly had time to absorb what they were hearing before they heard Ruth calling. "Did you say Mary, Mary Morgan is here?"

Ruth had found an inner strength that had eluded her for many days as she repeatedly asked for confirmation that Mary was in the house. Finally, Daianne went to her Mother's side and said, "Yes Mam, Mary is here but who is she and do you really want to see her?" Ruth explained in a weak and faltering voice that Mary was her only friend from her past. "Mary knows me better than you do" she said, "but I want to see her alone."

Mary was carefully helped up the stairs and taken to Ruth's bedside. As the family looked on, Mary took their dying mother in her arms, and as she did they saw their mother at peace for the first time in weeks. Not wishing to intrude any longer, the family quietly left the room and closed the door.

Life's journey for Ruth was now complete.

Lightning Source UK Ltd.
Milton Keynes UK
UKOW04f1424010218
317217UK00001B/3/P